The
Hanged Man's Noose

A Glass Dolphin Mystery

Judy Penz Sheluk

Barking Rain Press

The Hanged Man's Noose: A Glass Dophin Mystery, Book 1

Edited by Narielle Living (www.narielleliving.com)

Proofread by Rachel Roddy (www.creativeprose.com)

Cover artwork by Craig Jennion (www.craigjennion.com)

Barking Rain Press
PO Box 822674
Vancouver, WA 98682 USA
www.BarkingRainPress.org

ISBN Trade Paperback: 1-941295-24-X
ISBN eBook: 1-941295-25-8
Library of Congress Control Number: 2015937582

First Edition: July 2015

Printed in the United States of America

9 7 8 1 9 4 1 2 9 5 2 4 3

DEDICATION

For Mike, who never stopped believing.

CHAPTER 1

E mily Garland stared at the blank white page on her computer screen. Less than five hours to meet her *Urban Living* deadline, and she still hadn't come up with a new way to spin the same old condo stats.

She blamed the lack of concentration on her upcoming meeting with Michelle Ellis. Why would the editor-in-chief of Urban Living Publications want to meet with her in person? Outside of the obligatory appearances at builders' conventions and awards galas, Emily couldn't remember a time when she'd met with Michelle face-to-face. Certainly she'd never been invited to her office. She glanced at her Timex Ironman watch. 11:03 a.m. Time to get writing.

While it's common knowledge the Greater Toronto Area's (GTA) high-rise market is through the roof, most people don't realize how far along it has come: as of this reporting period, high-rise condominium suites make up approximately 60 percent of total new homes sold.

According to the Urban Building Association (U-BUILD), several factors are behind the condo surge, including a shortage of land. With limited supply, the cost of detached, semis, and townhouses has continued to escalate.

"Condominiums are a practical alternative," said Garrett Stonehaven, a prominent real estate developer and CEO of HavenSent Developments, Inc. "Builders are also 'right-sizing' to create more space-efficient and, thus affordable, units."

Right-sizing for affordability—what a bunch of hooey! After ten years of writing about the residential housing industry, Emily had been around Garrett Stonehaven enough to know he didn't have an altruistic bone in his handsome, six-foot tall body—at least not once the television cameras stopped rolling. But it didn't matter what *she* thought. The camera loved him. The readers of *Urban Living* loved him. Which was why Emily quoted him, every chance she got. It was called job security, a precious commodity to a freelance writer. She wrote a while longer until it was time to zero in on the closer.

"As the builder/developer of CondoHaven on the Park, we are interested in foreign and local investment potential," said Stonehaven. "But our primary focus is, and always will be, building homes for people to come home to."

- 30 -

Complete blather, Emily thought, entering the somewhat archaic -30- to denote The End. She looked at her watch. There was still plenty of time to get in a five-mile run.

———————

Emily arrived at the offices of Urban Living Publications at promptly 5:00 p.m., punctuality being both the curse and the reward of living life eternally on deadline. The offices took up a generous portion of the forty-fourth floor. Someone was doing okay. The going rate for commercial real estate in the financial sector was in the nosebleed section of dollars per square foot.

A petite fifty-something bottle blonde in a navy blue power suit marched out of a glass-walled office. "Emily, dear, so glad you could make it."

"Michelle. Good to see you." Emily held out her hand before Michelle could get into the whole hugging, air-pecking-on-the-cheek business.

"Come to my office. We need to talk."

The office was far more luxurious than Emily could have imagined. Emily had always thought editors and publishers were crammed into windowless, paper-infested cubbyholes. This was definitely a far cry from the cramped Queen Street quarters where she'd interned for a small press publisher right after graduation. Those offices had mounds of manuscripts threatening to buckle battle-scarred tables and bookcases overflowing with titles from past to present, bestsellers and busts and dreams turned to dust.

Michelle's office, on the other hand, featured a bank of windows with a view of the city's waterfront. A handful of sailboats dotted the late season waters. The remaining walls were covered in paintings, although none were immediately recognizable, at least to Emily's untrained eye. She suspected they might be by up-and-coming artists. She'd heard Michelle was heavily into the art scene. A massive mahogany desk—real mahogany, not the laminate look-alike she had in her own home office—held nothing but a twenty-seven-inch iMac, a twisty-looking acrylic sculpture in shades of gold and cobalt blue, and a silver-framed photograph of a fine-boned teenager, his straw-colored hair and peach fuzz whiskers glinting in the noonday sun, his clear blue eyes looking up with adoration at a tall, handsome teenager standing next to him.

"My son and his best friend," Michelle said. "The sculpture is from an Aboriginal artist in Northern Manitoba. But enough of the pleasantries. I'm sure you're curious to know why I asked you here, Emily, dear, instead of sending the usual email. Or calling."

"A little curious." *Hoping for the best, expecting the worst. Already a little tired of the "dear."*

"I'm assuming you've heard the Huntzberger acquisition rumors?"

Word on the street had Michelle and a couple of silent partners in negotiations to purchase Huntzberger Publications. Emily debated feigning ignorance but instead opted for the truth. Publishing was a small world. No way Michelle would believe she hadn't heard. "Yes."

"They're all true. Like many publishers these days, Huntzberger has been bleeding red ink. With the possible exception of tabloid journalism, people simply aren't buying print like they used to. But Huntzberger's loss is Urban Living's gain. My partners and I believe that properly managed, and with some innovative investments, publishing can be more than profitable, it can be lucrative."

Once again Emily wondered why she'd been summoned. As a freelance writer, she wasn't exactly privy to any corporate secrets. "I'm sure it's a wonderful opportunity." She straightened her posture and attempted to look suitably impressed.

"More than you can imagine. The official announcement of the acquisition was sent to all the media outlets earlier today, embargoed until tonight's six o'clock news. From that point onward, we'll be known as Urban-Huntzberger, Inc. My partners are in the process of preparing our IPO. These things take time, but we're hoping to get listed within a few months."

Preparing an Initial Public Offering, getting listed on the stock exchange. It had definite possibilities. Maybe Michelle was going to offer her a full-time job, one with benefits: dental, medical, paid vacation. A girl could dream. "Who are the partners?"

"They prefer to remain silent investors for the moment, though that will change when we go public. But you needn't let such things concern you. I'll remain editor-in-chief for all Urban-Huntzberger publications, and you'll continue to report directly to me on any assignments. Which brings me to today. We would like to offer you an assignment. But this one is a bit, hmmm, different."

Emily shifted forward in her seat. "Different?"

"It would involve relocating."

"Relocating?" Emily realized she was beginning to sound like a bit of a parrot. "To where? For how long?"

"To Lount's Landing. For as long as it takes. Probably three to six months. Possibly longer."

Lount's Landing? Emily searched her brain for any sign of recognition. None came. "Where exactly is Lount's Landing?"

"About ninety minutes northeast of Toronto. A charming little hamlet nestled along the shores of the Dutch River. We've arranged for a monthly lease on a Victorian row house within walking distance to the town's Main Street. Even better, we'll cover the rent for the course of the assignment."

Emily tried not to stare. Urban Living Publications, or rather, Urban-Huntzberger, had rented a Victorian row house? In a town called Lount's Landing? For a long-term assignment? What on earth?

"I know, dear. It's all rather overwhelming, but we specifically selected you for the assignment. You're a talented writer. A thorough researcher. A hard worker. Utterly reliable. More importantly, you know the business from top to bottom."

Maybe the last five years of trying to put a new spin on the same old condo stats hadn't gone unnoticed after all. "Thank you."

"You're welcome. But permit me to be perfectly frank. There was one other important consideration. You don't appear to have any ties to hold you here." Michelle turned to her computer, pulled up a document, and began reading. "No siblings. Both parents deceased. Father when you were fourteen. Stomach cancer. Mother two years ago." She paused. "Accidental overdose."

Emily went from stunned silence to outright indignation. They had been investigating her? Knew, or at least suspected, about her mother's suicide?

And what was all that nonsense about not having any ties in Toronto? Sure, Kevin might have dumped her for that blonde bimbo who called herself a personal trainer, but it wasn't like she didn't have a friend to her name. Besides, she'd known it was over with Kevin for a long time. But she'd invested so much time and energy in him, trying to make it work. And then for him to up and leave her, as if she had been nothing more than a meaningless diversion...

"If you're trying to portray me as a loner loser—"

"Not at all, dear, not at all. We understand the healing power of solitude. We also know you privately loathe Garrett Stonehaven. Not without cause, if our research into your mother's situation can be trusted. All things considered, we believe you're the perfect candidate for this assignment."

All things considered? What did that arrogant SOB Garrett Stonehaven have to do with an assignment in Lount's Landing? His turf had always been in Toronto's downtown core. More importantly, what did all this have to do with her mother's death, accidental or otherwise?

"We particularly enjoyed your exposé of the Kraft-Fergusson brownfield development," Michelle continued. "And you're always saying how much you enjoy the investigative side of journalism. We're simply willing to provide the opportunity, albeit at a much higher level. We're also willing to compensate you handsomely for the privilege, including benefits and stock options."

Emily thought back to her coverage of the brownfield scandal, the weeks of investigative research, trying to learn all she could about the types of hazardous waste and chemical pollutants industries like Kraft-Fergusson left behind. Remembered the long days of chasing down leads, the hours of writing and rewriting.

It had been one of the most rewarding—and frustrating—experiences of her career. Rewarding because she had finally been taken seriously as a journalist. Frustrating because, despite the fact that HavenSent Developments owned the

Kraft-Fergusson land, she'd never managed to pin any of the toxic dirt on Garrett Stonehaven. Thanks to his accountant, Eldon Thornbury, a vile man who slithered through loopholes and then sewed up the ends, HavenSent, and Stonehaven by association, had been completely exonerated of any wrongdoing. Had been lauded, in fact, for their utmost co-operation with all authorities.

"You have my attention."

Michelle reached into a drawer and pulled out a contract.

"First, Emily, we need you to agree to our terms and conditions, the usual confidentiality and exclusivity verbiage. I assure you, nothing sinister is behind the offer. We have only your best interests at heart. Of course, if you don't want the gig, there are plenty of other writers who would jump at the opportunity. Kerri St. Amour, for example."

Kerri say-no-more? They were comparing her to that backstabbing hack? Emily glanced at the numbers in front of her and thought hard. Get the goods on Stonehaven and get paid for the pleasure. There was enough money on the table to stop renting, put a down payment on a place of her own. Maybe take a few months off, write the historical romance she'd been dabbling with for years. It might be therapeutic to start over, go to a place where nobody knew her, a place where she wasn't Kevin's somewhat pathetic ex-fiancée. But was it all too good to be true? There had to be a catch. In her life, there was always a catch.

"What would I have to do?"

"HavenSent Developments is exploring a development opportunity in Lount's Landing. Nothing unusual, though it is a bit far afield, even for someone as ruthless as Garrett Stonehaven. But our source tells us there's more to Stonehaven's latest plan than meets the eye. Much more."

"Where do I fit in?"

"The town has a monthly magazine, *Inside the Landing*. It's a promotional glossy, similar to *Urban Living*, albeit on a much smaller scale, with stories about businesses in the community. Runs about forty pages, could be more if the ad revenue was there. It now falls under the Urban-Huntzberger umbrella. The previous owner had been ready to sell out and retire for some time."

"And my role?"

"You would be responsible for all the editorial content, make some much-needed improvements to the publication. In fact, we'd encourage it as part of your cover."

Aha! Catch number one. *Part of my cover*. Mind you, it did sound intriguing. "If I agree?"

"You'd move to Lount's Landing. Get to know the town, the people, make some friends. Find out what Garrett Stonehaven's up to. And write us an exclusive that will have Urban-Huntzberger's stock market value skyrocketing higher than the latest GTA condo."

Emily suspected this went way beyond a publisher trying to make money. What had Stonehaven done to warrant a Michelle Ellis sponsored witch-hunt? Who was Michelle's source of information? She cursed herself for wanting to find out, when every instinct told her to run.

"And the source?"

"Better you don't know. That way you can observe everyone with the same degree of neutrality, although we have arranged for you to connect with a Johnny Porter. He's the chairman of the Main Street Merchants' Association. He seems keen to keep *Inside the Landing* operational, although that's all he knows. It would be best for all concerned if you kept it that way."

Emily nodded. It certainly sounded as though Urban-Huntzberger had everything covered. She wondered whether she should study the contract, contact a lawyer. Take a moment to decide whether this was the opportunity of a lifetime or an act of insanity. "How long do I have?"

"We need an answer ASAP. You'd move in by the end of the month, sooner if possible. The rental house has been recently renovated and is currently available."

Michelle stood up. "Emily, you've been in this business long enough to know this kind of assignment doesn't come along every day. Work with us. Get rich with us. And help us to expose Garrett Stonehaven for the lying, cheating, bastard we both know he is."

Definitely more to this scenario than meets the eye. Emily pulled a gold-plated pen out of her handbag, a graduation gift from her mother a dozen years ago. She twirled it between her fingers, remembering how proud her mom had been, her daughter the first one in the family to go beyond high school. Remembered the way her mother had looked the last time Emily saw her, shell-shocked and shattered.

"Where do I sign?"

CHAPTER 2

Lount's Landing appeared to be a town in transition. Nestled among the Victorian architecture and the freshly painted shops with cutesy names like "Book Worm" and "Second Hand Rose"—the former a bookstore, the latter a consignment clothing shop filled with vintage and designer fashions—there were telltale signs of more radical change, starting with the "For Sale: Development Potential" real estate sign on an old elementary school at the foot of Main Street.

Emily's first order of business was a meeting with Johnny Porter, owner of It's a Colorful Life, chairman of the Main Street Merchants' Association, and her key contact—not that he knew the real reason behind her move to Lount's Landing. As far as Johnny was concerned, she was simply the new editor of *Inside the Landing*.

It's a Colorful Life was a throwback in time, the sort of store you'd expect to find Jimmy Stewart wandering into in Bedford Falls. Plastic paint trays hung from the ceiling like oversized Christmas ornaments. Every wall surface was covered with clusters of paint chips, a kaleidoscope of reds and blues and golds and ochers, of greens and purples and pinks and whites. She wedged her way between aisles of metal bins overflowing with rollers and brushes and sandpaper and masking tape, dodging paint cans piled high into pyramids.

The faint scent of vanilla filled her nostrils. "Pure vanilla extract, the real stuff, not the imitation kind," a man's voice called from the back of the store. "Stir one tablespoon into a gallon of paint and you get rid of that new paint smell. I add it to every gallon I sell." He came out into the open, held out his hand, and smiled. "Emily Garland, I presume."

The main thing Emily noticed about Johnny Porter, beyond the fact he was roughly her age and drop-dead movie star gorgeous, were his eyes. Eyes so dark brown they looked black. Miner's eyes, her old pals at boarding school would have called them, the kind of eyes that could dig their way into the depth of your soul. Emily made an effort to collect herself. Acting like an infatuated high school student was not the way to start off her new life in Lount's Landing.

"And you must be Johnny Porter." Emily shook his hand, noticing his grip was firm but gentle. Thought his hand lingered a moment longer than necessary. "It's a pleasure to meet you."

"Likewise," Johnny said, although Emily got the distinct feeling he was assessing her. She wondered if she made the grade.

"I wanted to thank you, Johnny, for all your efforts to make my transition from Toronto easier. Getting the office space ready, arranging for the house rental with Urban-Huntzberger, all your notes about the businesses and shops along Main Street. I can't imagine what I would have done without you."

"Nonsense," Johnny said, waving aside her accolades. "That's what we call good, old-fashioned small town hospitality. As chairman of the Main Street Merchants' Association, I consider it part of my responsibilities. It's in the Association's best interests to have the editor of *Inside the Landing* championing our cause."

"Thank you, anyway."

"You're welcome, anyway." Johnny smiled. "So I take it the house is good? You're the first renter. The owner, Camilla Mortimer-Gilroy, purchased it a few months ago, a bank foreclosure. It was in tough shape, and that's putting a gloss on things. She had it renovated from top to bottom, paint, new countertops and cabinets in the kitchen and bath, refinished all the floors."

"The living room walls are bit greener than I'd like, but it's nothing I can't live with. It's just a short term rental." Emily stopped. Day one and she had almost blown her cover. She would have to be more circumspect if she stood any chance of keeping her assignment a secret. "Then again, I may live there for quite some time. I'm hoping to save up some money and buy a fixer-upper of my own." No need to mention the planned fixer-upper was in Toronto.

"Then there's no reason to live with a paint color you don't care for. I told Camilla not to go with Warm Winter Wheat. Sounds lovely and soft and golden, but it always looks green in a north facing light. Hay Bale would have been a much better choice for the room's exposure. It would warm up the room completely."

"Wow, you know a lot about color."

"I should, owning a paint store," Johnny said with a grin. "But the truth is color has always fascinated me. Did you know that in Victorian times, flowers were used as a way for men to communicate their feelings to the women they were courting? Social conventions restricted conversations for a variety of reasons, but sending flowers of a certain color or type allowed secretive messages to be sent. There were even floriography dictionaries." Johnny laughed. "Listen to me, going on and on. What I'm trying to say is that people should enjoy their surroundings, and choosing the right paint color is one way of adding to that enjoyment."

"You've sold me on the Hay Bale, though I should probably check with the owner first."

"Don't you worry about Camilla. We go way back. I was a friend of her late husband, Graham. I can still remember when Camilla moved to Lount's Landing to become mistress of the Gilroy Mansion. Created quite a stir. Everyone had expected Graham to marry a woman with connections to the family and plenty of her own money."

"I gather she had neither."

"At least none that anyone was aware of. After Graham died, Camilla turned most of the mansion into a Bed and Breakfast. Created more talk, not that she had much of a choice. Graham liked to live large on the family legacy, and he didn't have much in the way of insurance."

"When did he die?" Always the journalist, a bit too pushy for her own good, but this time she needn't have worried. It appeared Johnny liked nothing better than to talk. She made a mental note to be careful of what she said around him.

"He died about five years ago, snowmobiling accident. Rode out on the Dutch River before the ice was safe and sliced straight through. By the time anyone found him, it was already too late."

"What a horrible way to die."

"Doing what you love?" Johnny shook his head. "No, Graham would rather have died snowmobiling than doing anything else. He was always a risk taker. And he'd been riding on thin ice for years—quite literally, and in more ways than one. It was just a matter of time. I've often wondered if his death really was an accident."

"But what about Camilla? She must have been devastated."

"She was, although to be honest I was never quite sure what devastated her more, Graham's death or the fact he left her penniless. They'd been married less than a couple of years, and I think Graham kept his financial affairs close to the vest. But Camilla's got a keen business sense. She started out by fixing up one room and bath and renting it out. Five years later, she's got one of the finest Bed and Breakfasts in this part of Ontario."

"I'm looking forward to meeting her. Camilla sounds like she'd be a great interview. Readers love those sorts of stories."

"I've suggested as much to her, but she's publicity shy. Says she had enough of the media hounding her after Graham died."

Emily could understand that. Some reporters—like Kerri St. Amour—were positively ruthless. She would wait, be sure to try a gentler approach when the time was right.

"I'll remember that when I call on her."

"Someone you definitely want to interview is Arabella Carpenter."

Emily thought back to the notes Johnny had provided. "The owner of the new antiques shop on Main Street?"

"The Glass Dolphin. The grand opening is this weekend."

"What good timing. Covering the opening will give me some material for the publication. Plus it would be a great networking opportunity. I'm assuming other business owners will come by to support her."

"They will—at least everyone who belongs to MSMA—but I have to warn you. Arabella's an expert when it comes to antiques, and she's a charming woman, but she can also be a tad irascible. Proceed with caution is all I'm saying. If she thinks you have an ulterior motive, you're toast."

An ulterior motive? What was Johnny hinting at? Surely he didn't suspect...

"I don't think networking is an ulterior motive, but thanks for the heads up." Emily looked at her watch. It was getting late in the day, and she wanted to reread her notes about Arabella before heading over there. "I'll pay Arabella a visit first thing tomorrow morning."

"As long as you're going there, can I ask you for a favor? Would you deliver this invitation to Arabella? It will save me the trip. Not to mention a confrontation." He handed her two cream-colored envelopes. "There's one for you, too."

A confrontation? Interesting. "What's it for?"

"A presentation about a proposed new development. I understand from your boss that you know the presenter. A man by the name of Garrett Stonehaven."

Her boss, Michelle Ellis, had assured her their agreement was confidential, but she couldn't escape the feeling that Johnny was testing her. She contemplated her options and decided to go for surprise.

"Stonehaven's in Lount's Landing? I've covered his condo developments in *Urban Living* for years. He never struck me as a small town kind of guy."

"Consider this your opportunity to find out more." Johnny smiled and Emily thought she detected a hint of relief in his eyes. "Oh, and one more word of warning."

"Yes?"

"It would be best if you gave Arabella the invitation as you were leaving."

"Why?"

"Let's just say Arabella has been more than vocal about her vision of what's right for Main Street. And I don't think Garrett Stonehaven's plans play any part of it."

CHAPTER 3

The alarm clock radio came on at exactly 7:00 a.m., the sounds of *Hey Joe* filling the room. Arabella Carpenter pushed the snooze button, not just for the extra ten minutes of sleep it might afford her, but to drown out the music. She mostly loved the Classic Rock Q107 played, but she had never understood the appeal of Hendrix. Especially at 7:00 a.m. on a Tuesday.

Arabella dragged herself up and into the shower before the allotted ten minutes were up, knowing she had a busy week ahead. Saturday was the grand opening of the Glass Dolphin, her new antiques shop on Main Street.

There were some, among them her know-it-all ex-husband, Levon, who might say this wasn't the time to invest heart and soul—not to mention her hard-fought life's savings—into brick and mortar when so much of today's antiques trade was negotiated online. But while Arabella had considered hiring a web design firm from Toronto to "enhance her online presence," replacing lemon oil and old leather with search engines and live bidding was as foreign to her as relinquishing the tactile feel of page and paper for a Kindle.

She squeezed into a pair of faded jeans and threw on a souvenir sweatshirt from the Royal Ontario Museum, then raked her fingers through chin-length auburn curls, glad she'd abandoned her fling with the flat iron. A pair of sneakers, a down-filled jacket, and she was out the door.

Arabella's walk from her midtown rental to the Glass Dolphin took about twenty minutes, including a breakfast stop at the Sunrise Café for a take-out coffee and a toasted cinnamon raisin bagel. She enjoyed the journey to and from each day, even if exercise wasn't exactly on her top ten to-do list. She'd also come to appreciate the finer points of the town, though when Levon had dragged her here from Toronto a dozen years ago she couldn't see it. Her favorite part of these walks was seeing the gradual transition of Lount's Landing, the way the town was embracing its history. She loved the idea of being part of the revival.

Her route took her past the Main Street Elementary School. Two years ago, the school board had put it on their deaccessioned list, claiming the early architecture was too costly to modernize for the few children in the area. A few months ago a "For Sale" sign had been posted on the property. Last week the sign had been replaced with a large billboard announcing, "Another Property Sold by Poppy Spencer."

Arabella hoped a cutting-edge developer would convert the space into loft condominiums. She could imagine herself living there, the school grounds home to green space, some picnic tables, a pond with ducks and geese, maybe a fountain that lit up at night. She'd read about other schools being repurposed. Why not in Lount's Landing?

She arrived at the Glass Dolphin to find a slender woman in a thin coat shivering by the front door. Arabella had made similar wardrobe miscalculations in November, a month where the prevailing Lount's Landing winds could be as unpredictable as an eBay auction.

"Sorry to keep you waiting, but we're not open until Saturday," Arabella said, pointing to a sign in the window. Something was vaguely familiar about the woman, though she couldn't stick a pin in it. Early thirties. Hazel eyes with a bit of a fleck. Dark brown hair tied into a ponytail, a red knit beret sloped back from her forehead. *She wears it well*, Arabella thought with a touch of envy. Her own attempts at beret wearing had resulted in the rather unflattering look of a Victorian shower cap crossed with a tea cozy.

Mind you, the Coach handbag Beret Girl carried was *definitely* a knockoff. The single rows of Coach's signature "C," and the way the C's didn't quite line up at the center. It was a dead giveaway.

Arabella prided herself on her ability to spot the real from the reproduction. The antiques world was full of fakes. But not the Glass Dolphin. Within her walls, everything would be original, from the exposed beam ceiling and the carefully restored pine plank floors to the merchandise she sold.

Authenticity mattered.

"I'm sorry to intrude," the woman said. "My name's Emily Garland. I'm—"

That's where she'd seen her before. "I thought I recognized you. You're the writer from *Urban Living*. They always include your photograph under the Contributors section." Arabella opened the door. "Come in, you're starting to look a tad blue. Ignore the myriad of boxes. This week is all about unpacking and setting up displays. The larger pieces of furniture will be delivered from storage on Thursday."

"Thanks, I'm frozen solid. I'm surprised you read the Contributors page. I always figured the only folks who looked at it were family members and envious writers. But what's an antiques shop owner in Lount's Landing doing reading *Urban Living?*"

"The better question would be, what's a writer for *Urban Living* doing in Lount's Landing?"

"Fair enough." Emily handed Arabella a business card. "Actually, I left *Urban Living*. I'm the new editor of *Inside the Landing.*"

"So *you're* the one. I heard the owner finally sold the magazine. Wanted to retire for a while, but it turned out to be a bit of a tough sell. Not surprising. It was a bit tired. Not many people bothered to read it; went straight from the porch to the blue bin." Arabella blushed. "I'm sorry. I shouldn't have been so blunt."

"No worries, you're absolutely right. I wouldn't have read the old magazine either. But I have big plans for a new format. More coverage of local events, plenty of photographs, in-depth interviews with local business owners. Give it a bit of a personality." Emily shrugged. "It seemed like a good opportunity."

"It sounds nice. Or at least nicer."

"I hope so. That's why I'm here. I was talking to Johnny Porter."

Arabella nodded. Johnny was good people, and a strong advocate for the businesses on Main Street. He'd even started the Main Street Merchants' Association, of which she was now a proud member. If she had her way, history would be making a comeback in the Landing.

Emily said, "Johnny tells me you're planning a grand opening on Saturday and Sunday. I'd like the Glass Dolphin to be *Inside the Landing*'s first big feature story. I could cover the entire weekend, include some background information. The story behind the store. What do you think? It's free PR for you, and it would give me the kick-start I need."

Arabella contemplated the offer. No question the Glass Dolphin could use the free press... as long as it was truly free. She'd heard of publications that offered free PR and then tried to upsell it with a paid advertising pitch. Then again, outside of the unfortunate choice of fake purse, Emily appeared to be perfectly legit. And she knew from personal experience how difficult it could be coming to a small town where everyone knew one another. If it hadn't been for Levon, she might have gone back to the city within a few short weeks.

"We can try it, Emily, see how it goes. I'm opening at eleven on Saturday, but I wouldn't mind showing you around on Friday. Everything will be set up by then. Why don't you come by after lunch, say about one o'clock? I can give you the grand tour. That way, come Saturday, I won't feel as if I have to entertain you, and you'll be able to meet other folks from town without worrying about following me around."

"Sounds like a plan. And I promise, there are absolutely no strings attached." It was as if she'd read Arabella's mind. "Now let me get out of your way."

Emily was halfway out the door when she turned around. "I'd forget my head if it wasn't attached. I have something for you from Johnny Porter." She reached into her purse and handed over a cream-colored envelope.

Arabella opened the envelope the minute Emily was gone. Inside was an invitation to a "Special Presentation" the following Tuesday, hosted by real estate developer Garrett Stonehaven of HavenSent Developments, Inc. A nice, handwritten note from Johnny encouraged her to attend.

Garrett Stonehaven. Wasn't he the Toronto developer Emily Garland was always writing about in *Urban Living*? Now the two of them were here in Lount's Landing, which could have been a coincidence... except for one thing.

Arabella didn't believe in coincidence.

CHAPTER 4

Garrett Stonehaven stepped away from the lectern to address the five people sitting in the room. "And that, ladies and gentlemen, is the dry run. What do you think? Are we ready for next Tuesday evening? Can we sell our plan to the good people of Lount's Landing?"

"Yes," all but Carter Dixon said in unison.

Stonehaven crossed his arms and studied the lone holdout through narrowed eyes. For a long time no one spoke.

"I still think the school is going to be problematic," Carter said eventually. "When the members of the Redevelopment Team were asked to consider properties, it was for a condominium conversion, not some big box store. Everyone agreed the Main Street Elementary School was perfect. Including you, at the time."

"We've been over this time and again," Stonehaven said, trying hard to maintain his composure. He clenched and unclenched his fists. What part of making money did this hick from Hicksville not understand?

"Converting the school into condos is not economically feasible, Carter. StoreHaven will require less capital outlay and encourage local business investment. Not to mention your personal takeaway as a profit-sharing member of the HavenSent Solutions team."

"I appreciate the monetary incentives, and I'm all for businesses becoming invested in historic Main Street. I'm merely suggesting we introduce the plans for StoreHaven a bit later on. Get revitalizing first."

"We have to be upfront if we're going to have any sense of credibility. Particularly if we're hoping to encourage investors, which, I might remind you, has always been the plan."

"But the school—"

"Hasn't been used for the last couple of years. Surely nobody expected it to stay vacant forever?"

"Vacant, no, but nobody's expecting this." Carter Dixon looked at the other team members. "Am I right?"

No one responded. A couple of the members looked down at their feet.

Nor will they respond, Stonehaven thought with satisfaction. Nothing and nobody would get in the way of this plan. Not as long as he was running things. And it was high time this rural renegade accepted it. Nonetheless, he had to at least give the appearance of concession. "What if we titled the presentation something like Neighbors Helping Neighbors?"

Carter snorted. "As opposed to neighbors screwing neighbors, Garrett? Or businesses screwing businesses? Because that's what it sounds like to me."

"Then you don't understand my concept, Carter. And if you don't, others might not either." Stonehaven closed his eyes and thought for a moment, snapped them back open when the idea came to him. How was it he hadn't thought of it before?

"What if we circle the entire concept back to the school, let folks know upfront that the school is the cornerstone of a renewed community." Stonehaven smiled. "What if we call it The ABC's of Revitalization: Neighbors Helping Neighbors."

"That might work," Carter conceded. "At least we're making the effort to be honest."

The other team members nodded.

"Not only will it work, it's bloody brilliant," Stonehaven said. His mind and body started to relax. *Time to start playing the game.*

Stonehaven watched the team leave the Community Center. He slipped a dollar into the hallway vending machine for a bottle of overpriced water, walked back into the conference room, and kicked the wall, hard. It didn't make him feel any better.

He collected his materials from the lectern, sat down at a long table at the side of the room, and considered his plan for the umpteenth time. Reread his notes, flipped through the PowerPoint, reviewed the handouts, looked over the blueprints and the architects' renderings, the financial analysis and the business case. It may have been a week until his official presentation to the townspeople, but he was nothing if not a perfectionist. You didn't get ranked as number one in *Urban Living's* first annual "Top 40 Before 40" by being sloppy. Didn't matter that he'd slid in under the deadline a week before his fortieth birthday, or that he'd greased a few palms to get the nod.

He expected—no, demanded—the same degree of dedication and discipline from everyone who worked for him. And Carter Dixon concerned him. Until now, he'd always had the same team based out of Toronto, people he could trust—as long as he paid them twice what the job was worth. Money could be a powerful motivator.

Coming to Lount's Landing meant getting in cozy with the community. So he'd gone against his instincts and brought a handpicked team of local business people on board, folks who had an interest in revitalizing historic Main Street, not to mention lining their own pockets. He'd been confident in his final decision. Everyone had appeared to buy into the concept, including Carter Dixon.

Sycophants.

Stonehaven wasn't fooled by the way Carter had acquiesced. He could sense trouble the same way a bloodhound could catch a scent. No question about it, he would have to terminate Carter's employment contract. The only decision was how and when to execute the termination. Everything about this project hinged on the Main Street merchants buying into it.

He should have seen it coming. Wasn't Lount's Landing named after Samuel Lount? What kind of town was named for a man who'd been hanged for treason?

Mind you, even Samuel Lount had his loyal supporters. The same would hold true for the traitorous Mr. Dixon, although arranging a hanging would be out of the question. An accidental death, on the other hand, might have possibilities.

Stonehaven got up and started to pace. He hated when things got complicated. It was time to talk things over with the one person he could trust, the one person who believed in him back when he was plain old Garry Stone. He picked up his cell and pressed 2-1-5, listened to the ringtone, one, two, three. Waited for the brief voice mail message to finish.

"Millie," Stonehaven said, after the beep. "We need to talk."

CHAPTER 5

Emily had spent the rest of Tuesday getting her house in order, buying a few groceries, and going for a one hour run. The best way for her to get the lay of the land, she had decided, was to traverse the streets on foot. In doing so, she got an immediate sense of the community and the people who lived there.

She'd also had a chance to think about her meeting with Arabella Carpenter, and she was more than satisfied with the results. Johnny had warned her that Arabella could be testy, but all Emily detected was a guardedness that could have come from a distrust of journalists in general. She didn't take it personally; years of freelancing had given her a hard shell. The Kerri St. Amours of the world gave the job a bad reputation.

Emily found herself feeling a tiny bit sorry for the antiques shop owner. Opening on Saturday and the furniture not coming out of storage until Thursday? Talk about working close to deadline. What about advertising? The sole form of advertising appeared to be a sign on the door and word of mouth. Maybe that kind of thing was enough in a small town, but a spread in *Inside the Landing* couldn't hurt.

Wednesday's first destination would be the Sunrise Café. According to her notes, it was also on Main Street, six blocks south of her office. The restaurant had been open for less than three months, but Johnny had said it was already a local magnet for decent coffee, home-style cooking, and a healthy dollop of local gossip.

The Sunrise Café was housed within a narrow, brown brick Victorian. A brass historical plaque indicated the building was once the establishment of Murdoch Gilroy, Esquire. Emily wondered if Murdoch Gilroy was any relation to her landlord's late husband, and suspected he was. A small wooden sign showed the hours as Monday through Saturday, 6:30 a.m. to 12:30 p.m., closed Sundays.

She tried to think of a restaurant in downtown Toronto that was only open for breakfast and closed on Sundays. None came to mind. Real estate was too expensive to rely only on bacon and eggs for income.

The front door was painted a bright, sunshiny yellow. Emily pulled on a brass handle and made her way inside. She was surprised to find the place packed.

The restaurant was charming in a country cozy way, with colorful prints of roosters and other farm life adorning the walls. Overhead, ceiling fans with alternating blades of bright yellow and orange spun lazily, circulating the smell of coffee, cinnamon, and buttered toast.

A tall, glass display case filled with fruit, homemade pies, and muffins separated the diners from an open-style kitchen. A basket of individually wrapped date squares and oversized chocolate chip cookies were strategically placed next to the cash register. Small town or not, whoever owned the Sunrise Café had business savvy.

A blonde waitress was the only server in sight. She was rail thin, early twenties, with inky blue eyes framed by heavily mascaraed lashes.

The tables were artfully arranged to maximize space while providing a modicum of privacy. A small bay window overlooked Main Street, a vase of bright yellow roses filling the nook.

She took a seat at the table for one and attempted to look inconspicuous. A burly man wearing a Toronto Maple Leafs hockey jersey glared at her, his down-filled ski jacket draped carelessly over the spare chair, the sleeves flopping on the floor.

Emily glared right back when the guy began grumbling loudly about "city slickers," the irony of supporting an NHL hockey team apparently lost on him. Last time she'd looked, Toronto was a city. A big one. She watched as the man tore a strip off the waitress for leaving peanut butter packets in the jam basket.

The poor thing tripped over the bulky ski jacket trying to get at the basket. Face red, lips trembling, the waitress pulled herself up, plucked the peanut butter packets from the offending basket, tossed them into her apron pocket, and muttered an apology. She took a deep breath, grabbed a plasticized menu from a stack on the counter, and made her way over to Emily's table.

"Welcome to the Sunrise Café, and my apologies for the show. My name's February. I'll be your server."

"Emily. I'm new in town. I took over *Inside the Landing*." She caught February's confused look. "It's a monthly magazine."

"Sorry about that. I'm fairly new here." February leaned over conspiratorially. "I'm also a writer."

Who wasn't? Emily wished she had a dollar for every time someone told her that. At least the girl wasn't claiming to be a poet. The worst was when they started spouting haiku.

"I'm not published," February acknowledged, as if sensing Emily's hesitation, "but I do have plenty of stories to tell." Her voice dropped to a whisper. "Working in a restaurant, you see and hear it all."

See and hear it all. This pasty-faced young woman might come in handy. "I'm sure you do, February. How about we talk when you're not so busy?" Emily riffled around in her wallet and pulled out a business card. "Here you go. Call me any time."

February glanced at the card and slipped it into her apron pocket. "Thanks. I better get a move on or Ms. Moroziuk—I mean Gloria—will have my hide." She motioned toward the kitchen, where a sturdily built woman, Gloria presumably, was working a hot grill laden with eggs, bacon, sausage, and pancakes. "Can I get you a tea or coffee to start?"

"Coffee would be great, thank you." Emily handed back the menu. "Do you have anything remotely vegetarian?"

"How's a BLT without the bacon sound?"

Emily considered. She'd been trying to make the switch to vegetarianism—mostly because of her ex-fiancé, Kevin—but she couldn't forget how good bacon tasted. Especially when it was all crispy. And all the veggies in the world hadn't stopped Kevin from dumping her. Eating bacon now and again couldn't hurt. Could it?

"I'll have the BLT, with the B."

February wrote the order on her pad before making her way toward the kitchen. Emily pulled out her tablet. It was always good to eavesdrop under the guise of reading, and she had Johnny Porter's PDF list of Main Street merchants on there. She could pass the time trying to figure out who was who.

Johnny was right. The Sunrise Café was a hotbed of gossip. It wasn't long before Stonehaven's upcoming presentation became the source of heated debate. Hockey Jersey kicked things off, a major league scowl spread across his face.

"I don't get where you're coming from, Chantal," Hockey Jersey said, addressing an athletic young woman sitting at the table next to him. "How can you possibly think a big city developer will know what's good for the town?"

"I didn't say it would be good for the town, Carter. I said we should keep an open mind." The woman's hair was black as a raven's back and cropped close. With the exception of a pair of diamond stud earrings, she appeared to be decked out in yoga wear from head to toe.

Emily referred to the PDF and pegged her as Chantal Van Schyndle, owner of the Serenity Spa and Yoga Studio. She assumed Hockey Jersey was Carter Dixon, owner of Slap Shot, a sporting goods store that Johnny wrote was "barely hanging on."

"Chantal's right," said another man. He had the ruddy complexion of someone who spent much of his life outdoors. "Let's wait until we hear the presentation next week and have all the facts."

"You think we'll get all the facts, Ned? You're a dreamer," said Carter. "Then again, maybe it takes a dreamer to open a store that sells nothing but bird seed."

Ned's complexion had gone from ruddy to raging, but he managed to keep his voice low. "Birdsong sells a lot more than bird seed, Carter. We sell supplies for backyard birders, something you would know if you weren't so wrapped up in your precious Maple Losers."

Emily checked the PDF again. Ned would be Ned Turcotte. "Bit of a temper," Johnny had written, "but keeps it under wraps most times."

"This will be the Leafs year," Carter said.

"Who's the dreamer now, eh, Carter?"

"Gentlemen, please, let's all take a chill pill." Gloria came out of the kitchen, wiping her hands on her apron. "This here's a respectable establishment. If you want to get rowdy, take it outside and don't find your way back."

Emily was surprised at how quickly Carter and Ned complied with Gloria's request. Clearly this was one woman nobody wanted to mess with.

<hr />

"What do you think, Emily?" February asked after Gloria had gone back to her grill. She gestured to the room at large. "Everyone, this here's Emily Garland, she recently moved to town. She's gonna be the editor of *Inside the Landing.*"

A murmur of "how's it goings," and "pleased to meet you's" filtered through the restaurant. Carter glared at her. Emily ignored him.

"What do I think about what?"

Dead silence. Emily looked around the room and knew she'd made a mistake. No one believed she hadn't been listening. She was grateful when a successful-looking businesswoman in her late forties came to her rescue. Steel gray eyes partially hidden behind dark designer frames, short brown hair artfully highlighted with glints of copper and gold.

"Poppy Spencer," the woman said by way of introduction. "We've been discussing Garrett Stonehaven's purchase of the Main Street Elementary School, and speculating on what he might do with it. Some forward-thinking folks believe he might bring business and investment opportunities to the town. Others, like Carter Dixon here, aren't quite ready to step out of the past."

"Spoken like the real estate agent who sold the school down the river," Carter said. His face had become red and bloated. He reminded Emily of a pot of borscht about to boil over.

"You're being ridiculous," Poppy said.

"Down the river," Carter said, his face getting redder.

Poppy let out an exasperated sigh. "If I hadn't sold the property to him, someone else would have."

"Paddling, paddling, paddling down the river."

"Grow up, Carter." Poppy turned to Emily. "What we should be debating is whether commercialism should trump traditional town values, or whether the two can co-exist. The answer is, it's not that simple, now that the mill at Miakoda Falls closed down."

Emily silently cursed Michelle Ellis for not mentioning a mill in Miakoda Falls. Or Miakoda Falls, come to that.

"Closed down and took away plenty of good paying jobs," Poppy continued. "Since then, most of the Main Street shop owners have been struggling to keep their heads above water. A successful real estate developer like Garrett Stonehaven might be able to help."

"Or drown us completely," Carter said, pulling at his collar. He began making loud gurgling noises. It might have been amusing except for one thing: by the time anyone realized Carter was going into anaphylactic shock, he was dead.

The atmosphere in the Café quickly turned from conversation to controlled chaos. Emily followed the action, keeping every detail fresh in her mind: Poppy Spencer called 9-1-1. Ned Turcotte attempted CPR. Gloria Moroziuk searched Carter Dixon's pockets for an EpiPen and found nothing but a wallet and a couple of butterscotch candies.

The paramedics made good time, assessed the situation, and told everyone to stand back, there might still be a chance of revival. Emily caught the look between the two EMTs as they loaded Carter onto the gurney. No amount of epinephrine was going to save Carter Dixon. But they weren't about to let Gloria's business hang in the balance. Gloria followed the paramedics, leaving a shaken and mascara-streaked February in charge of closing up. Meals were on the house.

Emily's journalistic instincts kicked in faster than a runner's high. There was bound to be an official investigation, and the closer she was to it, the better. "I think we should make of list of everyone who's here, along with our contact information. I'd be happy to take that on."

Poppy Spencer wasn't having it. "I realize you're a stranger in this town, Emily, but we're all friends here, in spite of what you may have surmised from our earlier debate. What you're suggesting is completely unnecessary and downright insulting."

"I'm not trying to insult anyone, Poppy. I'm suggesting it might be a good idea to have a list, in the event the police are called in."

"The police? You're not insinuating anything about this was deliberate?"

"Of course not. But if Carter dies, there's bound to be an investigation, if not by the police, then by the coroner's office."

"This isn't Toronto, Emily. If and when that is the case, each and every one of us will tell the police whatever we know. The workings of a small town are considerably different than those in a big city. You should remember that if you want to fit in."

Was that a warning? Emily glanced around the restaurant and saw the others nodding in agreement. Annoyed and more than a little embarrassed, she apologized with as much grace as she could muster, tossed some change on the table to cover February's tip, and hustled her way up Main Street to her office. She'd write up her own damn list when she got there, along with her best memory of what everyone had said and done.

CHAPTER 6

E mily was so lost in her thoughts that she collided face first into the ladder propped up against the front façade of It's a Colorful Life. Johnny Porter was standing on the top rung holding a string of Christmas lights.

"Penny for your thoughts." A warm smile lit up Johnny's face as he looked down. "Or should I say a nickel, since Canada gave up the penny?"

"God, I'm sorry, Johnny. My mind's off somewhere else."

"Anything wrong?"

"I just witnessed a horrible accident at the Sunrise Café."

"Accident?" Johnny dropped the string of lights, covering the sidewalk with splinters of blue and green glass.

Emily jumped back, narrowly missing the curb.

Johnny cursed under his breath and climbed down the ladder.

"What kind of accident? Is Gloria okay?"

"Gloria's fine, upset, obviously, but that's to be expected."

Good grief, she was making a complete bollix of this. She took a calming breath and recapped the events as succinctly as she could, starting with Carter's objection to Stonehaven's plan, and finishing with the paramedics.

"I got the impression they knew he was dead."

"They probably didn't want to leave Gloria stuck with a body in the restaurant, waiting for the coroner. In Lount's Landing, everyone has everyone's back, and Gloria's been a volunteer at the hospital's auxiliary for years. It would be a lot less complicated for all concerned if a doctor at the hospital pronounced him."

Emily had suspected as much, although she wasn't sure if she entirely approved. She recalled Poppy's warning and decided to keep her opinion to herself.

"I just wish I had done something to try to save Carter. But I thought he was being overly dramatic, mimicking a man drowning. I suppose we all did."

She remembered the way Carter had tugged at his collar, his face blown up like some sort of helium balloon, the horrible gurgling sounds coming from deep inside his throat.

"It must have been terrible to watch. Any idea what caused it?"

"Earlier, Carter had blasted the waitress, February, for leaving peanut butter packets in the jam basket. So I'm assuming he's allergic to peanut butter. But February took the packets away, so it couldn't have been that."

"It doesn't make sense. Gloria would have been careful. She knew about Carter's peanut allergy. Everybody did. He made certain of it. Carter could be extremely vocal. February Fassbender, on the other hand, is a relatively new recruit. She started working for Gloria a week or so ago. It's possible she wasn't aware. What I don't understand is why he didn't have an EpiPen. He always carried one. Another thing he thought everyone would want to know about."

"He might have forgotten it."

"That's one explanation," Johnny said, but he didn't seem convinced. "I need to make a couple of phone calls, starting with Gloria. But I want to hear your version of events again, if you're not in too much of a hurry."

Retelling it would help solidify her memory—and spending time with Johnny wasn't exactly a hardship. "I was heading up to my office, but I suppose another few minutes won't hurt," she said.

"Thank you. Now let's go inside. You can take a look around while I try to reach Gloria."

Johnny disappeared behind a door marked "Employees Only." Emily wandered around the store. Beyond the paint and supplies there wasn't much to see, although a small section of wall sporting a selection of plaques and photographs piqued her interest.

In addition to a plaque declaring It's a Colorful Life as a "Proud Member of the Main Street Merchants' Association," there were a number of plaques signifying sponsorship of local charities and team sports—everything from hockey and baseball to soccer and bowling—along with an assortment of signed photographs thanking Johnny for his support.

One photograph stood out from the rest, a faded color print of two teenaged boys standing on a wooden dock, a river behind them. Emily guessed their ages to be about fifteen and seventeen. The older boy had his arm slung protectively over the younger boy's shoulder.

Emily recognized a young Johnny Porter, shorter, scrawnier, a hint of adolescent acne, but the same dark eyes, black, smoldering, already sensuous. She figured the older boy for Johnny's brother. There was a strong likeness around the nose and chin. The two of them were smiling widely for the camera.

"My brother, Jake," Johnny said, startling Emily. She hadn't heard him coming.

"I spotted the resemblance. Are you still close?"

"He drowned the day after that photograph was taken."

"I'm sorry." Emily put her hand on Johnny's.

Johnny pulled away. "It was a long time ago."

"Some things don't heal with time."

Johnny changed the subject. "Gloria asked how you were doing. I told her you were here, that you filled me in, that you were fine."

"How is she doing?"

"She's a wreck. Carter didn't make it." Johnny pursed his lips. "There will be a police investigation. Carter's fiancée, Tiffany Branson, is accusing Gloria Moroziuk of murder."

"Why would Tiffany do that?"

Johnny considered Emily for a moment. "Ah hell, this is a small town. You'll find out soon enough. Gloria and Carter were part of Garrett Stonehaven's redevelopment team. Gloria and Carter had been arguing about it. Carter didn't trust Stonehaven. Apparently he didn't approve of Stonehaven's plans for the elementary school, though Gloria didn't get into details. Some sort of confidentiality agreement."

"That's no reason to suspect Gloria of murder."

"There's more. Gloria and Carter have been friends since childhood. A few years back, they purchased the low-rise apartment building next to the elementary school. They thought the apartment might be a good investment."

"Was it?"

"They manage, but not much more. There's always repair work to be done, and their tenants tend to be transient. Not all of them leave with the rent paid. Gloria was tired of being a landlord. It was the main reason she opened the Sunrise Café. She was looking for a way out."

"Let me guess. Garrett Stonehaven came along and made them a generous offer."

Johnny nodded. "Gloria wanted to sell. Carter didn't."

"And if one of them died?"

"The other would own the property outright."

Emily took a minute to process the information. She was about to speak when Johnny interrupted.

"I know what you're thinking. Gloria had the means, opportunity, and motive to murder Carter Dixon."

"Actually, I was going to ask if Stonehaven knew Carter's position."

"I'd have to say yes. Carter never had an opinion he wasn't willing to share. Why?"

"Just curious," Emily said. But she was thinking about her mother, the way she'd publicly battled with Stonehaven over his CondoHaven on the Park in downtown Toronto.

And her mother also happened to be dead.

CHAPTER 7

When she arrived at the office of *Inside the Landing*, Emily was still mulling over the events at the Café, along with everything Johnny had told her. Calling it an office might have been putting a shine on things, though, as it was basically a repurposed bedroom, eight by ten, housed inside a converted rooming house that had seen better days.

The other tenants included a guy who specialized in computer repairs and a husband and wife team who sold mail-order merchandise, mostly crap from what Emily could determine. Did anyone really believe a pair of overpriced spandex shorts could eliminate cellulite?

The owner of the row house was a thin, bald, bird-like man with heavily veined hands, sagging skin, and nicotine-stained teeth. He also occupied the largest space in the building with Print It! In addition to printing *Inside the Landing*, his presses produced everything from sales flyers to wedding invitations—and, in all likelihood, Garrett Stonehaven's brochures.

Emily sat down at her computer to record what she'd seen and heard. She was just about done when there was a knock on the door. Curious, she scurried to see who was paying her a visit. She was none too happy to see Garrett Stonehaven standing there.

"Garrett. To what do I owe the pleasure?"

Stonehaven pushed his way past her as if she were invisible, and promptly sank into her comfy, secondhand sofa. Emily resented that he had entered without being asked. She resented him sitting on her sofa even more.

She sat back into the chair at her desk. It was either sit there or stand. No chance in this lifetime was she going to sit down next to him. "What can I do for you?"

"What are you doing?"

So much for small talk. "Doing?"

"In Lount's Landing?"

"I'm the new editor of *Inside the Landing*—which you must know, since you managed to find me here."

"You never struck me as the small-town type."

"Ditto. And yet, here we both are."

"Did Michelle Ellis send you?"

Did he know about her deal with Michelle? And if so, how? "Why do you ask?"

"Don't play games. Did Michelle Ellis send you?"

"Indirectly."

"Why?"

"She hired me on behalf of Urban-Huntzberger."

"Again, the question would be why?"

"Why did Urban-Huntzberger hire me? Or why did I accept the job?" Emily fixed Stonehaven with what she hoped would pass for a steely-eyed glare.

"Both."

"I could ask why it's your business."

"Let's just say I have a vested interest in making sure my plans for Lount's Landing come to fruition. I would take a dim view of any interference, editorial or otherwise. A *very* dim view."

"Is that a threat?"

"Merely a statement of fact."

"You overestimate my fascination with you and your life, Garrett. I was offered the opportunity to take on a new job with career potential. I took it. I didn't know you were here until Johnny Porter handed me the invitation to your presentation."

"I suppose I have to take your word for it. But know this. There will be a heavy price to pay for anyone who attempts to sabotage either me or this project."

Emily bristled at the allegation. How dare Stonehaven come to her office and start bullying her? "And what will you do, Garrett? Ruin their reputation in the same way you managed to pulverize my mother's? Or maybe you can drive them to take their own life, arrange an accident?"

"Pulverize reputations? Drive people to suicide? Arrange an accident? What an overactive imagination you have, Emily. It sounds like you've been watching too many movies."

Emily fought the urge to drive the smug look on Stonehaven's face right into next week. "I've only been in town a couple of days, Garrett, but even *I* know that Carter Dixon wasn't exactly your biggest fan."

"So? What of it?"

"So Carter Dixon is also dead."

Stonehaven raised his eyebrows. "Carter's dead?"

Was he truly surprised by the news? A decade of interviewing and writing about the man and Emily still couldn't read him. "Yes. Earlier today. At the Sunrise Café. The police are investigating. Unfortunately, I was there to witness it."

"Death does seem to follow you around, doesn't it?" Stonehaven said. "First your mother and now Carter Dixon. You might want to heed my earlier warning. You know what they say. Things tend to come in threes."

"What the hell is *that* supposed to mean?" Emily asked, not sure she wanted the answer. She needn't have worried.

The bastard walked out without answering.

A confrontation with Stonehaven might have sent some folks to the nearest bar. Others might go in for chocolate or some other form of comfort food. Emily got her headspace back by going out for a five-mile run. By the time she returned to her office forty-five minutes later, she was feeling refreshed and ready to tackle what she'd come to think of as her investigation. Regardless of whether it was an accident or something more sinister, her nose smelled a story in Carter Dixon's death. But first she needed to do some research. Not knowing anything about Miakoda Falls had almost put her in an embarrassing position at the Sunrise Café. She was determined not to let it happen again.

A few hours spent online, supplemented by a couple more at the local library, filled in most of the blanks. Not only was the library stocked with volumes of the area's history, the head librarian, a silver-haired sexagenarian, was more than willing to share her knowledge.

The basic facts were this: Cedar County was a sprawling 975-square-mile stretch of land comprised of three burgeoning towns in the southernmost corridor, all within commuting distance to Toronto. Agricultural lands and gradually expanding villages lay in the middle. In the north were the tri-communities of Miakoda Falls, Lount's Landing, and Lakeside. The latter was largely considered cottage country, an enclave of summer vacation homes, albeit with a modest core of permanent residents, mostly retired.

Policing the area was the Cedar County Tri-Community Policing Center, affectionately known as the One-Trick-Pokey. Located inside the original train station in Miakoda Falls, the Center had been opened at a time when the towns had been growing in leaps and bounds, fueled by a buoyant economy, high paying jobs in the mill, and rumors of an automotive plant coming to the area.

The mill had closed down, just as Poppy Spencer had informed Emily, and the automaker had fallen upon recessionary times. Any plans for opening a new plant had been abandoned, causing much of the tri-town's workforce to seek housing and employment opportunities elsewhere.

Nonetheless, the One-Trick-Pokey remained, although its primary role now involved registering bicycles and handing out pamphlets on boating safety and Neighborhood Watch programs. The Lakeside cottagers expected—no demanded— a high standard of service for their maximized waterfront tax dollars and minimized part-time residential status.

As best as Emily could gather, getting assigned to the Cedar County Tri-Community Policing Center generally meant an officer's career had stagnated beyond redemption. She could imagine the response to Tiffany Branson's telephone call questioning her fiancé's death by peanut butter. According to the librarian, Tiffany wasn't a stranger to calling the police. "An active imagination, Tiff has.

Started when she discovered Nancy Drew. Liked to pretend Lount's Landing was River Heights."

Emily decided to talk to Gloria Moroziuk, February Fassbender, and Tiffany Branson. She figured Tiffany would be busy making funeral arrangements, and a call to the Sunrise Café resulted in nothing more than a recorded message saying the restaurant would be closed until the following Monday.

She could wait. In the meantime, there was one day until the dry run with Arabella at the Glass Dolphin. Tomorrow she'd try to learn a little bit about the antiques business, show Arabella she took her job seriously.

If Johnny was right—and there was no reason to doubt him—Arabella would be less than thrilled with anything Stonehaven might have up his sleeve, which suited Emily perfectly. She just had to find a way to ignite that particular fire, because the one thing Stonehaven didn't react well to was opposition.

Emily couldn't wait to give to him.

CHAPTER 8

Arabella surveyed the stack of unopened boxes. The thought of unpacking years of inventory might have been daunting to some, but not to her. She was determined to savor every moment.

She'd been dreaming about owning an antiques shop for ten years, first with Levon, and then without him. No one could take it away now.

But Levon had taught her well, Arabella realized with a trace of nostalgia. She remembered the days when they'd go picking together: estate sales, yard sales, auctions. Levon had an eye for finding a bargain in the rough. It was unfortunate his idea of picking things up went beyond antiques. For him, everything in life came down to the thrill of the hunt.

But he had taken her on as an apprentice when she had nowhere to go and no one to go to, and for that she would be forever grateful. Under Levon's tutelage, Arabella learned to love antiques for the history they told, the stories they shared. Take clocks. She could pinpoint the region a clock was made simply because of the primary and secondary woods selected. The same held true for antique furniture. No cheap "Made in China" knockoffs back in the nineteenth century. Craftsmen took pride in their work, unlike today's shoddy built-in obsolescence.

It was close to four o'clock before Arabella stopped, exhausted and hungry. She admired her wall of clocks. The styles were a nice assortment: regulators and banjos, schoolhouse and steeples, gingerbreads, and ogees. Tomorrow morning she'd hang up the vintage posters, the oil paintings and watercolors, the maps and mosaics, before the movers arrived with the furniture. Everything was going to be perfect.

She sat down on top of a stack of flattened boxes and began to cry.

"Am I crazy for thinking I can make a go of it on my own?" Arabella asked. She was perched on a wooden bar stool at The Hanged Man's Noose, munching morosely on an order of Full Noose Nachos, all gooey cheese and ground beef, sour cream and spicy salsa, guacamole and pimento olives. A half-empty glass of chardonnay was close at hand.

"Of course you're not crazy," said Betsy Ehrlich, deftly pouring draft beer for two men sitting at the end of the bar, watching television.

"Maybe I can still get my old job back."

"You're kidding, right? That job at McLelland Insurance was sucking the life out of you."

"You're right, you're right. I know you're right." Arabella took a generous sip of her wine.

"Do you really think I have a chance?"

"Arabella, you're going to be the pride of Main Street."

"You have to say that. You're my friend."

"True, but I also know what it takes to run a business on Main Street. And you, Arabella Carpenter, have the magic combination."

With the exception of the two men, the pub, for all its phenomenal nineteenth-century saloon décor, was deserted. Not exactly a magic combination, but Arabella decided it was best not to go there. "What's the magic combination?"

"Passion. Knowledge. Integrity. Plus you care about all those dusty old things."

"Those dusty old things are antiques," Arabella said, but she was smiling. Betsy could always lift her mood. Not to mention the Full Noose Nachos, which were to die for.

"Okay, so that's settled. Now you can do me a favor."

"Anything."

"I've been working on a signature drink, a house martini. I'd like you to try it."

Arabella was more into Australian chardonnay than hard liquor, no matter how fancied up it was, but she had to admit having a signature drink was trendy. And trendy couldn't hurt, even in a place like Lount's Landing.

"What's in it?"

"Blueberry vodka, triple sec, and blueberry juice."

"Sounds yummy. What are you going to call it?"

"A Treasontini."

"I love it," Arabella said, laughing. "Not only do you evoke images of a hanged man, you remind us why and how Samuel Lount met his death. But what's the occasion?"

"You know that real estate developer, Garrett Stonehaven? The one who's always in the news—that tall, dark, handsome HavenSent guy?"

Arabella nodded. She was no longer laughing.

"He's here. In Lount's Landing. Arrived a couple of weeks ago. He's staying at the Gilroy Mansion."

Arabella nodded again. She didn't trust herself to speak.

Betsy chattered away, mixing up a Treasontini at the same time. "He's been in here a few times, always alone. Always orders the same red wine, Châteauneuf-du-Pape."

"You stock Châteauneuf-du-Pape here? Isn't it a bit pricey?" Business must be better than she thought. Like most pubs, Betsy's markup on wine, beer, and liquor was substantial.

"Definitely pricier than my usual selection, but Johnny told me Châteauneuf-du-Pape is one of Stonehaven's few vices. So I took a flyer and bought a case at the liquor store. Figured worst-case scenario, I could always return them."

"Clever."

"I thought so," Betsy said, a self-satisfied expression on her face. "Stonehaven has a plan to revitalize Main Street. It sounds exciting."

"Have you seen the plans?"

"Not exactly," Betsy admitted, handing the Treasontini to Arabella. "But he told me it could help Main Street merchants. He's offering investment opportunities. What's not to like? He booked The Hanged Man's Noose for a post-presentation shindig. It will be great for business. Garrett's going to foot the bill for the entire evening."

Garrett. Trust Betsy to be on a first-name basis already. The woman would flirt with a corpse. Arabella attempted a weak smile.

"You *are* going to come, aren't you?" Betsy sounded concerned. "To the presentation? And the after-party?"

"I wouldn't miss either one for the world," Arabella said, and downed the Treasontini in one quick gulp.

CHAPTER 9

A rabella's sweatshirt and faded blue jeans had been replaced by a pair of black denim skinnies tucked inside knee-high riding boots, a crisp, white blouse, and a herringbone blazer. Red, green, and yellow Bakelite bangles clinked on her right hand. On her left hand, the tiny diamonds on the dial of her Art Nouveau-style wristwatch sparkled. Emily was proud of herself for recognizing both Bakelite and Art Nouveau. Her research had paid off.

The Glass Dolphin had also undergone a serious transformation. Every space was maximized; every nook and cranny filled with decorative pieces, from floor lamps and fireplace implements to fountain pens and furniture. Each wall conveyed a theme, from a comprehensive collection of clocks, to a wall of posters, prints and maps, to another wall filled with mirrors and sconces and girandoles. Throughout the space was the organized clutter of china and cabinets and chests and chairs, of quilts and coverlets, of paperweights and pretty things.

The back of the shop had been set up as an appraisal center, with a large oak desk, a stacking bookcase brimming with reference books, and a burgundy leather chair broken in by time. The only modern touch was a laptop computer.

The shop should have looked crammed and chaotic. Instead, Arabella had managed to make it look downright cozy. A place to explore, like some sort of magical world where time managed to stand still.

"It's magnificent, Arabella," Emily said, and meant it.

"Thank you. I'll admit I'm more than a bit nervous. I've planned this for so long."

"I know where you're coming from. My first issue of *Inside the Landing* has to be fantastic. That's why this is so important to me. How about you show me around and I'll ask questions as we go?"

"You're on."

"I have a few nineteenth-century maps," Arabella said, walking over to the wall of prints and posters. She pointed to a framed map with the inscription *Upper Canada, with all the Great Lakes*, the image size about eight-by-ten inches. It was priced at $275. "Notice how it's all hand-colored and engraved. This map is dated 1881, so it's an accurate depiction of the time. Earlier maps often have cartographic errors. For example, maps from the seventeenth and eighteenth centuries depict California as an island."

"California as an island?" Emily shook her head in wonder. "Would an error like that increase or decrease the value?"

"Maps with cartographic errors typically command a good deal more money than factual representations, however attractive the factual representation might be. There's a fascination with seeing the world the way some explorer charted it, albeit incorrectly, centuries ago."

"Do a lot of people collect maps?" Emily had never heard of such a thing, though she had to admit the story about California as an island was interesting. Even the map of Upper Canada had an appeal she couldn't quite explain.

"Certainly some folks do, but others buy one map and no more. Consider that for less than the price of a limited edition print you could own a unique piece of wall art."

Emily studied the map for a moment. Arabella was right. It *would* make a nice conversation piece. She thought back to yesterday's research.

"What about fakes and reproductions? I read that could be a concern if you aren't dealing with someone reputable."

"That's a good question, Emily, and a significant concern in the antiques trade, although the money and marketplace has to be strong enough for fakers to bother. The map of Upper Canada, for example, is priced at $275, but I'll likely end up selling it for around $250. Antiquers are born to haggle. As for reproductions..." Arabella paused for a moment. "Do you know the difference between fakes and reproductions?"

Emily was embarrassed to admit she did not.

"Let's look at the Sharon Temple, a national historic site in the Town of East Gwillimbury. A few years back, the Temple reprinted a late nineteenth-century map of the town for fundraising purposes. Quite a plain map, aesthetically, but of interest to local residents. Unframed reproductions were sold at the town's two libraries for five dollars apiece. But here's the thing. The reproductions were clearly marked. There was no intention to deceive."

Emily nodded. So far, so good.

"Now let's consider fakes. Some fakes start off life innocently enough, not as reproductions, but simply as another item made during a time when such things were popular, like a stained glass lamp from the early twentieth century, or a piece of pottery from the same period. Somewhere along the way, an unscrupulous seller adds a forged signature, like Tiffany Studios, or Rookwood Pottery, with the intention of deceiving the buyer to get far more money than the object is worth."

There's a lot more to this antiques business than I realized, Emily thought. She nodded again.

"Then we come to our deliberate fake, something that starts off life with every intention of deceiving. We are seeing more of this coming out of Asia, everything from totems and tribal masks to Chinese porcelain and bronze sculptures. If the market is hot, and the money is there, someone, somewhere, will try to exploit it. That's why it's important to work with a reputable dealer. Of course, the age-old caveat applies. If something seems too good to be true, it probably is." Arabella smiled. "Then there are knockoffs sold at a fraction of the cost of the real deal. You see it a lot with brand name clothes and accessories at flea markets."

Emily looked down at her fake Coach purse and blushed. Had Arabella noticed it was a knockoff? She made a mental note to ditch it as soon as she got home, replace it with her no-name leather satchel.

"I'm so sorry, I'm afraid I may have gotten carried away," Arabella said, her tone apologetic. "If I start pontificating again, feel free to kick me in the shin, or start snoring loudly. Some sign to let me know I'm being impossible."

Emily laughed. She couldn't help but like this woman.

"Actually, Arabella, I found it fascinating." She twisted the strap on her handbag. "Do you find yourself categorizing people the same way? As genuine, deliberate fakes, reproductions, or knockoffs?"

Arabella thought for a long moment before answering. "I suppose I do. But unlike objects, I like to believe everyone has a chance to become genuine again. At least people with a conscience."

CHAPTER 10

Emily was impressed with the sheer volume of knowledge Arabella possessed, but even more, she was impressed with the woman's passion for the objects in her shop, from the furniture, printed material and clocks, to a variety of goods which fell under the umbrella of "smalls," a catch-all phrase which referred to any small utilitarian or decorative item, excluding art. Emily had been admiring a red and white cameo glass perfume bottle with a sterling silver stopper, tagged as "English, Thomas Webb and Sons, circa 1900," when the doorbell rang.

"Not sure who that could be," Arabella said, making her way to the door.

It turned out to be Johnny Porter carrying an enormous bouquet of flowers: a mix of white carnations, daylilies, sunflowers, and assorted greenery. A tiny silver helium balloon with a "Congratulations!" message floated in the center.

"For your grand opening, Arabella," Johnny said, giving a little bow and handing her the bouquet. "Courtesy of the Main Street Merchants' Association." He looked around the shop. "The place looks great."

"Thanks, Johnny. I couldn't have done it without your support."

"Utter nonsense. It's all you." He turned to Emily. "It's nice to see you again, and I'm glad to say, under much more pleasant circumstances."

Emily felt her cheeks grow warm and caught Arabella's glance, a cross between amusement and bemusement.

"It's good to see you again, Johnny. I was going to call you later today. Have you heard any more from Gloria? I called the restaurant yesterday, but all I got was a message saying it's closed until Monday."

"Gloria's fine, though she's more than a little worried about how this might affect her business. Tiffany has been making some noises, but thankfully the police aren't taking her accusations seriously. Cried wolf too many times, is my guess."

"I was thinking of calling on Tiffany," Emily said, "but it sounds as if she wouldn't be the most reliable source."

"What's all this about Gloria and Tiffany and the police?" Arabella asked. "I usually stop at the Sunrise on my way here, but I've missed the last couple of days because I've been so busy getting everything ready. It's like I've been living in a vacuum. Is everyone all right?"

"Not exactly," Emily said, and filled Arabella in on the happenings at the diner. Johnny added what he knew. The coroner had ruled the cause of death as anaphylactic shock, and based on the stomach contents, peanuts appeared to be the culprit. The police interviewed both Gloria and February, but were treating Carter's death as an unfortunate accident.

"Apparently Carter had pancakes that morning," Johnny said. "Since Gloria only uses canola oil, something February and previous waitresses confirmed, they suspect the pancake mix had traces of peanuts."

"Poor Gloria," Arabella said. "Carter could be a first-class pill, but he and Gloria went way back, and they owned that apartment building together."

"I also feel badly for the waitress, February," Emily said. "From what I can gather, she only recently moved into town. What a situation to find herself in."

"I wondered how she wound up in Lount's Landing," Arabella said. "It's kind of a sleepy place for someone her age, and she didn't appear to have any friends or family here. Do you know, Johnny?"

"Gloria thinks February was trying to escape something in the city, like a bad relationship."

Emily thought back to her brief conversation with February at the restaurant. "She told me she wanted to be a writer. She might have thought a small town would be a good place to hunker down and write. She also said she had plenty of stories to tell, something about hearing and seeing things as a waitress."

"Did she, now?" Johnny smiled. "I enjoy a good story. Perhaps one of these days we'll get a chance to hear them."

CHAPTER 11

Emily left the Glass Dolphin a few minutes later, but instead of going straight home she headed north on Main Street towards Frankie's Fish and Chips. According to Johnny (who'd heard it from Gloria), February Fassbender lived in an apartment above the restaurant. And the reality was, Emily couldn't stop thinking about her.

She'd meant what she said to Johnny and Arabella. She felt badly for the waitress. There was bound to be an investigation, not to mention a liberal dose of small town gossip and unsubstantiated innuendo. A newcomer to town would be easy prey for both. Maybe it wasn't her place to do so, and maybe she wouldn't want company, but Emily felt compelled to pay the girl a visit, let her know that she had a friend if she wanted one.

Besides, that comment about seeing and hearing things as a waitress, about having stories to tell, kept spinning around in her head. *Who knows what February might have overheard about Garrett Stonehaven and his plan?* People ignored waitresses, the same way they ignored white panel vans and workers in nondescript uniforms. They became invisible.

Frankie's Fish and Chips was located at 467 Main Street North. Unit 1B was stenciled on a scarred wooden door adjacent to the restaurant's entrance. She knocked, and finding no answer, tentatively tried the handle. To her surprise it opened into a tiny vestibule with a mailbox, old-fashioned intercom system, and another door, this one glass. Emily pressed a small black button on the intercom. After a few moments, a tinny voice answered.

"Who is it?"

"Hi, February. It's Emily Garland."

"The woman from the newspaper?"

"One and the same."

A buzzer sounded and the glass door unlatched. Emily pushed the door open and made her way up a narrow flight of rickety stairs. February stood at the top, waif-like, a long Irish cable-knit sweater draped around her slender body and falling to her knees, her face so pale it was almost translucent in the dark hallway.

"C'mon in."

Even with the window wide open the place still reeked of deep fried fish and cooking oil. Emily wrinkled her nose and was embarrassed by the action.

"You almost get used to it after a while," February said. "The smell."

Emily nodded, stayed standing, and thought about her first apartment in the city, a shoebox backing onto the railway tracks, commuter trains running from before dawn to well past dusk. You *could* get used to anything, if money was tight and the rent was cheap enough. "I used to rent a place, you'd have thought the train was coming straight into my living room. I learned to adapt. Turned the TV on louder. Wore noise-blocking headphones when I wanted to read."

"Then you get it, though I'll admit my first few days here were nothing short of hell. Greasy bacon and eggs from the Sunrise, the stench of halibut and cod from Frankie's. It felt like every orifice of my body had been invaded, my pores, my clothes, my hair." February chuckled, a dry, dusty sound too big for her body. "I even tried washing with lemons, saw that on an episode of *CSI* when Sara Sidle tried to wash away the smell of death and decomp and dying. Do you watch *CSI*?"

Emily had to admit she did not.

"Doesn't matter," February said. "All that matters is the rent is dirt cheap, and the place is dead quiet. This time of night you could shoot a cannon along Main Street and no one would notice. That's comforting to someone in my line of work."

Emily frowned. "Your line of work? As a waitress?"

This time it was February's turn to frown.

"I believe I might have misjudged you, Emily Garland." February walked over to the door. "You should probably leave now. I'm expecting company later tonight and it wouldn't do for you to be here when they came."

"Maybe tomorrow—"

"I'll call you if I need you."

The door slammed before Emily made it halfway down the narrow stairway.

CHAPTER 12

No sooner had Arabella said goodbye to Emily than the doorbell rang again. She looked out the window and saw her ex-husband, Levon, standing there, hands in his pockets.

"I'd like to buy those candlesticks in the window," Levon said, sauntering into the shop. With the exception of a pair of work boots, he was completely dressed in denim, right down to a sheepskin-lined blue jean jacket and faded Levis.

Some men looked good in suits and ties. Levon, with his shaggy brown hair, indigo eyes, and lopsided smile, simply rocked in denim. Arabella resisted the urge to push a strand of hair away from his eyes.

"The candlesticks aren't for sale," she said instead, secretly pleased he'd made the comment. The Glass Dolphin had been named after her first antique find: a pair of sapphire blue Boston & Sandwich pressed glass candlesticks, circa 1840. She loved the way the dolphin's head rested on a slab glass base, the mermaid-like tail curling seductively upward to form a c-shaped scroll.

Levon had been with her at the estate sale. He'd walked right by the candlesticks, had saved the moment of discovery for her, knowing how special they were. She remembered the way they'd celebrated later that evening, starting with a bottle of cheap champagne and a large double cheese pizza.

"Not for sale?" Levon said, but he was smiling his lopsided smile. "Kind of hard to make a living if nothing is for sale, Bella baby. I take it you'll be able to part with one or two of your clocks? Or the John James Audubon print of the mourning doves you were always so crazy about?"

"The print is technically titled *Carolina Turtle Dove*, Plate 17 to be exact," Arabella said, but she couldn't help but laugh. There was a lot of truth in what Levon said. She had a hard time parting with things. She'd had a hard time parting with Levon, even after they both realized they made better friends than lovers. The truth of it was, Levon made a better friend than husband. She didn't care who her friends slept with. She *did* care who her husband slept with. It didn't matter that they'd hit a rough patch, or that he denied it.

But back to the present. The man had a point. What if she couldn't part with any of these things? She'd been a collector for so many years, only selling off what she had to, and always to buy more. What if she was kidding herself? What if the shop looked like a bunch of stuff collected by some neurotic antiques enthusiast?

"What do you think, Levon? Does the shop look ... does it look okay so far?"

Levon strolled over to the wall of clocks and caressed them, one by one, tracing the grain of oak and mahogany and pine gently with his fingertips, taking time to admire the reverse-painted glass front on the Seth Thomas ogee, the delicate floral pattern on the Ansonia Royal Bonn porcelain shelf clock, the intricate brass pendulum on the Gilbert "Number 12." After he made his way to the end of the display, he stood and faced the opposite wall, surveying the colorful posters, the watercolors and prints and old maps.

"Where'd you find the series of canvas-mounted Canadian Pacific Railway posters? And those ocean liner posters from Cunard and White Star?" he asked. "They're fantastic."

"A collector in Niagara Falls. In addition to the posters there's a fair selection of ephemera from various liners, postcards, menus, that kind of thing. I haven't decided yet how I'm going to display them. Thought I'd wait until someone inquired about one of the ship posters and then dazzle them with my knowledge and inventory."

"Clever marketing. But why is the person selling? This collection must have taken years to assemble."

"I think he needed the money to fund his latest passion."

"Which was?"

Arabella suppressed a giggle. "I believe her name was Charisma."

Levon burst out laughing. "Charisma, eh? Good on him."

"And her," Arabella said with a chuckle. "I guess you could say Charisma's ship came in."

"So will yours, Arabella. Everything looks absolutely incredible." Levon eyed her with a hint of sadness. "I think the student may have surpassed the teacher."

Arabella's uncertainty dissipated. It was the best compliment Levon could have possibly paid her.

CHAPTER 13

E mily arrived at the Glass Dolphin at nine o'clock sharp. She'd promised Arabella that she'd get there early enough to help out with any last minute preparations before the shop opened at eleven. They were in the middle of giving everything one final dust and straighten when the doorbell rang.

"That will be my friend, Betsy Ehrlich," Arabella said. "She owns The Hanged Man's Noose. Not sure if you've been there yet?"

Emily shook her head. She'd run by it a couple of times, but the idea of going into a bar on her own held limited appeal. Besides, she wasn't much of a drinker.

"You've got to go there, seriously, good food, good atmosphere, phenomenal nineteenth century saloon decor. It's totally not like one of those pickup joints you find in the city. Betsy's sister, Rebecca, runs Casual Catering and Bakery. I hired her to put together a few platters of nibblies for the grand opening. Betsy offered to deliver them and check out the shop at the same time."

After Arabella made the introductions, and Betsy got a quick run through of the shop, the trio went about setting up the food table. In addition to raw veggies, appetizers, and bite-sized desserts, she'd brought a variety of sparkling waters, and two large urns, one for coffee, and one for hot water. A multi-colored basket was filled with a selection of regular and assorted herbal teas. Another basket held a supply of non-dairy creamers, sugar and sugar substitutes. Emily had to give props to Rebecca Ehrlich. Everything appeared to be covered. There were cups, glasses and paper plates, all sporting the double "C" Casual Catering logo.

"I have to scoot, the pub opens in an hour," Betsy said when they'd finished. She gave her friend a quick hug. "I'd wish you luck, but you won't need it."

"Thanks, Betsy."

"Thank you for giving Rebecca the gig. She could use the business, especially once word gets out about Carter Dixon."

"What does Carter's death have to do with Rebecca?" Emily asked.

"Rebecca makes all the baked goods for Sunrise, has since it opened. She even makes the pancake mix, three different varieties. Gloria's a great short order cook but her baking is lethal." Betsy blushed scarlet. "Sorry, bad choice of words. But Rebecca never made any claim her goods were made in a nut-free facility. And she swears she was super-careful about cross contamination. Poor kid, she's worked so hard to make a go of the business."

"She can keep counting on me," Arabella said.

"And me, if I ever host an event for *Inside the Landing*," Emily said.

"Thanks, both of you. Now I totally have to scoot. But before I forget, Arabella, I told Garrett all about your grand opening. He's keen to see it." Betsy turned to Emily. "That's Garrett Stonehaven. He's a developer from Toronto with big plans for Lount's Landing. Positively *the* most amazing man I've ever met."

Amazing, Emily thought.

"Really," Arabella said.

"Really," Betsy said, a happy grin on her face. "I can't wait to hear what Garrett thinks of the Glass Dolphin. It's absolutely something to die for."

Arabella had unlocked the shop promptly at eleven and there'd been a steady stream of traffic from the moment the doors opened until five, when the doors closed. Not a mad rush, exactly, but Emily couldn't remember a moment when the store didn't have at least one customer browsing and another noshing on appetizers. Emily had done her best to chat with each and every one of them, taking photographs and getting quotes.

The day was pleasant if largely uneventful, a few sales made, some promises to come back and visit again, a couple of inquiries on possible consignments. Arabella took it all in stride with an easy grace and quiet confidence, answering questions, pointing out special features, all the while making casual introductions to Emily. She seemed to know everyone, not only by name, but by some sort of anecdote.

"Caitlyn Meadows. Caitie has the most incredible collection of vintage costume jewelry. I've been trying to pry a Sherman aurora borealis bracelet off her for years now." Introducing a dapper man in his early fifties. "Stanford McLelland, owner of McLelland Insurance Brokerage. Stanford's my ex-boss. He encouraged me to open the Glass Dolphin. Promised me a good deal on insurance rates, too, didn't you Stan?"

Emily was grateful for the introductions. With the exception of Johnny Porter, the only people Emily had recognized were Ned Turcotte, the owner of Birdsong, still ruddy-faced and still wearing a red plaid lumber jacket, and Chantal Van Schyndle, the owner of the Serenity Spa and Yoga Studio.

As unlikely as the matchup seemed, Emily got the distinct impression the two were more than good friends. It was nothing overt, more the way they interacted, Chantal finishing off some of Ned's sentences, and vice versa. She managed to get a couple of good photos plus a decent quote from Chantal about running a business on Main Street before the two of them wandered off.

"Chantal Van Schyndle," Arabella had whispered to her as Ned and Chantal examined a New Brunswick butternut desk. "Everyone calls her Van Swindle behind her back, because of the outrageous prices she charges." Emily had bitten her lip to keep from laughing out loud.

If Saturday was uneventful, Sunday more than made up for it. Things started smoothly enough. Betsy's sister, Rebecca Ehrlich, arrived first thing to collect Saturday's leftovers. She replaced them with freshly prepared platters, topped up the tea and coffee supplies, and added another bundle of napkins.

Emily was struck by the similarity in the two women. Rebecca was younger by about five years, no hint of crow's feet, her face not yet broadened by age. But there was no mistaking the two for sisters, at least when it came to appearance. Ironically, the younger sibling was much more "all about business," pulling out a checklist, and making certain Arabella initialed each item, coming and going, before signing off at the bottom of a sheet marked "Invoice."

Then again, Rebecca wasn't Arabella's close friend. Emily wondered if there was more behind Betsy's decision not to deliver the food on Sunday beyond a late night at the bar. She realized that as much as she had taken a liking to the antiques shop owner, she knew virtually nothing about her personal life, let alone her finances.

The trouble started when Poppy Spencer entered the shop carrying a large flower bouquet prepared with fresh fruit and chocolate. Watermelon slices were cut to form a number of poppies, and dark chocolate wafers had been used for the centers.

"Poppy Spencer, real estate agent," Arabella said to Emily. "Poppy, this is Emily Garland, the new editor of *Inside the Landing*."

"We met at the Sunrise Café," Emily said.

"How could I forget? Positively dreadful, what happened to Carter, though I understand from Johnny it's been ruled as an accident."

"That's my understanding, too, although no one from the police has called me."

"Nor me, Emily, although they still might. But today, I prefer not to think about horrid things. Today is all about the Glass Dolphin." Poppy strutted about the shop, randomly picking up the odd bit of china and glass. "The space is perfect, Arabella, as I told you it would be."

"You were right," Arabella said, turning to Emily. "Poppy found this place and she negotiated a three-year lease at a price I could afford."

"Don't forget the option to buy."

"As if you'd let me." Arabella's voice held a hint of irritation. "We all know how persuasive you can be, Poppy. Heck, if giant billboards are any indication of the truth, you were also the agent of record on the Main Street Elementary School. The one Garrett Stonehaven is apparently going to convert into some mega-box monstrosity."

Poppy's eyes narrowed into ice gray slits. "Grow up, Arabella. My job was to sell the schoolhouse property, not to turn away qualified buyers because they may or may not fit in with your—or my—personal vision for Lount's Landing. Plus, the Main Street Elementary School has been on the Board's deaccessioned list for years. It hasn't been used in the past two. Surely you realized it wouldn't sit vacant forever?"

"Of course I didn't think it would sit vacant forever, Poppy. I'm not an imbecile. I just hoped there might be a more compatible use for the property. Like converting the building to a condo."

"And that's my responsibility as an agent, how?"

"I'm saying that every sale shouldn't be all about the commission."

"You're still not getting it, Arabella. I'm not the only real estate agent in Cedar County. If I hadn't sold Garrett Stonehaven the property, someone else would have. He's been sniffing around Lount's Landing for the past two years."

"And you, no doubt, have been trailing after his scent like a dog after a bone."

"You'll soon learn, Arabella, that business is business. If you don't, you won't have one. Enjoy the fruit arrangement." Poppy Spencer flounced out of the store, the red soles of her Louboutins flashing like stop signs.

"Sorry you had to witness that," Arabella said. "When I moved to Lount's Landing with Levon, Poppy took me under her wing. But that was a few years back. She started changing about three years ago. It was as if she was slowly trading compassion for commerce."

"Yet you hired her to find the space for your antiques shop."

"I guess I hoped she was still the person I first met. And she is a great negotiator." Arabella blushed. "I suppose I'm a bit of a hypocrite, expecting Poppy to get the best deal for me, and not for the School Board."

"You're human. I would have done the same thing." Emily paused. "Look, as much as it pains me to admit it, Poppy is right. Business is business. Her job was to sell the school property. That's exactly what she did."

"I expect you're right." Arabella attempted a weak smile. "C'mon, let's try some of those watermelon and chocolate poppies before the crowds come flocking in. I always feel better after eating chocolate."

Crowds might have been an overstatement, but traffic remained steady, and Arabella remained the consummate host, although from the way she played with her bangles and straightened out items that didn't need straightening, Emily suspected Arabella was more nervous than she let on. It wasn't until two men arrived that she visibly relaxed.

"Levon and Shuggie," she said, her face beaming. "I knew they'd come."

For the first time, Emily could understand how difficult it might be to completely let go of someone like Levon. There was something disarming about him, from the slightly shaggy brown hair to eyes so blue they could have been fabricated from the head-to-toe denim he was wearing. Not to mention his smile, a lopsided half-smile that gave the impression the full-on deal was in reserve. For a special occasion. Johnny Porter might be drop-dead movie star gorgeous, but Levon Larroquette was charisma personified and dipped in chocolate.

"Levon, Shuggie, this is Emily Garland, editor, *Inside the Landing*," Arabella said. "She's here to cover the grand opening."

"Pleased to make your acquaintance, Emily Garland, editor," Levon said, with a slight bow. "Levon Larroquette, picker." He turned to the young man standing next to him, a tall, skinny twenty-something with a gap-toothed smile and dreadlocks spilling out from under a green and red knitted tam. "Shuggie St. Pierre, apprentice picker."

"It's nice to meet you both," Emily said. "I see you brought a camera. Am I to have some competition?"

Levon laughed. "Not bloody likely. No, we're here because we have a potential client who might be interested in a couple of the railway posters. I'll take the pictures, and Shuggie will do the measurements."

Emily figured a "picker picks poster" angle might add something to the feature. She was about to broach the idea when the front door chimed, announcing another visitor. Emily looked up and barely suppressed a gasp. Because standing there, all six feet of smug superiority, was Garrett Stonehaven.

If Stonehaven was surprised to see Emily, he didn't show it. Instead he favored her with a curt nod and immediately approached Levon.

"It's been a long time, Larry." Emily noticed he made no effort to shake hands.

"I've been more than okay with the separation, *Garry*."

Stonehaven chuckled softly. "Touché on both counts, Levon. Good to see the years haven't dulled your sense of clever repartee, especially since you're still doing that picking thing to earn a living. Not that there's anything wrong with it, although some of us have managed to move on to bigger and better things." He made an elaborate display of looking at his wristwatch. "Where might I find the owner of this charming establishment? I'd like to personally invite her to my presentation on Tuesday evening."

Emily didn't know much about wristwatches, but she could recognize a Rolex when she saw one. It was also clear Levon wasn't impressed, with the watch or with Stonehaven. He made his way over to Arabella, who was showing a young couple a colorful display of Depression glass. He put a hand on her shoulder and whispered something in her ear. She nodded and made her way over. Emily made a pretense of studying some crystal goblets and prepared to eavesdrop.

"Arabella Carpenter. I understand from Levon that you wanted to meet me?"

"Garrett Stonehaven. Betsy has been telling me all about your wonderful shop."

"Betsy's a good friend."

"And Johnny Porter has told me all about your commitment to revitalizing Lount's Landing, specifically historic Main Street." Stonehaven handed Arabella an invitation. "I wanted to personally deliver this to you."

"I have one already, thank you."

"So you'll be at the presentation?"

"I wouldn't dream of missing it." Spoken softly, smiling politely, but with an edge to her voice.

"Do I detect a hint of animosity, Ms. Carpenter?"

"Let's say I don't believe your vision for the school will align with mine."

"You should hear all the details before you judge me too harshly, Ms. Carpenter." Stonehaven walked over to the window and pulled out one of the cobalt blue glass dolphin candlesticks. "How much for these?"

"The candlesticks are in the window of the Glass Dolphin for decoration, Mr. Stonehaven. They are not for sale."

Emily suppressed a grin as Arabella took the candlestick from Stonehaven's hand. Her moment of merriment didn't last long.

"Nonsense, Ms. Carpenter. Everything is for sale at the right price. Everything and everybody. Even you."

"I think you'll find, Mr. Stonehaven, that small-town values cannot be bartered away quite so easily. You'd be wise to remember that."

"Is that some sort of veiled threat? Because I assure you, I don't take kindly to threats, veiled or otherwise."

"It would appear we have at least that much in common. Now if you'll excuse me, I have a grand opening to attend to and customers who require my attention. Unless there is something else in the shop you'd be interested in buying."

"Not today, Ms. Carpenter. But I'll be back for those candlesticks." He flashed an ultra-white smile. "I always get what I want."

CHAPTER 14

Arabella began to tremble the minute Stonehaven left. From the moment Betsy had mentioned StoreHaven, she'd tried to convince herself his plans might not be as horrific as she feared. Hoped he might be willing to listen to other options. After all, Johnny Porter had sent a handwritten invitation to the presentation and she trusted Johnny.

But the man she'd just met would stop at nothing to get his way. There was something dark and dangerous about him, something sinister under the layer of handsome civility. The way he smiled, revealing teeth bleached so white they looked false.

Arabella had been reminded of an old joke from her high school days. *Your teeth are like stars; they come out every night.* She suspected Stonehaven's blistering white smile wasn't the only thing false about him.

She took a deep, cleansing breath, the kind Chantal had encouraged at yoga class on the two occasions she'd summoned up the patience to try it, had almost managed to get a grip when Camilla Mortimer-Gilroy strutted in. As usual, everything about Camilla rubbed Arabella the wrong way, and it wasn't because she could eat like a starving sailor and maintain the figure of a runway model. Nor was it the perfectly highlighted blonde hair with wisps and tendrils framing a deceptively innocent, heart-shaped face, or the marine blue eyes men could drown in. Although Levon drowning in them had been rather the last straw.

What really bugged her was the way Camilla carried herself, as if she'd been born with a silver spoon in her mouth and a nanny in her nursery. She couldn't prove it, but Arabella suspected Camilla's background was far more humble. For all her posh and polish, she never spoke about her life before Lount's Landing. Another thing she and Levon had in common.

Camilla had made out like a bandit when she'd latched her French-manicured fingernails into Graham Gilroy. Or at least she thought she had. Arabella had heard rumors that Graham was close to bankruptcy when he died.

Most of all, it was that holier-than-though attitude of hers, as if everyone else in Lount's Landing was a Class-A hick. Recently, Arabella had heard Camilla was searching for small antiques and collectibles to decorate the walls and halls of the Gilroy Mansion. It had sounded like good news for the Glass Dolphin, until

Arabella found out Camilla had hired some chichi designer in Toronto to carry out the acquisitions.

"Arabella," Camilla said, her tone implying she'd been standing there for hours.

"Camilla, so kind of you to come slumming to the poor side of town."

"You are a droll one, Arabella. I'm here on the advice of my interior designer, Shakyra. You know, *the* Shakyra. I'm sure you've seen her fabulous decorating show on HGTV, *Shopping with Shakyra?* Shakyra says it never hurts to poke around a shop. Shakyra says even places like the Sally Anne and Goodwill occasionally have things of interest." Camilla preened. "I've been working exclusively with Shakyra's firm in Toronto to accessorize the Mansion."

Camilla was comparing the Glass Dolphin to charity thrift stores like the Salvation Army and Goodwill? Arabella eyed a platter of appetizers and contemplated throwing the lot at her.

"Shakyra, you say? Can't say I'm familiar with the name, but then I don't watch reality television, always seems so staged. Not that I'm accusing this Shakyra of anything. I'm sure she's simply marvelous at accessorizing. And for your purposes at the Gilroy Mansion, I'm sure that's quite enough. It's not as if the guests of a small town B and B are expecting the proprietor to be knowledgeable about antiques."

Arabella knew it was petty of her, but she was delighted to see the self-satisfied smirk all but wiped off Camilla's face. Time to insert the dagger and twist it. "But certainly, Camilla, do feel free to poke around, as you so eloquently put it. Everything in the shop is available."

She smiled sweetly and pointed to her ex-husband.

"Even Levon."

Chapter 15

E mily flipped the sign in the window from "Open" to "Closed" while Arabella opened the top drawer of an oak filing cabinet and pulled out a bottle of Courvoisier cognac along with two Waterford crystal brandy snifters.

"I must make a note to buy a small wine refrigerator," Arabella said, sinking into a velvet-covered chaise lounge. "In the meantime, your choice is cognac or cognac. Courvoisier. A shop-warming gift from Betsy. Can I pour you a drink?" She motioned for Emily to pull up a high-backed chair labeled as "wingback chair with walnut cabriole legs, circa 1885, possibly New England, sateen fabric, recently reupholstered."

"I'd love a shot of cognac." Emily was grateful for the invitation to sit. Her feet were as tired as the time she'd run the Toronto Marathon—and that was twenty-six point two miles. "I have to admit I had my doubts you'd get everything done when I first met you, Arabella, but you pulled it off, and in fine style, may I add."

"Thanks, though it felt a bit like an open house where all the nosey neighbors come to look and not to buy." Arabella poured a generous shot and handed it to Emily.

Emily smiled at the oddly appropriate analogy. She swilled the cognac in the snifter, warming it with her hands. "You did sell a few things, though, didn't you? I saw you wrap some Depression glass, and there's a space where you had one of your ocean liner posters. And there was a lot of interest in the pair of stacking oak bookcases you have over there. Plus, I'm sure I see a sold sign on the New Brunswick butternut desk." She had kind of liked the desk, herself, not that she needed another desk.

"Don't get me wrong, I'm delighted with the turnout, and the sales. I've got promises of return visits, and I made two appointments for appraisals next week. One is a nineteenth century tintype of a poodle. I'm really looking forward to that one. I love vintage photography. The other is an old clock the owner hopes to consign. All things considered, the weekend was as good as or better than expected."

"All things considered?"

"I could have done without the visit by Garrett Stonehaven, and I didn't appreciate the way he bullied me over the candlesticks." Arabella studied Emily with open curiosity. "Something tells me you could have done without his visit as well."

"It's a long story for another day," Emily said, taking a sip of cognac. She felt the warmth of it ease her tired muscles. "Speaking of unwanted guests, I got the impression Camilla Mortimer-Gilroy was even less welcome than Garrett Stonehaven." *And it went far deeper than accessorizing with Shakyra.*

Arabella's lips thinned to a straight line. "You've got that right."

"Anything you want to share?"

"No, can't say I do."

"Fair enough," Emily said, not wanting to ruin the moment of celebration. "Now, Levon, he seems like a nice guy. Very supportive of you."

"That he is."

"You seem to be good friends."

"He's my best friend."

"And yet he's your ex?" Emily saw Arabella tense. "Look, I don't mean to pry, it's the nature of being a journalist. We're an eternally curious bunch. Tell me to sod off and I'll stop the inquisition."

Arabella gave a weary smile. "It's okay. You're bound to find out sooner or later, you might as well hear the true story from me." She finished her cognac and poured herself another generous shot.

"Levon spent what we both euphemistically refer to as 'some time' at the Gilroy Mansion. He claimed it was perfectly innocent. The two of us had hit a rough patch and he needed some space. But Camilla was quick to tell me 'it' didn't mean a thing to either of them, emphasis on the 'it.' She claimed that she didn't want me to get blindsided with small-town gossip and nasty rumors."

"How charitable of her."

"Yeah, Camilla practically won the good neighbor of the year award."

Emily laughed, then turned serious. "But you're friends with Levon again. How on earth did that happen?"

"It took a while," Arabella admitted. "Levon has always maintained that nothing happened. In the end, I found it almost didn't matter, 'almost' being the operative word. We'd had issues. Nothing major. Working together, living together, it all got to be a bit too much 'togetherness.' We started thinking our marriage was a mistake. I'm not sure who decided it was finally over."

Emily wasn't so sure it was over, but she knew better than to offer an opinion. "And so?"

"We were friends for a long time before we became lovers. We had a history. And I suppose we both missed the friendship too much to let it go. Plus, we make good business associates. It might not be perfect, but for now, at least, it's working." Arabella conjured up a sad smile. "Enough about me. What about you? Any significant other back in Toronto?"

"An ex-fiancé. Kevin."

"A recent breakup?"

"Fairly recent," Emily said. "A couple of months ago."

"What happened? Or should I ask?"

"A personal trainer named Chloe happened. Very platinum blonde, very busty, all fake tan and toned legs."

"How did you find out?"

"Kevin. He used to come to my place every Saturday night for dinner. I'd make a gourmet dinner, appetizer, entrée, dessert, a nice bottle of wine. I enjoy trying new recipes."

"And one Saturday night he didn't come over?"

"He came over, all right, except that Saturday night he brought me a present."

"What was it?"

"A cookbook."

"What's so bad about giving someone who likes to cook a cookbook?"

"It was called *Cooking for One*."

"Geez, that's cold," Arabella said, and shivered.

"Ya think?" Emily downed the rest of her brandy. Her rental house was a fifteen-minute walk away. Worst-case scenario, she could crawl home. Maybe if she ate something it would help. She couldn't remember the last time she'd eaten anything but Poppy's watermelon bouquet. And that had been hours ago.

She got up and made her way to the front of the shop, where the selection of appetizers and bite-sized desserts had been set up for customers. She grabbed a couple of picked-over platters and set them on a small table next to the chaise lounge.

"The raw veggies are down to a few brownish looking mushrooms and some stringy looking celery. But there's still plenty of stuff here to eat if you don't mind your carrots in the form of miniature cupcakes with cream cheese icing."

"I like your style," Arabella said, and proceeded to pour them each another shot of cognac. "Now, what's the story with you and Garrett Stonehaven?"

CHAPTER 16

Emily headed north on Main Street to her office first thing Monday morning. Her head ached from too much crap food and cognac, and she could have benefitted from another couple of hours of sleep, but she needed to transcribe her rough notes from the grand opening while they were still fresh in her mind. She could always download the photos later.

Once again her walk took her past Frankie's Fish and Chips, and she thought about February's odd behavior a couple of days before. Maybe her landlord could shed some light on it. Johnny's notes had mentioned that the current owner, a man named Nigel Watters, had purchased the restaurant a few months back, kept the name to save on changing the menus and outdoor signage. "A bit of a gossip," Johnny had written. If anyone knew anything about February and her mysterious "line of work," Nigel just might be the man.

Emily's stomach roiled at the thought of fish and chips, but her curiosity about February overcame her reluctance. She could always just order coffee. In fact, coffee sounded good right about now, the stronger the better.

The inside of Frankie's Fish and Chips was long and narrow, with dark, wood-paneled walls punctuated by faux portholes and taxidermy fish reproductions. A center aisle separated a row of booths, the bench seats upholstered in red leatherette, the tabletops covered in red and white checkered plastic. Laminated menus were tucked behind stainless steel napkin holders and bottles of malt and white vinegar. There was a faint odor, as if some fish had gone off. Emily renewed her decision to stick with coffee only.

In his notes, Johnny had described Nigel Watters as a tall, knobby-looking man, mid-to-late forties, with a receding hairline, large aquiline nose, and pale blue eyes. What he'd missed was the aura of defeat that permeated from the restaurateur's pores like hot grease on a griddle. Emily slid into a booth and waited as he trundled over to greet her, his steps heavy, his shoulders slumped.

"Welcome to Frankie's. Let me guess. You're the new editor of *Inside the Landing* everyone's been talking about."

So folks had already been talking. That didn't take long. Emily found herself missing the anonymity of the city. It would have been a lot easier to go undercover in Toronto. She summoned up a warm smile.

"Emily Garland, editor, at your service. And you must be Nigel Watters. Johnny Porter told me to stop by." Emily crossed her fingers underneath the table. "He tells me this is the best fish and chips place in town."

"The only fish and chips place in town, actually. Not that it's helped business." Nigel gave a weary smile and waved his hands around the empty restaurant. "Hopefully you'll have more success with your acquisition than I have."

"Maybe I can help you by doing a write-up on the restaurant."

"I suppose it couldn't hurt."

"Thanks for the vote of confidence."

"I'm sorry. That was rude. I'm not usually rude."

Emily shrugged. "Don't give it a second thought. I'll have coffee, black is fine."

"It's just that I've been worried," Nigel said, making no effort to get the coffee.

"Worried? About the restaurant?" Being rude to the customers wasn't going to remedy that any time soon.

"No, well, yes, that too, but I'm more concerned about February. My tenant. Lives upstairs."

Emily perked up. Now *this* was interesting.

"I know February. I was in the Sunrise Café when Carter Dixon died."

"Feb mentioned a newspaper lady being there." Nigel shook his head. "I should have made the connection. I really am off my game."

"No reason for you to have done so. Why are you worried about February?"

"She promised to cover for me yesterday afternoon." Nigel sighed heavily. "I haven't had a minute off since I bought this money pit. With Gloria's place temporarily closed, I thought Feb could use the shift. But she never showed up. Not so much as a phone call or a quick pop-by."

"I saw her Friday evening. She told me she was expecting company. Maybe she went out of town and it was too late to tell you. When did you make your arrangement with her?"

"Late Saturday." Nigel bit his bottom lip. "I'll admit she seemed a bit off, as though something was weighing on her, but I put it down to the whole Carter Dixon business."

So Nigel had seen February after Friday night. Which meant that whoever had visited her hadn't posed a threat... unless they'd come back. Emily mulled the possibilities over in her head. That whole "her line of work" business continued to bother her. It was possible February had put herself in danger.

"Maybe you should go check on her. Make sure everything's okay. I can come with you, if you'd like."

If Nigel thought anything was odd about Emily wanting to check on February, he gave no indication. Instead, he seemed relieved. "That would be great. Let me put a 'Back in Ten' sign on the door on the off-chance another customer comes along."

The putrid stench of rotting meat permeated the hallway outside of February's apartment.

"She must have left something on the counter," Nigel said, his face taking on a greenish tinge.

Emily nodded, but she'd watched enough episodes of *Law and Order* to have her doubts. "Let's hope that's all it is." She shivered as they reached the apartment door. "Damn, it's freezing up here. I think it's warmer outside."

"February always kept the window open to keep the smell of the fish and chips from the restaurant out, then she'd complain about how cold the apartment was," Nigel said, knocking. There was no answer. He put his ear against the door and listened. "I'm not hearing anything." He knocked again.

"Do you have a key?"

"I do."

"I think you should use it."

Nigel's face went from green to chalk white, but he pulled a key out of his pants pocket and inserted it into the lock, his movements slow and methodical as he swung the door open.

"Oh. My. God." Nigel lurched forward, then stopped himself by grabbing onto the door jamb.

Emily looked over Nigel's shoulder, then felt her knees buckle and the bile rise up in her throat. What was rotting in the apartment was February Fassbender's dead body.

CHAPTER 17

Emily stepped out into the hallway. "We need to call the police," she said. The police wouldn't want them contaminating the scene.

Nigel followed her and leaned against the wall across from the apartment. He swallowed hard, his Adam's apple bobbing up and down. "How long do you think she's been dead?"

"I don't know. You said you saw her late Saturday afternoon. So sometime after that."

Nigel bent over and held his nose. For a minute Emily worried he was going to vomit. "God, the smell is awful. Overpowering. It's hard to believe I didn't notice anything in the restaurant."

Emily had noticed a slightly "off" smell, but she wasn't about to say so now. "The open window probably kept the odor from filtering downstairs." It might also have kept the body from decomposing more than it had, though admittedly her only knowledge came from what she'd seen on TV. As it was, the parts of February's face she could see looked all blue and squishy and distorted, like something you might see in a funhouse mirror. Thankfully, the girl's long blonde hair hung covered most of it. There had been an empty syringe by her right hand.

"Did you notice the syringe?" Nigel was getting more agitated by the minute. "I know she was thin, but I never took her for a junkie."

"Neither did I."

"Do you think the police will suspect me of anything?"

"There's no reason to think so," Emily said, although truthfully she had no idea.

The first police officers arrived about fifteen minutes after Nigel called them. They cordoned off the entrance at Main Street, and asked Emily and Nigel to wait inside the restaurant. Emily wished she didn't feel quite so hung over. Cognac headaches and finding dead bodies didn't mix.

A Detective Sheridan Merryfield interviewed Nigel and Emily, first separately, and then together, and then separately again. Handsome and muscular, with skin the color of Kraft caramels, a thick neck, shaved head, and hands the size of goalie gloves, he reminded Emily a bit of the actor on *NCIS Los Angeles*, the one who licked his lips a lot when he was hosting or presenting on awards shows.

Merryfield walked her through the events leading up to finding the body, from the "incident" at the Sunrise Café, to the finding of the body. He asked the same questions in a dozen different ways. Emily kept her answers brief and to the point. With the exception of telling him about February's "line of work" statement, she didn't leave anything out. Mention that "line of work" business and the police would lose interest in finding out the truth. She'd seen that firsthand with her mother, the way the police abandoned ship if they suspected the victim was involved in something illegal, regardless of whether the suspicion was in any way accurate.

"Right now it looks like an overdose," Merryfield said when it was clear neither she nor Nigel had anything left to add, "but of course we'll have to wait for the coroner's report. In the meantime, I'm going to ask you to keep this to yourselves. And Mr. Watters?"

"Yes?"

"We're going to ask that you keep Frankie's Fish and Chips closed for a few days."

Nigel slouched forward in his seat. "Sure, why not? It's not like I'm doing any better than Frankie."

Nigel might have promised the police to keep quiet about February's overdose, but Merryfield was no sooner out the door when he called Gloria Moroziuk. Restaurant owners had to stick together, he informed Emily. Besides, he'd swear Gloria to secrecy. Gloria could be trusted.

Emily left before she could be party to his gossip.

CHAPTER 18

Emily headed back to her office, her mind going over the scene at February's apartment with every step. Beyond the obvious horror of seeing a young woman dead, something about it bothered her. But what? Maybe if she had something to eat she could think better. Not that she was especially hungry, but it had been several hours since she'd had food—if you could call leftover appetizers food.

She popped into the Hasty-Tasty Mart a few doors down from her building and grabbed a pre-made salad, trying not to dwell on the preservatives that could be in it to keep it "fresh" for a week. Added a bag of kettle-cooked chips and a bottle of ginger ale. It wasn't exactly gourmet, but it would have to do.

She wolfed down the salad and chips and chased down a couple more ibuprofen within minutes of reaching her office. Feeling almost human, and refusing to think any more about February until she got some work done, Emily fired up her computer and starting sifting through photos from Arabella's grand opening. She'd barely made a dent when there was a knock on the door. Who would visit her here?

It turned out to be Nigel, though what he could possibly want was anyone's guess.

"Nigel, what is it?"

"Can I come in?"

"Of course."

He shuffled over to the leather sofa and flumped into the seat.

"What's up?"

"Maybe I shouldn't have said anything to Gloria."

"Considering you promised not to tell anyone, probably not. But you did." Emily studied Nigel through narrowed eyes. "Why the regret? Did Gloria say something that bothered you?"

"Humph." Nigel folded his knobby arms in front of him. "It's what she didn't say. To be perfectly honest, I was a bit disappointed in her reaction. Gloria sounded more worried than shocked."

"That's understandable. First Carter dies in her restaurant, and now her waitress is found dead. That's bound to start a few tongues wagging. Not exactly a boon to her business."

"I hadn't thought of it like that." Nigel bit his lower lip. "God, that means people will connect Feb's death with *my* restaurant. Just what I don't need."

Emily decided to overlook the insensitivity of the comment. Besides, there were questions she wanted the answers to, questions she didn't want to ask in front of the police.

"You told Detective Merryfield that February never mentioned any family. Are you sure she never mentioned anyone?"

"Positive, although I always got the impression February wasn't planning on staying in town long. She used to tell me this was all temporary, that she had a plan."

"A plan? What sort of plan?"

"One time she let a first name slip. She was talking about how this person was her ticket to the good life." Nigel licked his lips, a quick, flicking motion. "I didn't remember until the detective and his partner had left. I suppose I should call them back, let them know."

"That's probably best." Emily tried to keep her tone casual. "Out of curiosity, do you remember the name?"

"I think I do. It was Michelle."

Emily made herself a cup of coffee the minute Nigel left. She needed a clear head to process the facts. February had been a waitress in Toronto. She had moved to Lount's Landing with a get-rich-quick plan, apparently orchestrated by a woman named Michelle.

Could be the woman wasn't Michelle Ellis, but the odds were Las Vegas long. February had told Emily that she'd seen and heard things as a waitress. Had Michelle hired her to find out about Stonehaven's plan? But why would Michelle trust a druggie? She was considering ways to confront Michelle when the doorbell rang.

Exasperated by the interruption, Emily flung the door open. Her expression changed from frustration to pleasure when she saw Johnny Porter standing there. He held a glass vase filled with lavender roses and baby's breath, presumably purchased from Flower Power across the street.

"Johnny! What brings you here?"

"I wanted to give you a proper welcome in your new office." He handed her the flowers and grinned. "Actually, I wanted to see you again, and I thought the flowers might be a nice touch. You know, seeing as I delivered a bouquet to Arabella and all."

"They're beautiful, thank you," Emily said, thinking about what Johnny had told her about men and giving flowers during the Victorian era. She could feel her face flush scarlet and wanted to kick herself for it. What was it about Johnny that turned her into a high school senior?

"Would you care to come in?"

"Thanks. I'm here because I have a favor to ask."

"Sure, what is it?" She set the flowers down on the window ledge.

"Gloria Moroziuk called me. She told me that you and Nigel Watters found February Fassbender's body. And that it looks like a drug overdose of some sort."

"I'm sorry to say that it's all true, although Nigel had no business calling Gloria, and I can't give you any details. The police asked us to keep the information to ourselves until they finished with their investigation."

Johnny smiled. "I did mention, in my notes, that Nigel was a gossip."

Emily smiled back, though this time it took an effort. "An accurate assessment. But it sounds like Gloria couldn't wait to call you and share the news. And that you couldn't wait to come here and ask for more information."

"It isn't like that. It's just that it doesn't look good for Gloria, with two dead bodies associated with the Sunrise Café. I'd like to protect her from any unnecessary press, if that's possible."

"I wasn't about to print it. But it's a small town. The news is bound to get out, whether I print it or not. As has already been proven."

"I suppose I just want to reassure myself that as the editor of *Inside the Landing* you want to promote business, not hurt it with negative press."

"I do," Emily said, trying to keep her temper in check.

"I'm sorry if I offended you, but revitalizing Main Street is important to me. I have visions of it becoming vibrant again. It used to be, you know, before the mill closed down and folks moved away."

"I understand that, and I want to be part of the solution, not part of the problem."

"Thank you." Johnny stood up. "Will I see you at Stonehaven's presentation tomorrow evening?"

"I wouldn't miss it. I plan to take some photos, include them in the first issue."

"Somehow I don't think Arabella will be pleased about sharing space with Stonehaven." There was a twinkle in Johnny's black-brown eyes.

"I hear you. But I'm planning to take some photos at The Hanged Man's Noose to help promote Betsy's business. Arabella will like that. The two of them are good friends." A thought struck her. "Would you be willing to be interviewed after the presentation to offer your perspective? Speaking as the chairman of the Main Street Merchants' Association?"

"Love to, as long as we're friends again."

"We are."

"And you give me permission to tell you about the Association first."

"Permission granted," Emily said with a grin.

"Then why don't we arrange to meet on Wednesday morning for breakfast at the Sunrise Café. Unless you have an objection to mixing business with pleasure?"

"No objection. How's 8:00 a.m.?"

"It's a date. Now I better get back to the store." Johnny smiled. "Enjoy the roses."

Emily googled "meanings behind the color of roses" as soon as Johnny left. Her search revealed plenty of websites. She selected one that appeared to have an air of legitimacy, and blushed to her roots when she read the description.

"The unique beauty of the lavender rose has captured many hearts and imaginations, making them a perfect symbol of enchantment. The lavender rose is traditionally used to express feelings of love at first sight."

Johnny had told her that he was fascinated by color. Emily wondered if he was aware of this particular meaning. She wasn't entirely sure she was ready for the answer.

She also wasn't entirely sure she was ready to confront Michelle Ellis. She summoned up her nerve after drinking another cup of coffee, tidying her paperclip tray, and going through the rest of the photos from the Glass Dolphin grand opening.

Michelle answered on the first ring.

"It's Emily."

"Emily, dear. I wasn't expecting your report until after Stonehaven's presentation. Is everything okay?"

"Depends on your version of okay. There's been another death."

"Another death? I know you mentioned one of the diners at the Sunrise Café had some sort of allergic reaction and died, but I didn't think it was suspicious."

"Neither did I at the time. Now I'm not so sure. The waitress at the same restaurant, a young woman by the name of February Fassbender, has been found dead in her apartment."

Emily heard Michelle's sharp intake of breath, then, "How did she die?"

"Apparently it was a drug overdose. But here's the thing, Michelle. Her landlord, a man by the name of Nigel Watters, tells me she mentioned a woman named Michelle was going to help her live the good life. And I got to thinking. A woman named Michelle sent me to Lount's Landing with a similar pitch. Somehow I don't think it's a coincidence."

Michelle sighed. "I should have told you about February. She was a waitress at a restaurant near our office, worked there for about a year. I dined there a lot, usually alone after a long day at work. February always had gossip to share about various builders and developers from conversations she'd overheard. I tipped her handsomely for the information. And then one day she told me she needed to get out of the city in a hurry, asked me if I knew of any opportunities."

"Did you?"

"I promised her I'd look into it. That's when I got the idea to send her to Lount's Landing. She had eavesdropping down to a science. I figured she'd be a valuable asset."

"And as luck would have it, the waitress at the Sunrise Café had handed in her notice."

"It was a bit more complicated. I've known Camilla Mortimer-Gilroy for years. She was the one who first told me about Stonehaven coming to Lount's Landing."

"So you asked Camilla to hire the waitress away from the Sunrise Café, leaving Gloria in need of a waitress. But wouldn't it have been easier to have February go and work for Camilla? After all, Stonehaven is staying at the Gilroy Mansion."

"Camilla told me Gloria Moroziuk and Carter Dixon had managed to get onto Stonehaven's redevelopment team. She figured the reason he'd picked the two of them was to get his hands on their apartment, though from what Camilla tells me, Carter was having none of it. Whatever the story, from my perspective, February had a greater chance of finding out what was going on from Gloria than she would have working at the Mansion."

Emily believed her. "So you told February about the opening at the Sunrise Café, told her if she could get the job, you'd offer her a side deal, a way she could live the good life."

"You make it all sound so tawdry. The girl wanted a fresh start. If I could find a way to benefit both of us, what was the harm?"

"She's dead now, so you could say that she came to harm."

"That's a low blow. I certainly had no idea the girl was into drugs. I would never have hired her if I did."

"What I don't understand is why you still felt the need to bring me on board. You had February and you had Camilla."

"I needed someone who was a consummate professional but loathed Garrett Stonehaven enough to dig deep. February was in it for the money, and I knew she'd sell me out to the highest bidder if someone else came along. As for Camilla, I've never completely trusted her. I've always suspected her of playing both ends against the middle."

"Meaning she might also be working with Stonehaven?"

"I think it's entirely possible."

"That might explain it."

"Explain what?"

"Stonehaven came by the office a little while ago. He came right out and asked if you had sent me here."

"What did you tell him?"

"The truth, or at least a version of it. I told him you had sent me on behalf of Urban-Huntzberger to run *Inside the Landing*. I'm not convinced he bought it. He made a not-so-veiled threat, said he would take a dim view of anyone who tried to sabotage his plans." Emily thought about Carter Dixon. Had his death been an accident? Or murder?

"Don't let him intimidate you, Emily, dear. He doesn't know anything."

"What about Johnny Porter?"

"The chairman of the Main Street Merchants' Association? What about him?"

"Is he involved?"

"I doubt his interest goes beyond getting what's best for Main Street. Certainly he has no connection to me, other than what I've already told you. Why?"

"No reason," Emily said, looking at the lavender roses. "I just need to know who I can trust going forward."

"That's easy," Michelle said. "Trust no one."

It wasn't until Emily hung up that the thing that had been bothering her all along finally filtered into her consciousness.

The syringe had been next to February's right hand.

But February had written Emily's order down with her left. Emily was sure of it.

Which meant February's death probably wasn't an accident.

CHAPTER 19

Arabella settled into a carved oak booth at The Hanged Man's Noose and ordered a club soda with lime, desperately hoping the soda would settle her stomach. Her head still pounded from too much cognac, even after taking a couple of extra-strength ibuprofen liquid gels, and her mouth felt like it was coated with cotton wool.

Not that she'd been able to crack Emily on the subject of Garrett Stonehaven, regardless of how much cognac had flowed. When it came to playing the game of true confessions, Emily was all about getting them and not so much about giving them.

She wondered what Levon wanted. He'd phoned first thing this morning and asked to meet for lunch. Her curiosity had gotten the better of her. Last night, Emily mentioned the Larry/Garry business, thinking Arabella might know something. It was infuriating to admit she did not. As much as she hated to admit it, entire chapters of Levon's life remained closed to her.

The tavern door swung open, and Levon entered. "Sorry I'm late," he said, not bothering to offer an excuse. He took a seat and called out to Betsy for a Sleeman Honey Brown Lager, bottle, no glass, and turned his attention back to Arabella. "Thanks for coming."

"I appreciate the invite, but didn't I see you last week and then again on the weekend? People will start talking." Arabella said it lightly, but she knew there was truth to the statement. Lount's Landing was a hotbed for gossip-mongering. As much as she cared for Levon, she couldn't go through it all again.

"I wanted to congratulate you on what a good job you did setting up shop, and on a successful grand opening. It looked like you sold quite a few things."

"I did, and thanks, but you've done that already. So 'fess up. What's the real reason you wanted to see me?"

"I wanted to apologize for the Garrett Stonehaven incident," Levon said, looking none too happy about it.

"It was uncomfortable, but I don't see how you're to blame for his bad manners." She took another sip of her soda and decided to plunge in. "I am curious about one thing. What's the deal with the Larry/Garry business?"

"It's a long story."

"You're the one who called me, remember?"

Levon slumped further into the booth. "I know. It's complicated."

"Levon, the man plans to convert the elementary school into one of those hideous mega-box stores. The kind you see in bedroom communities where everyone commutes ninety minutes to get to a job they hate, in a city they don't want to live in. And maybe we can stop him from building it, and maybe we can't, and maybe it isn't as bad as it looks on the surface, but in the meantime, if you two don't go back a ways, I'll eat my hat."

"You're not wearing a hat."

"Don't deflect, Levon. I hate it when you deflect."

"Okay, so what if we do? Go back a ways."

"Maybe you can convince him to take his megastore somewhere else."

Levon gave her a full-on smile, the kind that used to work on her, back when they were a couple.

"Have I mentioned how much I love your new hairstyle? All those fluffy copper curls around your face suit you. Much better than the straightened look you were going for before."

"Don't mess with me." Arabella resisted the temptation to play with her hair, which was, by the way, auburn, not copper. Not that Levon had ever sweated the small details. "Now tell me about Garrett Stonehaven."

"All right, already, you win. Yes, Garrett Stonehaven and I go back a ways."

"Now we're getting somewhere. Exactly how far back is 'a ways'?"

"A few years." Levon took a long sip of his beer. "I guess it's about time I told you. Especially since Stonehaven has come here with his latest dog-and-pony show. Sooner or later, something or someone is going to slip. It's better if you hear it from me."

"I appreciate the courtesy this time around."

Levon resisted the dig. "Do you want the full story, or not?"

"Tell me everything."

"The unvarnished everything?"

Arabella hoped she was ready. "The unvarnished everything."

CHAPTER 20

Emily spent a sleepless Monday night, visions of the syringe lying next to February's lifeless body haunting her. The police might believe her death was the result of an overdose, but Emily didn't, and she was determined to find out the truth. She went over the facts and possibilities for the tenth time in as many hours.

Point one: February had been the waitress who served Carter the pancakes that killed him. But what if the pancakes weren't the cause? Betsy Ehrlich swore her sister, Rebecca, had been ultra-careful about cross-contamination. How else could Carter have been exposed to peanuts? And why didn't he have his EpiPen with him? Emily thought back to the moment when February had tripped over Carter's jacket. She had looked embarrassed, but what if it had all been an act? What if she had tampered with his food in some way, taken the EpiPen from his pocket when she'd stumbled? But if so, why? Had someone hired her to kill Carter? Emily shook her head. The idea seemed implausible, at best.

Point two: Michelle said that February had eavesdropping down to a science. February admitted that she "saw and heard things as a waitress." Had she seen something suspicious that day in the Café? What if February's mysterious "line of work" was blackmail? What if the person she'd been waiting for was the person she planned to blackmail? Maybe that person had agreed to her demands, only to come back a couple of days later with a syringe full of drugs?

But who could that person be? Gloria? If she wanted Carter dead, surely she wouldn't use her own restaurant as the place to do it. Michelle? She was in Toronto, and besides, what reason could she possibly have for wanting Carter Dixon dead? That left any one of the others who'd been in the Sunrise Café that morning. Chantal Van Schyndle, owner of the Serenity Spa and Yoga Studio. Ned Turcotte, owner of Birdsong. Poppy Spencer, the real estate agent who'd sold the elementary school property to Garrett Stonehaven.

Garrett Stonehaven, whose plan Carter Dixon had been publicly dissing. Could Stonehaven have hired February to give peanuts to Carter?

Emily rubbed her temples, trying to ward off the headache she could feel coming on from lack of sleep and an overactive imagination. Was her hatred of Stonehaven clouding her judgment? She checked her watch, surprised at how much time had gone by. It was time to get ready for his presentation.

The conference room was jam-packed, the last-minute arrivals forced to stand at the back of the room. Emily noticed Levon and Shuggie were among the unfortunate standees. She caught Levon's eye and smiled in recognition. He gave her one of his trademark lopsided smiles, then turned to say something to Shuggie. The young man looked up and waved to Emily, a swift gesture warmed by his gap-toothed grin.

Arabella sat across the aisle, in the third row, Stanford McLelland by her side. Emily had considered saving a seat for her, but she'd been a little embarrassed to do so, worried it might seem a bit high school juvenile. Seeing Stanford sitting next to her, she was glad she hadn't given in to the feeling. She wouldn't have thought to save two seats, would have felt foolish if Arabella had made some sort of excuse. She and Arabella might have spent a night drinking too much cognac and telling too many tales, but it wasn't like they were best buddies.

Emily was also feeling vaguely disquieted by her own duplicity. She didn't like to think about what the antiques shop owner would say if she discovered Emily's arrangement with Urban-Huntzberger and Michelle Ellis. She had the distinct impression Arabella didn't tolerate phony people in her life, any more than she'd tolerate fakes and reproductions in her shop. And now Emily had the burden of knowing about Michelle's relationship with Arabella's nemesis, Camilla Mortimer-Gilroy, and the drug-addicted February.

It was all getting way too complicated.

At least her mission involved exposing Garrett Stonehaven as a fraud, which in turn might mean stopping, or at least altering, his plan. Surely that good deed would counteract the sting of any deception.

Garrett Stonehaven strode into the conference room with the quiet confidence of a man used to making presentations. Emily had seen him in action enough times to know he never showed so much as a hint of nerves. True to form, he looked like he'd stepped off the runway at a Canali trunk show, right down to his black leather lace-up shoes.

Today's ensemble included a black suit with a fine pinstripe, a white-on-white shirt and a cornflower blue silk tie. Even his hair was perfect, thick, dark waves with a hint of gray at the temples.

The noise level in the conference room had gone from near deafening decibels to dead quiet. Emily realized most of the people here had only seen Stonehaven on television newscasts, or read about him in home and condo magazines, the real estate section of newspapers. Never mind what he might or might not have to say, it was a bit like a celebrity had come to their town.

He made his way to a small table next to the podium, powered up a laptop, and nodded to a young man standing at the side of the room. The lights dimmed, plunging the room into semi-darkness.

"NIMBY." Stonehaven's voice reverberated through the silence. An oversized screen lit up at the back of the stage, casting a soft shadow across his face. A kaleidoscope of before-and-after Main Street images began flashing by: brick storefronts sandblasted to their former glory, old warehouses painted and prettified with awnings and gilt lettering, the rutted stretch of asphalt road replaced with cobblestone pavers, the sidewalks lined with cast iron lampposts and planter boxes overflowing with lush foliage and fresh flowers. Red, white, and gold flags were emblazoned with a singular message: "Welcome to Historic Main Street."

"NIMBY." The voice softer now, a shade above a whisper. "Not. In. My. Back. Yard." His dark eyes scanned the room as if daring someone to speak. No one did.

"I know what you may be thinking. What does NIMBY-ism have to do with a beautifully revitalized Main Street? And the artist's conception of what could be *is* beautiful, don't you agree?"

Murmurs of assent filtered through the room. Emily shifted in her seat and looked around the dimly lit surroundings. Stonehaven had these people in the palm of his hand. Even Arabella looked mesmerized.

Stonehaven waited a few moments, glancing from person to person, as if hypnotizing the audience into silent submission. Once again, they complied. The screen faded to black, then slowly filled with a picture of the Main Street Elementary School. The audience gasped.

Because this school looked sadly dilapidated, the roof missing more than a few shingles, the windows boarded up, the plywood spray-painted with graffiti, the lawn unkempt, balding patches of grass squeezed out by a field of weeds, the gravel baseball diamond washed away by wind and weather, the basketball hoop rusted and bent, its net missing save for a solitary shred of white rope.

"The Main Street Elementary School, another two years down the line. If it continues to sit vacant and abandoned," Stonehaven said, his voice somber. "And it will only worsen as time goes on."

Another slide, this one showing the back of the school. More boarded-up windows, more dilapidation, more graffiti.

"Let's look at the facts," Stonehaven continued. "The elementary school property has been vacant for the last two years, because the Cedar County District School Board deemed modernization too costly. It was cheaper to build a new school on the outskirts of town."

Emily looked around again. Several people were nodding.

"But this is nothing new to any of you. I daresay if you have children or grandchildren of elementary school age, you were glad to find them attending a nice, new, modern school with wireless technology and classroom modules that can be customized to fit varying class sizes and curriculums. We've all heard the horror stories about mold and asbestos in other schools built way back when. Who knows what could be lurking behind the walls of this tired old Main Street property? Simply put, the Cedar County District School Board couldn't take a chance."

Far be it for Stonehaven to prove there was any air quality or environmental concerns at the Main Street Elementary School, but he'd managed to plant the seed, dark and deep, Emily thought. She watched as Stonehaven seized the moment.

"That's where HavenSent Development comes in. Because that's one of the things HavenSent does. We try to save old buildings, breathe new life into them, resuscitate them if you will. When my team heard about an abandoned old elementary school in dire need of rescue, in a charming community ninety minutes northeast of Toronto, I knew I had to see it for myself."

A joyous expression came over Stonehaven's face. "I fell in love with the town, the building, the property, and historic Main Street. I asked my team of engineers and environmental experts to assess the structure. After weeks of waiting, we got the green light. Now we get to the part where you, the people of Lount's Landing, come in."

Another slide of the Main Street Elementary School, this time bearing the caption "Letting Go of NIMBY." Except in the artist's renderings, it didn't look much like the dilapidated school from the earlier slides, nor did it resemble the school currently sitting vacant and in reasonably good repair.

It looked like the pictures of the mega-box store in the *ABCs of Revitalization* brochure: the basketball court, the baseball diamond, the playground all paved over to make room for row upon row of parking.

The cynic in Emily noticed the artist had managed to keep a bit of green space, including the ancient oak on the front lawn, the grounds surrounding it filled with acorns and fallen autumn leaves, a picnic table a few feet away.

No chance that tree would make the final cut, not if Stonehaven's track record stood pat. There would be some sort of excuse, a disruptive root system, a problem with getting equipment in and out. It was always something. Later, he'd bring in a local nursery, have them plant a handful of blue spruce saplings, make sure the media was there in full force while he spouted off about environmental responsibility and his love of nature.

At the moment, however, Stonehaven was busy unveiling a new series of slides, each one depicting a cheerful employee clad in a bright red, white, and gold smock, the color scheme identical to the flags shown in the earlier slides of historic Main Street. The employees were directing smiling shoppers and their oversized carts towards aisles packed with merchandise. Each slide offered up some sort of positive message, phrases like "Exciting Full- and Part-time Employment Opportunities," and "Bringing Business Back to Main Street." One slide in particular piqued Emily's curiosity. The one that read "Investment Potential."

The presentation ended with one last artist's rendering, this time of the store's proposed exterior, the words "StoreHaven: Another HavenSent Solution" superimposed over it, bold lettering at the bottom of the slide proclaiming, "The ABCs of REVITALIZION: Neighbors Helping Neighbors."

The screen gradually faded into blackness as the overhead lights came back on, one by one. Stonehaven flashed a brilliant smile and bowed to his audience.

Emily couldn't believe her eyes. Not only did the pompous ass take a bow as if he was on stage for some sort of Broadway play, but more than half of the room stood up and clapped. She turned around and saw Levon and Shuggie standing at the back of the room. From the dour look on Levon's face, he hadn't been any too impressed with Stonehaven's performance. Arabella also remained seated, her expression stony.

She watched as Stonehaven motioned everyone to sit, a contrived look of humility on his handsome face. At least Emily assumed it was contrived. He'd never struck her as the humble type.

"Thank you," Stonehaven said. "Thank you, all. Now, are there any questions? All I ask is that you stand up and introduce yourself first."

Emily watched as Arabella bolted up from her seat, her face flushed.

"Arabella Carpenter, owner of the Glass Dolphin antiques, and my question is, how will a mega-box store like StoreHaven help the businesses on Main Street? How will it result in the kind of transformation your before-and-after slideshow presented?"

There were a few random mutterings of "yeah, how's that going to help us?" and similar comments, but the vast majority merely glanced around the room to see what everyone else was doing.

"Two excellent questions, Arabella," Stonehaven said, with complete composure. "Now I'm going to ask the audience one. Did anyone notice the positive messaging in the StoreHaven slides? The signs that read 'Investment Potential' and 'Employment Opportunities' and 'Bringing Business Back to Main Street?'"

"A lot of meaningless mumbo jumbo," Arabella said, still standing, her voice icy. "It doesn't explain how StoreHaven is going to help *us*. To put it bluntly, I'm not seeing Team Main Street winning against a mega-box monstrosity."

Stonehaven shook his head, a mournful expression on his face. "It's that kind of narrow thinking, this 'us versus them' mentality, that's harming this town's economic viability. Frankly, I expected more from you, Arabella. I would have thought a new shop owner would have a broader vision."

"Let's try to keep this to the facts at hand, Mr. Stonehaven. Oh, wait a second. There are no facts at hand. No wonder my vision isn't quite as broad as it could be."

Score one for Arabella, Emily thought, as the audience laughed.

"There may not be a lot of dollars available now, but once people start coming here from the Greater Toronto Area, there will be increasing amounts of disposable income."

"You're suggesting a mega-box store in Lount's Landing will bring people up from the GTA?" Arabella gave a dry chuckle. "Forgive me for being obtuse, but I don't see it. Those kinds of places are a dime a dozen in the city."

Stonehaven scowled. "StoreHaven will not be any mega-box store, where one corporation owns everything. My concept is a store co-owned by members of the tri-area community, with a carefully appointed management team, led by myself, at least initially, to supervise the overall project and the day-to-day operations."

"Supervised by you?" Arabella said. "How bloody convenient."

"Please sit down, Arabella, and let me explain."

Arabella sat, her face blotchy with anger.

"Thank you." Stonehaven turned his attention to the rest of the room. "For a modest investment fee, shops and businesses will be allowed to stock a limited selection of their inventory in StoreHaven, a vignette if you will. The store will be staffed with professionally trained sales associates, available to sell the merchandise within the store, and to provide them with full information on your shops."

"Can you explain what you mean by an investment fee?" For once it wasn't Arabella doing the asking, it was Johnny Porter. Emily looked around the room and saw a lot of nodding heads.

"An excellent question, Johnny. Part of the investment fee would go toward the revitalization of Main Street, to turn it into a destination for tourists and local shoppers, a place to congregate and shop for fine things. We could start with sidewalk planters, or by replacing portion by portion of the paved road with cobblestones, at least at the crosswalks. Or sandblast some old brick, add some awnings. This sort of vision won't happen overnight, but the opportunities for improvement are endless."

"Who makes the decisions on how the investment fees are allocated?"

"Another excellent question, Johnny. The investors will be put in priority sequence, which means the first investors will have the first say in how the pot is distributed, once sufficient funds have been accumulated. A win-win situation. Neighbors Helping Neighbors."

Emily couldn't believe her ears when people starting speaking at once, everyone asking how they might become an investor. The man could sell air-conditioning for igloos.

"There's no need for panic," Stonehaven said, now smiling broadly. "I'll be taking appointments to discuss the fine print with any interested investors starting tomorrow, no obligation. Main Street merchants will be given top priority, although I will accept investors from Miakoda Falls and Lakeside until such time there is no more availability."

Stonehaven motioned to the room at large. "Anyone who wishes an appointment can book one through Camilla Mortimer-Gilroy at the Gilroy Mansion, where I have had the pleasure of staying, and where I will continue to conduct business for the foreseeable future. Camilla will be booking appointments daily from noon to 5:00 p.m."

He turned to acknowledge Camilla, and gave another bow. "In the meantime, enough talk of business and industry. I've planned a post-presentation celebration at The Hanged Man's Noose, my treat. I believe the pub's lovely proprietor, Betsy Ehrlich, is waiting for us as we speak."

Most of the room stood up and cheered while Stonehaven gathered his belongings and strode purposefully out of the conference room. A hoard of people flocked after him, including, Emily noticed, a pale and tense-looking Stanford McLelland.

"Honestly, there are more horses' asses than horses in this town," Arabella shouted over the applause. "How can you people buy what that man is selling?"

CHAPTER 21

Emily managed to catch up with Arabella in the hallway. "I thought we could go to The Hanged Man's Noose together. I figured you might need a friend after your showdown with Stonehaven."

"Was it a showdown, Emily? I thought I was asking questions everyone had the right to know the answer to."

"Stonehaven doesn't take kindly to having his authority challenged." Emily thought back to the time her mother had dared to try.

"Emily's right, Bella," Levon said, sauntering up beside them. "This is one guy you don't want to cross."

"So we're just supposed to let him march into town and bastardize the integrity of Main Street while ripping us off in the process? I don't think so."

"No one's suggesting that, Arabella," Levon said. "But I don't think being confrontational is the answer."

"Whatever you say, Levon," Arabella said, rolling her eyes. "Where's Shuggie?"

"I sent him ahead to save us a table. Mention free booze and food and the place will be packed, and good on Betsy for getting Stonehaven to foot the bill. But you need to calm down before we go there. I know how you can get when you're riled up. Hell, I've been on the receiving end a time or two."

"I'm not riled up, Levon, and you deserved to be on the receiving end more than a time or two, and you know it."

"I'm just saying—"

"And I'm just saying I don't trust the man, and don't tell me that you do." Arabella glared at Levon, then turned to face Emily. "What was your impression, Emily? You must have heard Stonehaven speak before."

"I have, plenty of times, but I've never heard one quite so investment-focused. Seriously, I don't know what to think, although it sounds as if Camilla is involved, at least peripherally. What do you think, Levon? You don't have a business on Main Street. Maybe you can view this through the eyes of an impartial observer."

"I'm not sure how impartial I am, Emily," Levon said, exchanging a look with Arabella. "Do you have any other suggestions?"

Emily did, but she needed help to pull it off.

"I do have one idea."

"What is it?" Arabella asked.

"Someone needs to make an appointment with Stonehaven to find out what the fine print is all about. Until we sort that out, we don't know what we're dealing with. It could, after all, be completely legit." Not that Emily believed it for a moment, given her assignment. But she couldn't tip her hand, at least not yet. "Whatever Garrett Stonehaven is up to, good, bad, illegal, or indifferent, three heads are definitely better than one. We find out the facts, and get together to discuss what we've learned."

"Sort of like our own little task force?" Arabella asked, her face flushed with excitement.

"Exactly like our own little task force," Emily said.

"Who makes the appointment?" Levon asked.

"I think it has to be Arabella," Emily said. "You don't operate a storefront on Main Street, and I've been reporting on Garrett Stonehaven's activities for years now. Unless it's for an interview, he'll view my request with suspicion. Besides, after the fuss Arabella made, he'll be expecting her call."

"Emily's right," Levon said.

"Since when was asking questions considered making a fuss?" Arabella asked. "Though I have to admit that what you say makes sense."

"So you'll make an appointment?" Emily asked

"First thing tomorrow."

"Perfect. I'll do the same thing, except I'll set it up as if it's an interview for *Inside the Landing*."

"So what's next?" Levon asked.

"We head over to The Hanged Man's Noose, and enjoy some free food and cocktails," Emily said. "They'll taste all the better knowing that it's Stonehaven's dime. Eat, drink, and be merry, guys. If we play our cards right, we might win this one."

The Hanged Man's Noose was buzzing by the time they arrived. Shuggie had managed to find a table crammed into a corner softly lit by a neon sign advertising Labatt's Blue Light. Emily suspected the table had been added at the last minute to accommodate a few more people. The laminate top didn't fit with the rest of the nineteenth-century saloon-style décor.

Betsy saw them walking in and waved enthusiastically, a wide smile crossing her gamin-like face. She was wearing a black turtleneck, black leggings, black leather over-the-knee boots, and a blood red apron. Her dark brown hair had been twisted back into a bun, revealing diamond-studded ears and a long, thin neck. She was quite lovely, reminded Emily of Audrey Hepburn in *My Fair Lady*. It had been her mother's favorite old movie musical. The two of them had watched it over and over again.

Emily looked around the room. Everyone had a blue drink in a martini glass, along with small plates of appetizers. She noticed Chantal and Ned were sitting at a table with a morose-looking Gloria. Johnny was sitting with Poppy and Camilla, the three of them deep in conversation. There was no sign of the man of the hour.

Emily was considering how to best approach Gloria when a server came by with a tray of appetizers and four blue drinks in martini glasses. "This should get you guys started. Shuggie had me wait until you got here before serving him, such a gentleman."

"Thanks," Emily said. "But what's with the blue martini?"

"It's Betsy's secret concoction. She calls it a Treasontini. Came up with it specifically for Stonehaven's post-presentation celebration, says every good bar needs a signature drink." The server laughed. "I sure hope you guys like blueberries."

"She had me sample a Treasontini last week," Arabella said. "It's quite good. Betsy told me it was made with blueberry vodka, triple sec, and blueberry juice. But I'm sure we can order anything we want. Betsy wanted to do something special. I have a feeling she's sleeping with Stonehaven, not that she's said anything. But I've known Betsy long enough to know the signs."

"He does have a way with most women," Emily said, taking a tentative sip of the blue martini. "But I don't get it. Why Treasontini?"

"That would be Betsy's idea of humor," Arabella said. "She's quite a history buff, although most folks around these parts know the basic story. Lount's Landing is named after Samuel Lount. He was a blacksmith and a farmer, but he was also a political activist. Not exactly a safe career choice in the nineteenth century. He was hanged for treason in 1838."

"Treason. Treasontini. Cute," Emily said. "But why would anyone name a town after a traitor?"

"He's not considered a traitor anymore," Arabella said. "He's considered a patriot, and an important part of Upper Canada's history. You see, Lount was also a member of a Quaker sect called the Children of Peace. They were known for their fair dealings with the First Nations and their strong stand against slavery. Lount was revered in the community, although he resisted public office for a long time. His compassion for the poor and disenfranchised ended up getting him killed."

"Now Arabella, that's not entirely accurate," Levon said. "Lount's desire for justice is what led him to William Lyon Mackenzie's Reformers."

"Yes, but that decision ultimately led to his death."

"The Reformers?" Emily asked, hoping to avoid an argument between the exes.

"It was a political party determined to derail a capitalist market economy, something the Reformers blamed for impoverishing farms and families while landowners prospered," Levon said. "Lount ran for Assembly in 1834, and won handily."

"I'm not seeing the problem," Emily said.

"Everything changed in 1836, when Francis Bond Head led the Conservatives to an overwhelming victory," Arabella said. "Bond Head's platform was 'loyalty to the crown and bread and butter on the table.' The Reformers, including Lount and William Lyon Mackenzie, were crushed in defeat. There were all sorts of unethical practices at the polls, including intimidation for any man daring to vote Reformer. Mackenzie and Lount started to question whether democratic change was possible within the existing political system. They, along with several other disillusioned Reformers, planned a rebellion to literally throw Bond Head and his Conservatives out of power."

"I'm guessing that didn't end well," Emily said.

"You could say that. Lount was hanged for treason. Lount is reported to have said, 'We die in a good cause, Canada will yet be free,' as he passed fellow prisoners on the way to the scaffold."

"It sounds fascinating," Emily said. "I'm a bit embarrassed I don't know about the area's history. Canada's history, come to that. Outside of World War I and II, all I remember learning about is the War of 1812."

Arabella grinned. "I'm quite sure Betsy would be happy to fill you in on all the sordid details of Samuel Lount and his failed rebellion, if you're a willing candidate."

"Warning, warning, danger, danger," Levon said, chuckling. "Be prepared for a lecture on everything you never wanted to know about Samuel Lount and were too smart to ask."

Shuggie laughed. "I made that mistake, once. It was innocent enough. All I asked was why Betsy decided to name this place The Hanged Man's Noose. I was a couple of beers in, so I was able to sort of glaze over most of the details."

"You guys are bad," Emily said, but she found herself laughing, too.

"Speaking of drinks," Levon said. "I'm going to sidle my way up to the bar and get myself a Sleeman Honey Brown. Does anyone else want anything? Another Treasontini? A glass of wine?"

"I'll come with you," Shuggie said. "I need to stretch my legs. Too much sitting."

"Chardonnay, and ask Betsy for a generous pour," Arabella said.

"I kinda like the Treasontini," Emily said. "I'll have another one of those. And more of these appetizers, if you can snag some of those, Levon."

"Yeah, those brie and cranberry puff pastry thingies are to die for," Arabella said. "Definitely more of those."

"One chardonnay, one Treasontini, one platter of appetizers, heavy on the brie and cranberry puff pastry thingies," Levon said. "We're on it."

Emily watched as the two men ambled over to the bar, Levon stopping at the occasional table to offer a quick smile and a short chat. She glanced over at Arabella and saw the antiques shop owner was also watching him work the room, a look of admiration on her face. Divorced or not, there was definitely still chemistry between those two, feelings that went beyond friendship, even if they were both too stubborn to admit it.

"Totally like Stonehaven to make a grand entrance, he always has to be the center of attention," Emily whispered to Arabella. They'd been in the pub coming on forty-five minutes and the developer still hadn't turned up. "If he's true to form, he'll pop in for a quick minute, make a toast, and be on his way."

"I'd like to know who is on his team. Gloria's apparently on it, and my guess is so are Chantal and Ned. They're always together, and they're sitting with Gloria."

"I think you're right. I can also make an educated guess. Carter Dixon. If I know Stonehaven, he'll want to own the property next to the school. What better way to convince Gloria and Carter to sell their apartment building than to bring them onto his team?"

"Carter Dixon?" Arabella's face turned pale. "And now he's dead. You don't think Stonehaven is responsible?"

"All I know is those who cross Stonehaven tend to come to harm's way," Emily said, thinking of her own mother, the way she publicly battled him when it came to CondoHaven on the Park. "Levon was right, Arabella. You must be more cautious in what you say to him."

"What about February? Surely she didn't cross Stonehaven."

"I'm still mulling that one over," Emily said, "but I do have a theory."

"I have a theory too, about Stonehaven's plan. But I have to run it by Levon first."

"You have to run your theory by Levon first? Seriously?"

"Not the theory, but the reason for having the theory. It stems from something Levon told me in confidence. It wouldn't be right to share that with you unless he was okay with it."

"You think he will be?"

"I think so, if it means stopping Stonehaven. In the meantime, what do you think about Johnny Porter?"

"I think his role is strictly in the interest of the Main Street Merchants' Association." Emily sipped her Treasontini. "I could be swayed by the fact I find him drop-dead gorgeous and utterly charming. He brought me roses, you know. Lavender ones."

"Lavender roses, eh? You could do a lot worse, and it would be nice to see Johnny settled down and happy. Outside of a casual date here and there, he's never shown much interest in anyone."

"They were roses, Arabella, not an engagement ring. He hasn't even asked me on a date yet." Emily didn't think a breakfast meeting at the Sunrise Café counted. She looked at her watch. "Look, Stonehaven is nothing if not predictable. He always waits about an hour before coming to one of these post-presentation parties. I should go before he shows up and sees us together. We don't want him to think you're making an appointment as anything but an interested and apologetic business owner."

"Apologetic?" Arabella wrinkled her nose in distaste. "I suppose I can do apologetic if it means getting some answers. Tomorrow we'll both make appointments, and I'll be sure to ask Levon about telling his story. Let's get together at some point to compare notes."

"I have an appointment tomorrow morning," Emily said, trying not to blush, and not quite succeeding. "I'll make an appointment with Stonehaven when I get back to my office, call you once it's all said and done."

"Fair enough."

"And Arabella, when Stonehaven comes in, please try to play nice. For our plan to work, he has to believe you're sincere." She got up before Arabella could argue, walking out of the pub as Stonehaven walked in.

CHAPTER 22

Stonehaven's entrance was met with a round of applause orchestrated by Betsy, and it gradually filtered through the room as people stood up, cheering and clapping. He started making his way around the pub, shaking hands and chatting amiably about little bits of nothing. Every now and again, he'd glance over at Betsy and give her wink and a smile, and she'd smile back with a look that was part conspiratorial and part minx.

Definitely sleeping together, Arabella thought, acknowledging Stonehaven's presence with a glacial stare.

Instead of putting him off, Stonehaven seemed to take it as an invitation, pulling up a seat at her table. *Play nice,* Emily had said. Did playing nice mean she actually had to *be* nice? Before either of them had a chance to speak, Betsy was over at their table, a large wine glass and a bottle of Châteauneuf-du-Pape in her hands.

"This one's on the house, Garrett," Betsy said.

"Thank you, Betsy, but please, don't pour it for me now. I'd much rather take it to my room at the Gilroy Mansion, where I can enjoy it in solitude." He grinned. "Or possibly with some company later on."

"I'm afraid alcoholic beverages have to be consumed on the premises," Betsy said, her face flushed scarlet. "Liquor Control Board regulations."

"I won't tell if you won't tell." Another wink.

"Don't be an ass, Stonehaven," Arabella said. "Betsy could lose her license."

"That's true, Garrett, I could. In any case, I arranged with Camilla to have a bottle open and breathing in your room."

"How thoughtful of you."

Betsy smiled and shrugged, somehow managing to make the gesture seem seductive. "So you'll stay, have a glass of wine?"

Stonehaven nodded. "I will."

"I've got an idea, Betsy," Arabella said. "Why don't you make up a batch of Treasontinis for a toast?"

"That's a great idea," Betsy said, and practically sprinted to the bar.

"I have to say, I'm more than a bit surprised at the gesture, Arabella," Stonehaven said. "I had the distinct impression you don't care for me."

"It is your money, after all, Garrett." Arabella smiled sweetly. "And, seriously, I can't think of a more appropriate drink to toast you or your presentation."

"You mock me. I find that entertaining. But I'm not a traitor, no matter what you or your new friend Emily might think."

"Neither, according to history, was Samuel Lount. Yet he was hanged all the same. Tried and convicted by a jury of his peers."

"Is that a threat?"

"Merely an observation. Folks here have a way of pulling together."

"So do people who want to make money, Arabella."

Arabella was still thinking of a witty retort when the wait staff began delivering trays of Treasontinis around the bar. She was deciding between "What about those of us who want to keep our money?" and "What about those of us who want to keep your hands out of our pockets?" when Betsy started chanting, "Here, here, toast, toast." Before long the room was chanting with her. The moment for a witty retort had passed.

Stonehaven stood up, bowed to the room in general, picked up his glass of red wine, and turned to face the five people sitting at the bar. Arabella took note of who was sitting there: Gloria, Poppy, Levon, Camilla, and Johnny, each one smiling, each holding a Treasontini. Betsy stood behind the bar, her face radiating happiness.

"Before I begin my toast, I'd like to thank Betsy Ehrlich for putting on a tremendous post-presentation party," Stonehaven said.

The announcement was met with boisterous cheers.

"And now for my toast, let me begin with a quote from Samuel Lount. 'Be of good courage boys, I am not ashamed of anything I have done, I trust in God and I am going to die like a man.'" Stonehaven raised his glass to the people standing at the bar.

He may have been ready to say something else, but Arabella wasn't about to wait to hear it. She saw the confusion on the faces of the people all around her. Not ashamed of anything he'd done. Die like a man? What the hell? He didn't have any right to ruin Betsy's party, even if he was sleeping with her. Even if he was the one paying for it. She stood up and faced Stonehaven.

"Be careful what you wish for, Mr. Stonehaven, you just may get it." Arabella picked up her Treasontini and held it up high. "Come on everybody. Let's all drink to the newest traitor in our town." She downed her drink in one fell swoop. By the time she put her glass down, Garrett Stonehaven had left the building.

CHAPTER 23

I n the cold, cruel light of morning, Arabella's witty toast to Stonehaven the night before seemed a lot less clever. How was she ever going to gain the man's trust if she did nothing but antagonize him? Not to mention that Betsy had been beyond furious, confronting Arabella after Stonehaven had stormed out of the pub with his bottle of red wine.

"For God's sake, Arabella, Garrett was reciting the last words of Samuel Lount," Betsy had said, her usually placid face flushed a violent shade of crimson. "He had a whole speech planned. He rehearsed it with me so I'd be ready. It was all about how we didn't have to die for our freedom today, but that it still took a person with real courage to start a venture like The Hanged Man's Noose. He was going to say how proud he was to be associated with someone like me, someone who respected history but was still willing to embrace the future. How others could learn from me by investing in StoreHaven. And you had to butt in with your stupid toast and ruin everything."

Arabella had apologized profusely, but Betsy wasn't having any. Levon looked embarrassed, not that it had anything to do with him. Arabella had slunk out of the pub and made her way home, sobered by the crisp night air and the possibility she'd ruined a longstanding friendship.

Thank heavens Emily hadn't been around to see her in action, though she knew it was just a matter of time until word spread. Betsy would be sure to tell anyone who asked how Arabella had taunted the generous developer who had paid for the party. As much as the thought made her skin crawl, there was only one viable solution. She had to go to the Gilroy Mansion, swallow her pride, and apologize to Garrett Stonehaven.

Arabella arrived at the Gilroy Mansion a few minutes before ten. Thankfully Garrett's black Lexus was in the parking lot, which meant he was at the Mansion, no doubt preparing for his appointments with investors.

She timed her visit knowing Camilla would be out for her Wednesday morning yoga class at Chantal's studio. It was bad enough she had to face Stonehaven. Having to face Camilla would have been too much to take.

It wasn't as though Arabella was privy to Camilla's comings and goings. Everyone in town knew about Camilla's commitment to her Monday, Wednesday, and Friday morning yoga classes. She'd been a devotee to the discipline since Graham had died.

"Yoga and meditation got me through the dark times," Camilla would say to anyone who cared to listen. Not that many did, at least in Arabella's humble opinion. The cynic in Arabella also wondered how long and how dark those times had been, given the speedy renovation of the Gilroy Mansion into a Bed and Breakfast, but she managed to hold her tongue. There had been more than enough gossip going around after Levon had "temporarily" moved out of their house and into the B&B for "some space."

The Gilroy Mansion was an old Victorian row house that had, in more prosperous times, been converted into one large home. Following Graham's death, Camilla had restored and re-divided the home back into three wings: a central wing of generous proportions, where Camilla lived, an east wing which housed one upper story and one main floor luxury suite, each with private bed, bath, and kitchenette, and a west wing which housed an opulent two-story suite, with a master en suite, walk-in closet, and full kitchen.

Stonehaven had taken up residence in the west wing. Levon had told her it was filled with fine furniture, art, and antiques. If he had helped Camilla with her selection, he'd been wise enough not to mention it to Arabella. Nonetheless, she gathered that Camilla had spared no expense. Mind you, given the prices she charged, her guests would expect nothing less.

Arabella made her way to a gleaming red front door marked "West Mansion" and lifted the heavy brass knocker, once, twice. No answer. Tried again. Once, twice. Still no answer. She tried to sneak a peek in the window, but the blinds were still drawn. Surely a man like Garrett Stonehaven wouldn't still be asleep at this time of morning? She was ready to give up when, on the off chance of getting lucky, she decided to try the door.

It was unlocked. Arabella slipped into the foyer and closed the door behind her, starting at the sound of the latch clicking into place. "Mr. Stonehaven? Are you home?"

No answer. She surveyed the formal living room, her eyes flicking from corner to corner. A broad, high-backed wing chair had been placed in front of a cast iron fireplace, the blackened embers showing no signs of life. A small wooden table stood next to it. It held a Tiffany-style reading lamp—a Made in China special—a half-empty glass of red wine, a prescription bottle, and a file folder. She caught a glimpse of Stonehaven's shoulder and swallowed hard.

Pills and booze. Had he passed out?

"Garrett?"

Sure that the pounding of her heart could be heard three blocks away.

Sure that he was going to wake up, turn around, and blast her into next week.

Except he didn't wake up.

He didn't turn around.

He didn't hear her heart pounding.

Because Garrett Stonehaven wasn't passed out in his chair. He was blue and rigid and sightless.

And very much dead.

CHAPTER 24

E mily arrived at the Sunrise Café on Wednesday morning a few minutes early, despite having changed her outfit a half dozen times. She eventually decided on casual but stylish. Blue jeans, brown suede boots, and a moss green wool sweater. She grabbed the first available table for two and settled in to wait. She didn't have to wait long.

"You got the memo," Johnny said, laughing. He took off a dark blue, down-filled jacket and hung it on the back of his chair. He was also wearing jeans and a moss green wool sweater.

"Great minds think alike."

"They do indeed. Sorry to keep you waiting. Have you ordered?"

"Not yet, and there's no need to apologize. I've been here less than a minute."

The new waitress shuffled over, a tall, angular woman, mid-to-late forties, with tired eyes, wide hips, and short, mousy brown hair bereft of any particular style. Emily remembered February, so young, so pale, so blonde, so different from this woman. She'd heard from Nigel that the police were ruling the girl's death as an accident, not that she knew where Nigel had gotten his information

The syringe in the wrong hand still nagged at her, as did Michelle's assertion that she had no idea February was a druggie. Surely a serious drug addiction would be hard to hide. Emily wondered if there was a way to get the autopsy report, knew it was a long shot. But maybe if she approached Detective Merryfield...

"What'll it be, folks?" The waitress interrupted her thoughts. "The special today is a toasted Western, home fries, and coffee or tea."

"I'll have the special, with coffee," Johnny said, "and hopefully Emily will join me back into the present."

"I'm sorry. I was just remembering..."

Johnny nodded and put his hand over hers. "I know."

Emily felt her stomach flip over and her cheeks get warm. Seriously, she had to stop behaving like a schoolgirl with a bad crush. She pulled her fingers away from Johnny's and handed the menu back to the waitress. "Just coffee for me, thank you."

"No wonder you're so thin. You don't eat," Johnny said after the waitress left.

"I had breakfast already."

"An early riser."

"I like to run five-miles most mornings, come home, have a protein shake. But enough about me. Tell me about last night. What did you think?"

"About the presentation? Or the bizarre exchange between Stonehaven and Arabella?"

"What bizarre exchange?"

"Sorry, I forgot you had left by then. I was about to come over and sit with you two when you up and left."

"I had some things to take care of," she said, wishing now she'd stayed. "So what happened?"

"First off, Stonehaven sat with Arabella. I couldn't hear what they were saying, but it was clear he was taunting her."

Damn. And she'd told Arabella to be nice. "Sounds like his *modus operandi.*"

"I take it you don't care for him? Past history?"

"It's a long story."

"I have the time if you ever want to fill me in." Johnny flashed an affectionate smile. "I've been told I'm a good listener."

I'm sure you are. "Another time. Right now, I'd like to hear more about what happened last night."

Johnny was about to fill her in when her cell phone rang. Emily cursed herself for forgetting to turn it off. She hated people who answered their phones in restaurants. She glanced at the screen. Arabella. She let it go to voicemail, was about to turn her phone off when a text came through. "Call me. URGENT. Arabella."

"I know I'm being incredibly rude, but I need to call this person back. It seems there's some sort of emergency. I'll be right back."

"I'll be waiting."

Emily stood outside the Sunrise Café, shivering in the cold winter air. She'd slipped on her gloves, but like a fool she'd left her jacket inside, thinking the wool sweater would be warm enough. It wasn't.

"Arabella, it's Emily. What's the emergency?"

"I was at Garrett Stonehaven's room at the Gilroy Mansion this morning."

"They gave you an appointment already?"

"Not exactly."

"Then what exactly?"

"I may have said and done some things last night at the Noose. Some things that in hindsight I shouldn't have." Arabella paused. "I was worried I might have blown my chance to get the scoop on the investment side of the plan, figured if I went to see Stonehaven before he took appointments, groveled a bit..."

Emily knew how much Stonehaven despised weakness. "Let me guess. Stonehaven dismissed you."

"Worse."

"He wouldn't let you in?"

"He didn't answer. So I tried the handle and the door was open. I thought I could do some snooping around if he wasn't there."

"It didn't occur to you that you might be taking rather big risk? What if he'd stepped out for a moment?"

"In retrospect, it might have been a bit impulsive."

"A *bit* impulsive?"

"It gets worse."

"Worse?"

"Uh-huh. It turned out he was in."

Emily could imagine Stonehaven's response when he saw Arabella trundle through the door. "What did he do?"

"He didn't say or anything." Arabella's voice broke. "He was already dead."

CHAPTER 25

E mily hated to ask, but she'd been in the news business long enough to know that if you didn't pose the question, no one was volunteering the answer. And as much as she was growing to like her, Arabella could be a bit of a hot head. "Did you kill him?"

Arabella sighed. "Seriously, Emily. Would I have called you if I did?"

"I don't know." There it was, spoken out loud. Emily wanted to believe Arabella was innocent, wanted to trust the person she'd begun to view as a friend, but how much did she really know about the antiques shop owner?

"Thanks for the vote of confidence. He could have died of natural causes, did you ever think of that? He was sitting there, slumped over in an armchair. He could have had a heart attack or something. Or it could have been an accident. A prescription bottle was on the end table next to him, an empty glass, along with a bottle of red wine."

"Have you called the police?"

"No. I don't think anyone saw me. Camilla's car was gone. To be honest, I figured she'd be at yoga. And as far as I know, there isn't anyone else staying at the Mansion right now. I hightailed it out of there, came to the shop, and called you. I thought of calling Levon, but I knew he'd go all 'what the hell were you thinking' on me, and frankly, I couldn't deal with it."

What the hell had she been thinking? Emily waved at Johnny again, signaled another two minutes, and crossed her heart the way kids did when they were making a promise. He nodded and smiled. It was a warm smile, with no sign of irritation. She smiled back, feeling ridiculously pleased. "So then you thought of me?"

"I didn't know what else to do. I wouldn't have known Stonehaven was dead unless I entered his room uninvited. And after last night—"

"What about last night?"

Arabella gave Emily a recap.

"I see your point," Emily said when Arabella had finished.

"So what should I do?"

"Give me a minute." Emily shut her eyes and tried to think. "Are you absolutely sure nobody saw you?"

"Positive."

"Okay, then. Go back to the Gilroy Mansion, knock on the door, call his name, try the door. You see him there and call the police."

"What if they ask why I didn't call them right away?"

Emily sighed. "How will they know unless you tell them?"

"Right, you're right. Okay, I'll do it. Will you come over when I'm finished with the police?"

"Text me when you're back at the Glass Dolphin. I'll come by as soon as I can."

"Thanks for believing me."

"I hope I'm not making a mistake."

"You're not. I promise."

Emily wished she could be as sure. How much did she know about Arabella Carpenter? She hung up without saying anything more, dragging her half-frozen body back into the warmth of the Café and Johnny's smile.

"Sorry about that," Emily said, taking her seat. "I hate when people do that to me. Take calls while we're in a restaurant. It always seems so incredibly self-absorbed."

"I don't think you're self-absorbed." Johnny pushed aside a plate that held the remnants of a toasted western and home fries. "Anything I can do to help?"

"Thanks, but it's a personal matter. Something's come up. Back in Toronto. With an old friend." Emily realized she was babbling. The kind of babbling liars did when they didn't have a good cover story and were making things up on the fly.

Emily could tell by the sudden tightness in his jaw that her story didn't fool Johnny. Had he seen the name of the mystery caller flash on her cell? Seen the "ARA" before she'd slipped the phone back into her purse?

Maybe. Probably. Almost certainly.

She cursed silently. Why hadn't she just told the truth? Admitted it was Arabella, upset about the evening before. Now Johnny would assume they were hiding something.

Which of course, they were. Even the reason for this breakfast was moot, now that Stonehaven was dead. But Johnny didn't know that yet, and neither should she.

"Let's get back to the interview, shall we? Tell me about the Main Street Merchants' Association, and what StoreHaven could mean to its members and the town."

The tension left Johnny's face, and he smiled, his dark eyes warm and inviting.

"I thought you'd never ask."

CHAPTER 26

A rabella went on a food-finding mission the minute she got back to the Glass Dolphin. She whipped open drawers and cupboards throughout the shop, looking for something, anything. A stale Snickers bar, some mints, a pack of saltines. There had to be more than the tin of Walker's Scottish shortbread she saved for visitors. Unfortunately, there wasn't. She thought back to her "interview" with Detective Merryfield at the Gilroy Mansion. The man had the most enormous hands she'd ever seen, not to mention the biceps of a professional bodybuilder. He'd been more than kind, taking down her statement, explaining it would be a while before they determined the cause of death. "This isn't like television where everything happens in an hour," Merryfield had said, and his partner nodded in agreement.

But the sniff of suspicion was out there. Because she had to admit, if Garrett Stonehaven had been murdered, things didn't look good for her. Not after the way she'd stood up to him at the presentation, and certainly not after her toast. What if they found out she'd been at the Gilroy Mansion earlier this morning? She couldn't bear to think about it. And there was something more worrisome. When she got there, the second time, the red wine and the half-empty glass had still been sitting on the end table where she'd seen them last. But the bottle of pills she'd told Emily about was missing.

Which left two possibilities. Either someone had been in the room after her and taken the pills away, or when she had wandered in someone had been in the suite, hidden, and waited until she left.

Either scenario was less than desirable. But how could she tell the police something was missing without telling them she'd left and come back?

Arabella desperately hoped she could trust Emily. Emily would know what to do. Because Stonehaven's plan, she was convinced, was at the core of everything. She may have been used to weeding out fakes and forgeries, but as a journalist, Emily would have contacts, ways to get at information.

And at least once Emily got here she could break out the shortbread.

Emily took notes as Johnny talked. She learned he wasn't born in Lount's Landing ("another Toronto transplant"), and that he had moved here after his older brother died at camp.

"I was still in high school, but my parents were too grief-stricken to deal with me after Jake drowned," Johnny said. "Graham Gilroy had been at the same camp as Jake, and his folks took pity on me and let me stay with them a while. I did a few odd jobs after graduation, and about ten years ago I opened It's a Colorful Life."

"It must have been hard on you when Graham died in the snowmobiling accident."

"Wicked hard. Camilla and I pulled one another through. It's funny, I never cared for Camilla before that. I always thought she married Graham for his money and his status. And frankly, I don't think she thought much of me either. But Graham's death brought us closer. We finally had something in common."

"Your grief."

Johnny nodded. "I know you're becoming friends with Arabella Carpenter, and I'm sure you're aware there's some history between them. But Camilla isn't the monster Arabella makes her out to be. Truth be told, Arabella can be a bit of a hothead."

"And Levon?"

"Is still in love with Arabella, always has been, always will be." Johnny smiled. "It's the reason Camilla tries so hard to push Arabella's buttons. Camilla is used to getting what, and who, she wants. But we're getting off track. You wanted to know about the Main Street Merchants' Association."

"I did. What prompted you to start it?"

"Shops started closing up after the mill closed in Miakoda Falls. Main Street was at risk of becoming one of those dilapidated old streets no one bothers to visit, let alone shop at. I started researching towns that had transformed their own Main Streets."

"What did you discover?"

"The most successful ones had formed associations or corporations, with the end goal of strengthening the economic, historic, and cultural characteristics of their respective communities. That's exactly what I wanted to do."

"You seem to be succeeding. There are a few new businesses. The Hanged Man's Noose, the Sunrise Café, the Glass Dolphin."

"Thanks. Poppy Spencer has been a great asset. She's worked tirelessly with landlords to get vacant properties leased." Johnny grinned. "Poppy can be persuasive. She's also the one who brought Garrett Stonehaven into the picture."

Interesting. Emily would have to pay Poppy a visit.

"There seems to be some controversy about his plan."

"Change is always difficult, perhaps all the more so in a small town."

"So you believe StoreHaven will be good for Main Street?"

"I believe the potential is there, otherwise I wouldn't be supporting the project. But ultimately its success or failure will depend upon the amount of investor interest." Johnny looked at his watch. "I need to open the store. Can we pick this up at a later date? Possibly over dinner?"

"A girl has to eat," Emily said, and tried not to blush.

CHAPTER 27

E mily arrived at the Glass Dolphin to find Arabella pacing the floor, a tin of shortbread in her hands.

"Have a cookie," Arabella said. "Scottish shortbread. Not quite as good as homemade, but darned good for tinned biscuits."

Cookies? The woman had discovered Garrett Stonehaven dead, fled the scene, and was concerned about cookies?

"Thanks, but I just finished eating."

"Do you mind if I have a couple?"

"They're *your* cookies," Emily said, smiling.

"I eat when I'm stressed. But these are supposed to be for visitors."

"Have my cookie then."

"Now there's an idea." Arabella reached for a cookie.

"So, fill me in."

Arabella told Emily how the police had taken her statement. From her description of Detective Merryfield, Emily figured him for the man in the front row at Stonehaven's presentation, which was interesting—and worth exploring—but at the moment, Arabella's predicament took precedence.

"They didn't say much. Took down the details, said they wouldn't know the cause of death right away," Arabella said. "I told them about last night at the Noose. I figured if I didn't someone else would. I also told them I'd gone over to the Gilroy Mansion this morning to talk to Stonehaven like a rational human being. But the reality is if his death wasn't an accident, I'm definitely going to be a suspect." She chewed on her thumbnail. "There's something else."

"What?"

"The pills I told you about, the ones on the table next to him."

"Uh-huh?"

"They weren't there when I got back."

"Not there? What do you mean they weren't there? Are you saying someone came and took them?"

"It looks that way." Arabella looked miserable. "The thing is, Emily, if I tell the police something is missing, then it means I have to tell them I was there earlier. And if I do that, they'll wonder why I didn't call before."

It was a dilemma. But there was more to it. Arabella was possibly in danger—*if* whoever was responsible for Stonehaven's death spotted her the first time round. A thought struck her. "Was Camilla back by the time the police arrived?"

"Not at first. She drove up while they were taking my statement, came strutting over in her size zero yoga gear, demanding to know what was going on. Detective Merryfield told her I'd discovered Stonehaven dead in his room, that they'd need to interview her."

"How'd she take the news?"

"At first she stood there, looking stunned. Then she started attacking me, said this sort of thing could ruin the Mansion's reputation." Arabella grinned at the memory. "I admit I used that to my advantage. I asked her point blank if I should have just left, not called the police. That shut her up."

"Quick thinking. Still, the missing pills are problematic."

"I know." Arabella took out another cookie.

"What are you going to do?"

"I'm hoping it's what *we* plan to do."

"We?"

"Yes, we. The way I figure it, everything revolves around Garrett Stonehaven's plan."

"You could be right. But where do I come in?"

"I thought with your experience as an investigative reporter and a journalist you might be able to help me find out the truth." Arabella flushed scarlet. "Help me clear my name. If it needs clearing."

Emily knew she should call Michelle Ellis before promising anything. With Stonehaven dead, the assignment might be over, though Michelle might ask her to stay and report on the police investigation. She thought about Johnny, his vision for Main Street, the businesses and people that depended upon him and the Association he had founded. Businesses like The Hanged Man's Noose, like the Glass Dolphin. For owners like Betsy Ehrlich and Arabella Carpenter.

She thought about Carter Dixon. Not the easiest man to like, at least not the version she'd met, but a man who, at least according to the local buzz, had the best interests of Main Street at heart. Or at least he thought he did. She remembered February Fassbender, the invisible girl who "saw and heard things." And in that moment Emily knew what she had to do.

"I'll help you find out the truth, Arabella. Or at least I'll try."

"Thank heavens that's settled." Arabella closed the tin of shortbread, but not before taking out one more cookie.

"You should call Levon and tell him everything before Camilla does."

"I know. Not that I'm looking forward to it."

"Are you going to tell him you were at the Gilroy Mansion earlier?"

"I don't think so. He's bound to overreact. He has a tendency to do that when it comes to me. The fewer people who know, the better."

"I have to agree with you there. But if you're calling Levon—"

"Yes?"

"You told me at The Hanged Man's Noose you had a theory, but you needed to clear it with Levon first."

"I don't have to clear the theory with Levon. I have to clear telling his story, which was the reason for the theory. Though now that Stonehaven's dead, I'm not so sure about any of it."

"Do you think, if you were to be there, that Levon would tell me his story? Let me decide it it's plausible?"

"I can ask him, see what he says."

"Then that's our next step."

CHAPTER 28

They ended up meeting Levon at The Hanged Man's Noose the next afternoon. Emily knew Arabella was reluctant to revisit the pub, given her recent run-in with Betsy over Stonehaven, but Levon had insisted, telling her Betsy and Arabella needed to kiss and make up.

Emily had sided with Levon on the location, although her reasons were far less altruistic. She was primarily interested in Betsy's side of everything that had transpired. Outnumbered, a reluctant Arabella had agreed. But judging by the way two women hugged one another, each one crying and apologizing at the same time, Emily was sure their friendship would survive the Stonehaven tsunami.

"I don't like the idea of you getting any more involved in this than you already are," Levon said. "Let the police do their job, and keep your nose out of it."

"Emily is going to help me," Arabella said, a haughty tone to her voice.

"Gee, now I feel better."

Emily was about to respond when a puffy-eyed Betsy arrived at their table with a Sleeman Honey Brown lager for Levon, a chardonnay for Arabella, and a merlot for Emily. Telltale splotches of someone who'd been crying on and off for hours stained her cheeks.

"How are you holding up, Betsy?" Emily asked. "I understand from Arabella that you were seeing Sto ... Garrett. It must make it doubly difficult for you."

Betsy attempted a smile, didn't quite succeed. "You can't begin to imagine. I realize not everyone was on board with what he was planning for Main Street, Arabella especially, but I loved him, you know? And I know he loved me. Garrett wouldn't have done anything to hurt me."

Emily wasn't so sure, but she knew better than to say so, and thankfully Arabella stayed silent while Levon studied the foam on his beer.

"Garrett wouldn't have done anything to hurt me," Betsy repeated, her voice breaking. She wiped back a tear and glanced from Emily to Arabella to Levon and back to Emily. "You want to know the hardest part of all this? The thing that really haunts me? His murderer might have... might have been here on the night of the presentation party."

"Do you remember everyone who was here that night?"

"I need to make a list for the police. They left here about an hour ago. But why do you care?"

"Emily's going to help us find out the truth," Arabella said, with a pointed glance at Levon.

"I'm all for that," Betsy said, her face brightening. "If you want, Emily, I can give you a copy of the list once I've finished."

"A copy of the list would be great. We should each make a list. Who knows, one of us might remember someone the other didn't."

"Speaking of people who were here that evening, I don't remember seeing Stanford McLelland at the post-presentation party," Levon said.

"He wasn't here," Betsy said. "I was a bit surprised, because he's been such a supporter of the pub. He spent a lot of time with me so I'd understand all the types of insurance I'd need, and he worked hard to get me an affordable rate. But then again, Stanford's never been one for crowds." She glanced around the pub. "Customers waiting, gotta go. I'll get you that list, Emily."

"Weren't you sitting with Stanford at the presentation?" Emily asked after Betsy had left.

"I was going to tell you about Stan," Arabella said, her eyes lighting up. "The night of the presentation, after Stonehaven left, he told me that he felt a migraine coming on."

"I suppose that's possible," Emily said, not quite getting Arabella's excitement. So what if the man had a headache?

Arabella shook her head. "I worked for Stan for years. I've never known him to complain of so much as a mild headache, let alone a migraine. But there was something he said that struck me as odd at the time. He said something about taking care of everything. He told me not to worry."

"You have to call him," Emily said. "Find out what he meant."

"I'm way ahead of you," Arabella said. "I called Stan as soon as I got into the shop this morning. I told him about the Treasontini business, about Stonehaven's death, about the police interviewing me. He came to see me within the hour. I thought it was to lend me support, but the truth was he came to tell me something."

"Which was?"

"He'd been part of Stonehaven's team." Arabella leaned back, a self-satisfied smirk on her face.

"Wow, I didn't see that one coming," Emily said, shaking her head. "Stanford McLelland and Garrett Stonehaven. I don't really know Stanford, but he didn't strike me as the sort of guy who'd support someone like Stonehaven."

"Can't say I saw it coming either," Levon said. "How'd Stan manage to get on Stonehaven's team?"

"He told me that he'd been recruited. To be fair, Stanford thought it was about revitalizing Main Street and finding a location for a condo. He didn't think there was anything ... untoward."

"A condo in Lount's Landing?" Levon sounded skeptical.

"I could see it," Arabella said, a defensive tone in her voice. "I always thought the schoolhouse could be converted with a little bit of imagination."

"And I have seen it, even written about it in *Urban Living*," Emily said. "Besides, Stonehaven was known for his condo developments. It all makes sense if you look at the bigger picture."

"Fine, right, whatever," Levon said. "Who else did he recruit, did Stan tell you?"

"Gloria and Carter. They also recruited Chantal and Ned. According to Stanford, no one on the team was aware of StoreHaven until Stonehaven held a pre-presentation meeting."

"Nice," Levon said.

"Typical," Emily said.

"There's more. Carter Dixon challenged Stonehaven on it, in front of everyone, told him he should start revitalizing Main Street before springing the idea of StoreHaven onto folks. From what I can gather, things got tense. No overt threats, but it was clear Stonehaven was not impressed. Then he suggested circling the revitalization of Main Street back to the school, and Carter said that could probably work. Stanford said it calmed Stonehaven down some."

"I sense a 'but'," Emily said.

Arabella nodded. "Stanford said he saw this look of fury in Stonehaven's eyes. And now Carter is dead. He didn't come right out and say it, but I'm sure Stanford thinks Stonehaven was behind Carter's death in some way. Except Stonehaven wasn't at the Café that day, was he?"

"No, but that doesn't mean he wasn't behind it," Emily said. "Remember when I told you I had an idea?"

"Yes, but you said you weren't quite ready to talk about it," Arabella said.

"That's because there's a fair bit of conjecture on my part."

"We'll take that into consideration," Levon said.

"I think February might have done something." She told Arabella and Levon about the way February had stumbled and fell.

"Everyone said Carter always kept an EpiPen in his jacket pocket, but he didn't have one on him that day. What if February knew he'd have an allergic reaction? Somehow had tampered with his food? What if when she stumbled, it wasn't by accident but rather to grab the EpiPen from his pocket?"

"That's a whole lot of what-ifs," Levon said. "It's more plausible that February stumbled because she was stoned."

"You're right on all counts. That's why I've been reluctant to say anything. But the fact is, February stayed behind after Gloria left to follow Carter to the hospital. She said she'd do all the cleaning up before closing. So she had plenty of time to get rid of any evidence."

"Okay, let's assume for argument's sake that February is responsible for Carter's death, and that Stonehaven put her up to it in some way," Arabella said. "And let's assume she couldn't deal with it, so she decided to shoot some heroin, and that the overdose may or may not have been intentional. It still leaves us with the question of who killed Garret Stonehaven. If it turns out not to be an accident."

"And why," Emily said.

"Levon might have a theory," Arabella said.

"What sort of theory?"

"It's a long story, and it goes a long way back," Levon said.

"Okay, so tell me already," Emily said. "But first, let's order some real food. The wine is starting to go to my head."

CHAPTER 29

Levon and Arabella each settled on the Jailhouse Club, bacon extra crispy for her, not so crispy for him, and a side order of sweet potato fries split two ways. "Make sure you give us each our own plate," Arabella said to Betsy. "Levon can be a bit territorial when it comes to his food."

"Just because I don't like someone picking food off my plate while I'm eating doesn't mean I'm territorial," Levon said.

"A picker who doesn't like to be picked," Arabella said.

Emily decided to stay out of it. She studied the menu for a minute—typical pub fare, without a lot of vegetarian meal options, unless you considered potato skins and deep-fried mozzarella-jalapeno poppers as vegetarian meals. In the end, she ordered a BLT—surely a couple of strips of well-done bacon couldn't hurt—and a club soda with lime. "If I drink any more wine, I won't be able to concentrate," she said, pushing the empty wine glass away from her. Arabella asked for a diet cola. Levon ordered another beer.

"So, what's the long story?" Emily asked, after they had finished eating.

It took Levon a few moments of shifting in his seat and exchanging looks with Arabella, but eventually he got started.

"I grew up in the suburbs, Scarborough to be exact, street upon street of virtually identical 1950s bungalows. Three bedrooms, one bathroom, kitchen, a living room, dining room combo, all crammed into a thousand square feet. If you were lucky you had a wood-paneled basement recreation room."

Levon paused to take a sip of his beer. "The neighborhood started off as one of Toronto's first shiny, new post-war suburbs, gradually transitioning from fresh dreams to blue collar to new immigrants to drugs and decay. But it wasn't a bad place to grow up. We had decent-sized yards and, I don't know, I guess you'd call it a sense of community."

"I know the area," Emily said. "I grew up a few miles north of you, in Agincourt."

"We used to say Agincourt was on the right side of the 401," Levon said with a grin. "My dad left a few weeks shy of my sixteenth birthday. Left for a pack of smokes and never came back. My mom spun out of control. Started drinking, taking tranquilizers, dating whoever came by, the furnace repairman, the neighbor down the street. I became the invisible kid. A child psychologist might say I acted out to get attention. Whatever the reason, I started hanging out with a group of equally screwed up teenagers. Before long, I was flunking out of school."

"What did your mom do?"

"She was too far gone by then to realize anything was wrong. At midterm, I changed a couple of F's on my report card to B's. Shouldn't have fooled anyone, but my mom had no real interest in her own life, let alone mine. The school guidance counselor was equally useless. Back then, wasn't a lot of bubble wrapping of kids."

"What did you end up doing?"

"Did I straighten out, do you mean?" Levon shook his head. "I started taking stuff from the house, little things, knickknacks and vases and old junk my father had left piled up in the attic, stuff I knew my mom wouldn't miss. Then I'd take them into Pete's Pawn Shop and get a bit of money. I convinced myself I was doing my mother a favor, de-cluttering the place."

"But your mom couldn't have had enough stuff to keep you going for long."

"She didn't, but before long spring came, and with it, a plethora of neighborhood yard sales. I used what little money I had to start buying the kind of stuff Pete sold, jewelry, old wristwatches, paintings, furniture, china, you name it."

"Sounds like you were born to be a picker," Emily said.

Levon smiled. "Maybe I was. For a while, things looked promising. I had a hobby that more or less kept me out of trouble and into a bit of money. Pete was a crusty old curmudgeon, but he started to take time with me, mentor me. I managed to pull my marks together, enough to squeak through the year with a pass. And then winter happened."

"Winter?" Emily couldn't see the connection.

"Winter. No more yard sales to feed my habit. Remember, there was no Internet back then, no eBay or craigslist. It wasn't like today. You basically had those *Super Shopper* kinds of publications and newspaper ads. One afternoon, I was at the local hardware store and decided to try for the five-finger discount. Took a set of socket wrenches, stuffed them inside my jacket."

"But it turned out okay? You got away with it?"

"Not exactly. But the owner was a decent guy. He called the police, I think more to scare me than anything else, because in the end he didn't want to press charges."

"What did the police do?"

"The officer on duty was a decent sort. His last name was Death, spelled D-E-A-T-H, but he pronounced it Deeth, said if Mr. Murphy wouldn't press charges, there wasn't much he could do, beyond having a long, hard talk with my mom. When she didn't answer the phone, he drove over to our house. To this day, I don't know why he insisted on going there without me. Could be he'd seen it all before, or could be he had a policeman's premonition."

"A premonition?"

"Officer Death found her in the car garage, inside her beat up car, the engine still running. The kid next door saw the whole thing, couldn't wait to tell me all about it, how her face was bright cherry red." Levon swallowed hard. "Officer Death called it in right away, and an ambulance was there in no time, but it was too late to save her. She was pronounced DOA at the hospital, a clear case of suicide by carbon monoxide poisoning."

Emily knew firsthand how suicide impacted the surviving family. She also knew spouting off a bunch of platitudes wouldn't make it any better. "I'm sorry."

"It was long time ago. Twenty years and counting. The good news is another kid today shouldn't have to face that sort of horror show. Catalytic converters found on modern automobiles eliminate over ninety-nine per cent of carbon monoxide produced."

Arabella reached for Levon's hand.

Twenty years later and Levon was still reading up on CO2 poisoning, Emily thought. She wondered if the people left behind after a suicide ever got over the pain, the sense of abandonment.

Levon stopped and took a sip of his beer, grimacing slightly. "There are a few other details I'd rather not go into, but the bottom line was I was sent to a boot camp for young offenders who needed some direction in their life. It was called Camp Miakoda."

"I remember there had been talk of experimental boot camps for teens, but I hadn't realized there was one in Miakoda Falls," Emily said. "Is it still there?"

Levon shook his head. "It was about ten miles outside of Miakoda Falls, on the Dutch River, locked in between two sets of waterfalls and surrounded by forest. Quite remote, as you'd expect it to be. The government of the day sank a fair bit of money into it, but it faced a lot of public and political opposition. It was only open for that one summer. The land, including the buildings, was sold off about three years ago to a real estate developer."

"Let me guess," Emily said. "Garrett Stonehaven?"

"I'm not sure," Levon said. "I tried to trace it, but all the records circled back to a numbered company. Poppy Spencer would know. She was the realtor of record."

Arabella had mentioned that Poppy had started changing about three years ago. Getting involved with Stonehaven might explain it.

"It might be unethical for her to reveal the name of the purchaser, but I think your conclusion is solid, given her most recent dealings with Stonehaven," Emily said. "Plus, Johnny told me Poppy was the one who brought Stonehaven to Lount's Landing. Do you still have the information on the numbered company?"

"Sure, it's on my computer somewhere. If I email it to you, could you trace it?"

"I might be able to. It's interesting, though. If the Miakoda Falls camp was purchased by Stonehaven three years ago, then his plans for Lount's Landing went far deeper than StoreHaven." Emily studied Levon. "What was your interest in finding out who purchased the camp? Did you have plans to buy it?"

"No, but I'd heard the camp had been sold and I wondered if the buyer had been Garrett Stonehaven. I've followed his career with some interest. He was at camp with me that summer, though back in the day he was known as Garry Stone. He changed his name legally as soon as he turned eighteen. He thought Garrett Stonehaven sounded more sophisticated, the kind of name a big shot might have."

"Like Levon sounds a bit more glamorous than Larry," Arabella said.

"Nothing hiding there, Arabella. The whole Larry business was just Garrett being an ass, a riff on my last name. He knew it bugged the hell out of me, knew my deadbeat dad was known as Larry—I made the mistake of confiding that tidbit to him when I thought he was a friend. Trust him to throw it back in my face all these years later. His not-so-subtle reminder of our past."

"Fascinating," Emily said, thinking this was exactly the kind of dirt Michelle Ellis would be interested in. "Not only did Garrett Stonehaven have another name, he was a young offender. What was he in for?"

"He was busted for running a pyramid scheme. Ironically, while he was there, he tried to run another one."

Emily thought about Stonehaven's presentation, the neighbors helping neighbors angle. "Do you think StoreHaven was a pyramid scheme?"

"I think it's possible."

"And if it was a pyramid scheme, then he might be dead because he tried to swindle the wrong person or persons," Arabella said.

"That's certainly one theory," Levon said, "but I've been thinking about nothing else for the past few hours. I think the reason for his death might go farther back than StoreHaven. Possibly as far back as Camp Miakoda."

"Do tell," Emily said, leaning back to hear the rest of the story.

"Outside of group and individual counseling, Camp Miakoda wasn't what you'd expect of a boot camp for young offenders," Levon said. "It was more like a supervised summer camp. We were encouraged to partake in a variety of outdoor activities. That was their word, by the way, partake. Baseball and basketball, swimming and hiking. Kayaking and canoeing."

"I suppose they were trying to develop your teambuilding skills and keep you fit," Emily said, "but weren't they worried you'd try to run off?"

"Be a bit tough. The property was surrounded by high wire fencing, and the road leading into the camp was a good mile of winding road, leading up to yet another fence, this one guarded. Adjacent to the camp was a fast-flowing river, across the way, acres of densely wooded forest. If the river didn't stop you, the forest had your number. It wouldn't take much more than a few minutes to get lost in there."

"But you were on the water, with access to a canoe. Surely you could have tried to make a run for it."

Levon shook his head. "Arabella asked me the same thing. It would've been difficult, if not all but impossible. At that point the Dutch River has two fairly large waterfalls, one about three miles to the east and one about five miles to the west.

Nothing like Niagara Falls, but the one to the east had a partially open dam, used to be an old hydro generating station, helped power the mill upriver way back when. No one in a boat, or swimming, was going to survive the fall without breaking at least a few bones, and all kinds of stories were floating around about the fools who died trying. But even without all that, where were we going to escape to? Most of us didn't have anywhere else to go."

"So you became one big happy family?"

"I wouldn't exactly say one big happy family. Each of us was carrying more than our fair share of baggage. Not everyone got along every single day." He glanced over at Arabella.

"We all have our fair share of baggage," Arabella said.

Levon flashed a smile. "Some of us more than others, eh, Bella? Anyway, it wasn't long before friendships started forming. My first real friend there was Graham Gilroy. We met on the bus, sat next to one another."

"Graham Gilroy of the Gilroy Mansion?" Emily was surprised. Johnny hadn't mentioned anything about Levon and Graham being friends.

"The one and only, although back then he was just another kid with a sad story. He'd been caught stealing exams and selling them to other students, not to mention cheating on a few of his own exams. Claimed the constant pressure to achieve good grades drove him to it, but he'd also pocketed some serious coin selling those papers. His parents had enough money and power to pull some strings and save him from getting expelled or worse. The trade-off was a summer at Camp Miakoda."

"A poor little rich kid," Arabella said, with an affectionate glance at her ex. "And Levon, a poor little poor kid."

Levon smiled. "Something like that. I was also a bit in awe of Graham. Everyone at Camp Miakoda was, to one degree or another. Partly it was because he had the sort of self-assurance that comes with growing up wealthy, but it was more than that. Graham was always pushing the boundaries."

"What sort of boundaries?" Emily asked.

"Silly things. Like if we were supposed to swim across the river and back, Graham would dive in off the rock cliff, instead of off the dock. When he died in the snowmobiling accident it dawned on me. He'd always had a self-destructive streak. But back then, Graham seemed exciting. And to be perfectly honest, I figured getting chummy with a rich kid couldn't hurt my future chances."

"So you became fast friends with Graham," Emily said. She could see how that could happen.

"Yeah, but you know how these things are. First friendships form and then cliques develop. Before long there were five of us, with Garry the self-appointed leader of the pact." Levon shook his head. "I knew the minute I set eyes on Garry Stone that he was trouble. I should have trusted my instincts. I first met him on the school bus taking us to Camp Miakoda. We were picked up at various drop points, depending on where we lived. By the time I got in, the bus was pretty much full, row upon row of taciturn teens, most of them looking as scared as I felt. The lone exceptions were a dark-eyed kid with a semi-insolent stare and a guy sprawled out next to him. I can still remember the way he sat there, his impossibly long legs splayed out into the middle of the aisle. He muttered something like 'another loser,' and a couple of the kids snickered, though most of them kept their heads down and their mouths shut. The dark-eyed kid, he just kept on staring."

Levon's eyes narrowed at the memory, and his voice took on a hypnotic tone. Emily closed her eyes and found herself being transported to another time and place...

⫸►●◄⫷

Levon decided to take the seat across from them. "Takes one to know one," he said quietly, kicking one of those long legs, hard, as he pretended to trip over them. There would be a nice bruise there tomorrow. The driver turned around and shot him a warning look. The dark-eyed kid grinned. The sprawler studied Levon through narrowed eyes. After a moment he nodded and pulled his legs away. Levon wasn't sure if the guy was giving in, or thinking of a way to give it back. He'd be ready for either.

The drive to Camp Miakoda took forever. As a city kid, even one from the suburbs, Levon had never seen so many trees, let alone endless stretches of road dotted with nothing but the occasional one-horse town. The final stop before camp was in a godforsaken place called Lount's Landing. He was wondering what would possess anyone to live so far from civilization when a curly-haired teen with a kiss-my-ass swagger stepped onto the bus.

"Money," the long-legged kid said, under his breath.

Levon looked at the new arrival. Long-legs was right. Everything about this guy spelled money, from the brand new Levi's to the Tommy Hilfiger polo shirt. Who wore Tommy Hilfiger to boot camp? He moved over to the window seat and gestured for the new kid to sit next to him. Hilfiger boy muttered a quiet thanks and sat down. "Graham," he said. "Graham Gilroy."

"Levon. Larroquette."

"Garry Stone," long legs said, leaning over. "This here's Jacob Porter."

"Jake."

"Cut the chatter," the bus driver said, not bothering to turn around. Levon settled back into his seat and stared out the window. For the first time, he began to doubt Constable Death's plan. They couldn't talk on the bus? And this was supposed to be better than juvie hall or some do-gooder foster home?

After a very long ninety minutes, they turned into a narrow road all but obscured by a thicket of pines. A barbed wire fence came into view. Two security guards were there to unlock the padlocked gate and let them through. One pimply-faced kid at the back of the bus murmured, "Oh, shit," which prompted a few nervous titters, hastily stifled.

The narrow road continued, twisting and turning, with intermittent clearings off to one side, presumably to provide an allowance for an oncoming vehicle to pass. The clearings were already starting to grow over with a tangle of weeds and wild-flowers. If you tried to escape, Levon thought, the mosquitoes and black flies would eat you alive. The silence in the bus was deafening, the odor of sweat and stolen dreams palpable.

At long last they arrived at a gatehouse. The bus driver handed some sort of pass to the guard. A wooden arm inside the gate lifted and they drove through.

The first thing Levon noticed was a long red bunkhouse with small leaded glass windows. They were attractive until he realized the leaded glass acted like bars. The next thing he noticed was a narrow river, with a densely packed forest on the other side. So this was going to be home for the foreseeable future. An ominous chill fingered his spine.

"Welcome to Camp Miakoda," the bus driver said, his voice dripping with sarcasm. "Back rows go first. Come on boys, step lively."

CHAPTER 30

E mily wasn't sure where Levon's mind had wandered off, but she had been a journalist long enough to know when to push and when to wait. Arabella also knew
enough when to stay silent, at least when it came to her ex-husband. She gave Emily
a look as if to say, "He does this." It wasn't until Levon suggested they order coffee
that Emily knew he was ready to start talking again.

"So how did Garry Stone become part of your clique?" Emily asked after Betsy
had brought their coffee.

Levon didn't answer right away. Instead he took a tentative sip of his coffee.
"Betsy seriously needs to upgrade her coffee supply. Stuff could strip the stripes off a
zebra." He added two creamers and a packet of sugar, stirred, sipped, added another
packet of sugar. When he was satisfied, he looked up at Emily and Arabella and
began.

"Like I said, I first met Garry on the bus to Camp Miakoda. After Graham got
on in Lount's Landing, and Garry made a snide comment about how he looked like
money, I decided there and then that whoever this long-legged guy was, he was a
class-A jerk. When we got to camp I made a point of staying out of his way. But after
a few days, he sauntered over and reintroduced himself to me and Graham. He was
completely charming, apologized for his behavior on the bus."

Emily nodded. She knew how charming Stonehaven could be.

Levon continued. "We'd seen him around. He was hard to miss, a good head
taller than the rest of us, and loaded with the kind of looks women swoon over and
men admire. But it was more than that. He had this way of carrying himself, like he
had some sort of magical power."

"Even then?"

"Even then. I mentioned earlier he'd been busted for running a pyramid scheme,
a fairly lucrative one if he was to be believed, and we had no reason not to. All sorts
of pyramid schemes were going on at the time, with names like the Dinner Club or
the Empowering Women Club or the Airplane Club. You get the drift. But if you
got invited into one of the 'clubs,' no matter how naïve you might have been, you
knew it wasn't exactly legit."

"I've heard of pyramid schemes," Emily said, "but I'm not entirely sure how they
work. Is it the same as a Ponzi scheme? I remember reading about Bernie Madoff

and the way he bilked all sorts of celebrities and high society investors out of their life savings. The papers called it an elaborate Ponzi scheme."

"Bernie Madoff's an excellent recent example of a Ponzi scheme," Levon said. "Basically, it's a fraudulent investment plan where the money isn't actually invested. Instead, every new investment is used to pay off earlier investors. So when the investors stop coming in—"

"There's no money to pay off the earlier investors," Emily said.

"Exactly. But the thing to remember is Bernie Madoff didn't invent a new system. He simply took things to another level. Greed on steroids, if you will. The Ponzi scheme gets its name from a real life con artist by the name of Charles Ponzi. In 1920, Ponzi ran a scam promising New Englanders a fifty percent rate of return in forty-five days for a convoluted investment involving international mail coupons."

"Yet folks believed it," Emily said, thinking back to her conversation with Arabella on fakes and reproductions in the antiques world. "I guess the old adage, 'if it seems too good to be true, it probably is' comes into play."

Arabella smiled, and Emily knew they were both remembering the same conversation.

"There's another old saying, 'you can't cheat an honest man.' People fall victim to their own greed. Or desperation, if you want to put a shine on it," Levon said.

"So how does a pyramid scheme differ from a Ponzi scheme?" Arabella asked.

"In a Ponzi scheme the money collected from new investors is paid to previous investors, thereby providing a veneer of legitimacy. If you're one of the investors getting a great return on your investment, you aren't complaining, and a new investor is hoping for the same rate of return. In a pyramid scheme, every investor is expected to recruit further investors. Once that stops happening, the pyramid collapses."

"I still don't understand exactly how it works," Arabella said.

"Neither do I," Emily admitted. And she would need to when she reported back to Michelle Ellis. She had to prove she'd done her homework. Michelle would have zero tolerance for anything less.

"Okay," Levon said. "Let's take the classic 8-Ball Model, and let's say the game is called the Chef's Club. The head chef would be at the top of the pyramid. That's level one. The head chef recruits two people at level two, let's call that level the sous chef. So far, no money is changing hands, but both people at the sous chef level have an obligation to recruit two additional people for level three, let's call them kitchen assistants. And still no money is changing hands. Are you both with me so far?"

Arabella nodded.

"Not entirely," Emily said. "So far the pyramid has three tiers. The head chef, a second sous chef level with two people, and a third level with four kitchen assistants. But if no one has paid anybody any money, where's the scheme?"

"I'm getting to that. The four people recruited at the kitchen assistant level are each expected to recruit two new members for a fourth level, let's call it the wait-staff, but now the rules are changing. Those eight people can only join if they are willing to pay an entry fee to the head chef, let's say a thousand dollars. The head chef, or the founder of the pyramid, receives the entry fee from all eight people of level four, in this case, eight thousand dollars."

"Not a bad return for zero upfront capital investment," Emily said. "But what happens to the other levels? How do they make any money?"

"A great question, Emily. Once the head chef is paid, he leaves the pyramid, and the two sous chefs reach the top. At that point, the pyramid is split into two. Each sous chef becomes the head chef of their own pyramid, and the four kitchen assistants split off to become sous chefs, two in one pyramid, and two in the other. Then the eight members of the waitstaff split off, four in each pyramid, to become level three kitchen assistants."

"So as kitchen assistants, it's their job to each recruit two more people to fill out the now vacant eight spots at the level four waitstaff level," Emily said. "And once again, the waitstaff recruits are required to pay an entry fee of one thousand dollars."

"You've figured out the formula."

"But what happens to the original head chef?"

"He or she will join the waitstaff level in one of the other games, hoping to get to the top again. And by doing so, they add an air of legitimacy to the Chef's Club."

Emily thought for a moment. "And the pyramids keep splitting?"

"They do."

"So at some point, one or all of the pyramids have to collapse, don't they? Assuming each pyramid could go on for a while, there wouldn't be enough people in the world to keep it going in perpetuity."

"Right again. Often the only people who end up getting any money are the ones who never invested a dime, though the first recruits of level four sometimes get lucky."

"Wow," Emily said.

"Double wow," Arabella said.

"Double wow indeed. It's the allure of getting rich quick. Everyone figures they know two people, and it's in the best interest of the folks moving up the levels to help the newbies get fresh recruits." Levon shrugged. "Like I said, most people are victims of their own greed. And I'm sorry to say, Graham and I were no exception."

"Are you saying that you, Graham, and Garry ran a pyramid scheme at Camp Miakoda?" Emily thought about it. "Wouldn't that have been rather risky?"

"Graham was a risk-taker," Levon said. "And when Garry came up with the idea to run a pyramid scheme at the camp, he convinced us we could make enough money to start a new life once we got out. He called it graduating from Camp Miakoda, and in a way, he was right. We learned a lot about life there. On one occasion, we were taken on a heavily supervised bus trip to visit a maximum-security prison. Believe me, after that visit no one wanted to be a repeat offender."

"I know what you're thinking, Emily," Arabella chimed in. "Levon didn't want to be a repeat offender, and yet he was willing to risk running a pyramid scheme at a boot camp for young offenders."

"That was exactly what I was thinking," Emily said. "Though I expect a young Garry Stone could be every bit as convincing as Garrett Stonehaven."

"He's become more polished over the years, but you're right. He was very convincing. He managed to put together a team of six to form Club Miakoda. Garry was at the top of the pyramid. All the six of us had to do was recruit eight players who would pay $1,000 each and then split the money between us."

"Were you successful?"

"We could have been wildly successful, at least in the short term. Like I told Arabella, we were surrounded by kids who wanted to get rich quick, and they knew folks who wanted to get rich quicker. We found our first eight investors within a couple of days."

"You say you could have been successful," Emily said. "Meaning you weren't successful."

"Garry had promised us an even split, but when the money started coming in, he changed the rules, reverted it back to the traditional 8-Ball model where only the top gun got paid, and the pyramid split."

"What did you do?" Emily asked.

"What could we do? Go to the authorities and accuse Garry of cheating us on an illegal game? Before we were able to recruit another eight members, word got out there was a pyramid scheme going on and we had to shut it down. None of us could risk getting caught. And Garry Stone made off with eight grand."

"You suspected it was Garry Stone who did the talking," Emily said, her brow furrowing. "After all, he'd made his money and he wasn't about to risk getting caught to save any of you."

"I might have suspected Garry, but I could never prove it. As for the money, he claimed the guards took it, but I never believed him. As sure as I'm sitting here, he buried that money somewhere on the grounds, along with a list of everyone in the pyramid. Those names were his insurance policy."

"What about the others? What did they think?"

"I can't speak for everyone who was involved, but I do know Jake Porter was furious. For one thing, he'd dragged his kid brother, Johnny, into the scheme, and for another, he had this real sense of fair play, it didn't matter what the situation was."

"Hold up a second," Emily said, thinking of the photo of Johnny and his older brother hanging on the wall at It's a Colorful Life. "Are you saying Johnny's brother, Jake, was at *boot* camp? Versus, I don't know, a *regular* camp?"

"I forgot you didn't know the whole story," Levon said. "Yes, Jake was at Camp Miakoda."

Johnny had conveniently forgotten to mention that part. What else hadn't he told her?

"What about Johnny? Did you know him then?" Emily tried to imagine Johnny at fourteen, his older brother first sent away to camp, only to be found dead by the end of the summer. She couldn't reconcile the image with the man she knew.

Levon shook his head. "I wouldn't say any of us got to know Johnny, but we all respected his loyalty. We were allowed visitors on alternate Sundays, not that I ever had any. But Johnny, he never missed a single one. It was clear to everyone that Johnny idolized Jake, the way he followed him around like a lost puppy, hanging on his every word, laughing at his every joke, no matter how feeble. And for his part, Jake was determined to keep Johnny on the straight and narrow. He used to say he'd kill anyone who tried to mess with Johnny."

"And yet it was Jake who died," Arabella said.

"Go figure."

"How did Johnny take Jake's death?" Emily asked.

"How do you think? He was devastated. We all were. Graham and his heroics had galvanized the lot of us. Before Jake drowned, I think we all felt immortal."

"Every teenager feels immortal," Arabella said. "It's the best and worst part of adolescence."

Emily nodded. Arabella was right. But something else was niggling at her. "Johnny never mentioned a boot camp, but he did tell me his older brother drowned years ago. Did it happen at Camp Miakoda?"

Levon nodded. "Uh-huh. Jake died in a canoeing accident during a violent storm. I could never understand why he was so determined to go. I tried to stop him. Maybe if I had, things would have turned out differently."

"The wind was wild that night," Levon said. "Huge, nasty gusts that threatened to blow the lead right out of the leaded glass windows. Most of us were gathered in the communal living area, playing cards, board games, reading. Graham and Ambrose were working on a 3-D jigsaw puzzle of a gigantic castle, complete with moat."

"A jigsaw puzzle of a castle with a moat?" Emily grinned and winked at Arabella. "Was this summer camp or boot camp?"

Levon grinned back. "What can I say? Ambrose was younger than most of us by a good couple of years. He was still a bit of a mama's boy, a quality Garry had managed to manipulate into hero worship, along with a couple of other unsuspecting rubes." His eyes closed and his voice softened, taking on the hypnotic quality Emily had experienced earlier. Once again, she found herself seeing the scene through Levon's eyes.

An unplugged television in the corner stared blankly, the screen black, punishment for the second night at camp when a fight had broken out over who wanted to watch what. Now, nobody got to watch anything. Levon took comfort in the silence. His mother had been glued to the TV twenty-four seven. He didn't miss it.

He did, however, miss Jake, who was always up for a game of chess right about now. He was about to go check out Jake's room when a flash of lightning lit up the dark night, and he saw Jake's thin frame walking toward the boathouse. *What the hell?*

Levon got up slowly—it was vital he didn't alert the supervisor in charge—and made a point of yawning as he made his way out of the room. Garry glanced up. The guy had the instincts of a hawk. Levon mouthed, "Wiped." Garry went back to his prey. No one else paid him a lick of attention.

A guard sat by the side door, reading a newspaper. Levon straightened his shoulders and put on his most concerned expression. It wasn't hard to do.

"Sir, I'm a bit worried the deck chairs and canoes weren't put away properly. I thought I'd take a look down by the boathouse, make sure everything's in order."

The guard took his time considering the request. Finally, "Grab a flashlight. Wear your rain gear."

"No time to go back to my room. The storm is getting worse by the minute."

The guard shrugged. "Your body. Make sure you're back in ten. And be careful out there." He unlocked the deadbolt and opened the door.

The rain pelted down, hard, stinging jabs that drenched his clothes, his hair. Levon found his way along the pathway to the river by rote, felt someone's eyes on him, knew it would be Garry, forced himself not to look back.

He got to the dock as Jake was getting into a canoe, a life jacket tossed onto the floor.

"Jake, what the hell are you doing?" He reached over to grab the canoe, bring it back to safety.

Jake shoved him away, dark eyes defiant. "Get out of here, Levon. This isn't any of your concern."

"I'm making it my concern. Come on, whatever it is, surely it can wait until tomorrow."

"You don't understand. This can't wait."

"At least put on the life jacket."

"Stop acting like my mother."

"Then stop acting like an ass."

But he was calling to the wind. Jake had already pushed off and started paddling.

CHAPTER 31

E mily tried to draw Levon out of whatever world he'd fallen back into. "You blame yourself for Jake's death."

"That's what I've been telling him," Arabella said. "Jake was at Camp Miakoda because of anger management issues. What if he decided to take his anger out on the water?"

"That certainly seems possible," Emily said.

"I didn't buy it then and I don't now," Levon said. "Until that night, I'd never seen that side of Jake. Sure, he was cocky. We all were to varying degrees, but Jake was never belligerent. Frankly, I always assumed he'd done something to protect Johnny and it backfired. Jake had a real sense of fair play, and he would have done anything for Johnny."

"Johnny Porter has the same quality," Arabella said. "It's one of the reasons he started the Main Street Merchants' Association, to make sure all the businesses and business owners got a fair shake."

That sense of fair play concerned Emily. "What if Johnny saw history about to repeat itself," she asked, "only this time Stonehaven's pyramid scheme put a lot more than people at risk?"

"I talked to him," Levon said. "Johnny may have been misguided, but I think his motives for working with Stonehaven were pure. That properly managed, StoreHaven could be a good opportunity for Lount's Landing."

"I have to side with Levon on this one, Emily," Arabella said. "I know StoreHaven isn't my idea of what's best for the town, but Johnny would never do anything to intentionally harm Main Street."

"Okay, let's say you're both right," Emily said. "Something else has been niggling at me. To make the pyramid scheme work at Camp Miakoda, it would require seven people, Garry Stone at the top, Levon and Graham on the second level, and Jake and Johnny Porter on level three. That leaves two spots unaccounted for. You never said who the other two people were."

"Come to think of it, you didn't," Arabella said. "I don't know how I missed that."

Levon flushed. "I guess I didn't. Garry's girlfriend took one of the spots. They'd been together since grade nine, and she used to visit him regularly."

"What was her name?" Emily asked.

"Her name?"

"The girlfriend's name?"

"Went by Millie. The other was a kid by the name of Ambrose. He was Garry's recruit, a frail kid with a pasty complexion, straw-colored hair, and peach fuzz whiskers. I'm not sure why he ended up in Camp Miakoda, but whatever the infraction, it wasn't his idea. The boy was a follower, not a leader. I always thought that had a lot to do with his mother."

"What about his mother?" Emily asked.

"She used to visit him every other Sunday like clockwork, a tiny little thing, blonde hair, heavily into the art scene, and I seem to remember that she did something in publishing. She couldn't have been more than thirty at the time. Must have gotten pregnant while she was still in high school. Never any sign of a husband or a boyfriend, but she was certainly devoted to Ambrose."

"Was Ambrose equally devoted to her?" Emily asked.

Levon shrugged. "Devoted? I don't know how many teenage boys are openly devoted to their moms, but he didn't seem to mind her visits. And she always brought him treats. Candies, chips, chocolates, that sort of thing. Ambrose made some pocket change selling them to some of the other kids. Most of the time Millie and Garry would join in. Millie hit it off with Ambrose's mother, and Ambrose positively worshipped the ground Garry walked on."

"What happened to Ambrose?"

"Rumor had Ambrose moving to Toronto to work with Garry, though by that time he had transformed himself into Garrett Stonehaven. I have no idea whatever happened to Ambrose after that. Or his mother. This was long before email and texting and Twitter and Facebook and all the other instant connectivity we've come to expect."

Emily frowned. "I've been covering stories about HavenSent Development, Inc. and Garrett Stonehaven for the past decade, and I'm positive that I've never come across anyone called Ambrose. What was his last name?"

"It was Ellis, Ambrose Ellis."

Ambrose Ellis?

"What about his mother, you said she was into the art scene, maybe publishing. Do you happen to remember his mother's first name?"

"As a matter of fact, I do, because we used to torment Ambrose singing that old Beatles song, "Michelle". Used to drive him crazy." Levon chuckled at the memory.

"So her name was Michelle? Michelle Ellis?" Emily said.

"That's right. Michelle Ellis. Why, do you know her?"

Emily looked at Arabella and Levon and nodded miserably. "Not only do I know her, I work for her."

"You work for her?" Arabella stared at Emily with a look that sent shivers up her spine. "I thought you owned *Inside the Landing*. At least, that's the impression you gave everyone."

"I said that I was the new editor of *Inside the Landing*," Emily said, wishing she were anywhere but here. "I never claimed to be an owner."

"Nor did you try to dissuade anyone of the notion," Arabella said.

Emily could see her friendship with Arabella disintegrating, just another fake. She tried again. "That may be true, but it doesn't change the fact that I didn't lie about it."

Arabella rolled her eyes. Emily soldiered on. "*Inside the Landing* is owned by Urban-Huntzberger Publications. Michelle Ellis is one of the owners, and she hired me to find out the truth about Stonehaven's plans for Lount's Landing. That was my assignment. The editor job was a cover."

"Nice of you to enlighten me now," Arabella said. "You didn't think telling me might have been important after I found Stonehaven dead? After I trusted you enough to come to you?"

"I'm so sorry, Arabella. You can't imagine how much I've wanted to tell you the truth."

"And yet somehow you were able to continue with your deception," Arabella said, her tone frosty.

"I'd signed a confidentiality agreement. A lot was at stake."

"Like money?" Arabella asked.

"Sure, money was part of it. But that wasn't my main motivation for taking the assignment."

Arabella leaned back in the booth, arms folded, her expression dour.

"Cut the woman some slack," Levon said. "She's willing to break that confidence now, if it means finding out the truth. Isn't that right, Emily?"

Emily shot Levon a grateful smile. No wonder Arabella had never quite let him go. The man was a gem. "Yes, Levon, that's right." She looked earnestly at Arabella. "Hear me out before you pass judgment, that's all I ask. Will you do that?"

Arabella gave a reluctant nod.

"Do you both promise to keep what I tell you absolutely confidential?"

"I promise," Levon said.

"You have my word," Arabella said.

Emily thought for a moment. Could she trust these two? Maybe, maybe not, but at this point she had nothing more to lose. Once the police knew her whole story—and they were bound to find out eventually—she'd move right to the top of the suspect list.

And so, she told them. About Michelle Ellis. About the assignment. About Michelle sending February to work at the Sunrise Café. She told them everything—everything except the part about her mother's suicide.

Some things she wasn't ready to share.

CHAPTER 32

Emily's voice had a harsh edge to it. "I've discovered another one of your secrets today, Michelle. This time from Levon Larroquette. You might remember him from Camp Miakoda."

There was a lengthy silence before Michelle's voice came through, quiet and resigned. "I suppose part of me knew you'd find out about Ambrose. You're a good researcher. It's one of the reasons I hired you for this assignment. In a way, I'm relieved."

"Did you kill him?"

"Kill Ambrose? He was my son. I loved him with all my heart."

Levon hadn't said anything about Ambrose being dead. She'd been asking if Michelle killed Stonehaven.

"How did Ambrose die?"

"The how isn't relevant."

"But you suspect Stonehaven was involved in some way?"

"Yes."

"Now Stonehaven is dead, the police suspect murder, and I'm here, working on a bogus assignment, hired by a boss with a hidden agenda. For all I know, you might have hired someone to kill him."

"Don't be melodramatic, Emily. Let's suppose I wanted to hire someone. Which I did not. But if I did, how would I go about doing it? Advertise 'Murderer Wanted' in *Urban Living*? Take out a full page spread in *Inside the Landing*? I'm afraid you grossly overestimate my powers."

"Spare me the sarcasm. We both know you're not sorry he's dead."

"Not being sorry someone is dead is hardly the same thing as causing it to happen. I expect there's a long list of people who wanted Garrett Stonehaven dead, including you."

Emily wasn't sure how to respond to the allegation. Had she wanted Garrett Stonehaven dead? Or had she wanted payback for her mom's suicide? She evaded the question.

"Look, right now it doesn't matter what I did or didn't want, the man is dead. Are you telling me, with complete honesty, that you didn't have anything to do with his death? Not that I have any reason to trust you."

Michelle sighed. "Yes, Emily, that's what I'm telling you. I believe my exact words when I offered you this assignment were 'to help us expose Garrett Stonehaven for the lying, cheating bastard we both know he is.' I wanted to publicly humiliate him, and if we could get an exclusive story to sell more magazines, all the while increasing our stock value, more the better. Now he's dead and all sorts of reporters will be crawling around town looking for a story."

Emily hadn't thought of that. "Don't worry about other reporters. This town is full of secrets, and folks here don't take kindly to strangers. Anyway, I have a theory. If I can prove it, then we'll have a story."

"What sort of theory?"

"It's possible Stonehaven's death is a direct or indirect result of something, or some things, he did or didn't do, back when he was at Camp Miakoda. The same time your son, Ambrose, was there. I need you to tell me everything. Why Ambrose was sent to Camp Miakoda, his interaction with the other teens there, when and how he died."

"We should meet."

"Do you want me to come to Toronto?"

"No, you stay put. See what else you can find out. I'll come to your office tomorrow morning."

"Thank you, Michelle."

"You may not thank me when you hear what I have to say."

Emily hung up, a sense of unease cloaking her body like a shroud. It was the same choking feeling she'd had the day her mother had died. She pushed the thought aside. There was no point imagining the worst.

CHAPTER 33

Arabella hadn't completely forgiven Emily. She had a feeling some detail had been left out, something personal, beyond the money, beyond the chance to start over after getting dumped by her fiancé. She wouldn't belabor it. Emily promised to confront Michelle and get more information. She promised to help find out the truth. It was enough, at least for now. If she stopped talking to all the people who had deceived her, she'd be a very lonely woman indeed.

Which brought her back to Stanford McLelland. He admitted being part of Stonehaven's team, claimed he tried to stop the mega-box store, but he was sparse on the details. Not that she suspected Stanford of anything illegal, but those details might shed light on Stonehaven's plan. She checked her watch. If her ex-boss's routine hadn't changed, he'd be in the office, eating lunch at his desk while the rest of his staff went out.

She hung the "Back at" sign on the front door, setting the clock hands on two.

Arabella arrived at the McLelland Insurance Brokerage a few minutes after noon, her cheeks flushed from the brisk pace and late November air. Why was it the sunniest days were always the coldest? And it wasn't January yet. January and February, those were the worst.

As she expected, Stanford was sitting in his office, a half-eaten sandwich on his desk, his eyes glued to his computer monitor, his fingers flying across the keyboard. As usual he was impeccably groomed, navy blue suit, matching tie, white shirt. Stanford took his professional image very seriously. Small town broker he might be, but you wouldn't know it from his appearance, or the number of diplomas, certificates, and awards lining the walls.

He jumped slightly at her knock, then settled back in his seat and smiled warmly.

"Arabella. Good to see you. Come in, come in. Can I get you anything? Tea, coffee, water? Half a tuna salad sandwich?"

"Nothing, thanks," Arabella said. She took a seat.

"I'm glad you came by. I had the feeling you weren't any too happy with me."

"That's why I'm here. I need to know everything. Everything about your involvement with Garrett Stonehaven, his plans for the mega-box store." She fidgeted slightly. "So far, the police haven't ruled his death as suspicious, but three accidental deaths ... there's bound to be a thorough investigation. I'm worried I might be a suspect. Because of the way I stood up to Stonehaven at the presentation. And the toast I told you about."

"I'm sure they have plenty more suspects than you, Arabella. The man I knew would have made plenty of enemies over the years. I'm not sure what else I can tell you."

"Can you recap it for me? I might have missed something, some detail." *Something you didn't tell me the first time.*

"You always were thorough," Stanford said with an indulgent smile. "I heard Garrett Stonehaven was looking for local business people to join his development team. I agreed to join."

"But how did you hear about the team? Nobody invited me, and I'm a business owner on Main Street."

"I'm not surprised. Camilla Mortimer-Gilroy recruited me."

That explained it. Camilla would never consider asking her. "Who else did Camilla recruit?"

"No one, as far as I know. Gloria, Carter, Chantal, and Ned were all recruited by Johnny."

"So Johnny was part of Stonehaven's team?"

"From what I can understand, Stonehaven approached Johnny because he was the chairman of the Main Street Merchants' Association. You know Johnny. He'd do anything for this town. And like I said, originally we all thought we were looking for a property to convert into a condominium."

"So no one expected StoreHaven?"

"Heck, no. We expected some commercial space on the main floor, but nothing mega-box. Possibly a convenience store and a dental office or medical services. Chiropractor, physiotherapy, massage, stuff like that."

"But the plan changed."

"It did. Stonehaven sat us down, gave us a preview of his presentation. It was the first any of us had heard of StoreHaven. He claimed converting the school to a condo wasn't economically viable."

"And Carter Dixon challenged him on it."

"He did. Fat lot of good it did him."

"What about you? Did you believe Stonehaven?"

"No, but I also saw the way he dismissed Carter. I knew confronting Stonehaven in front of the others would lead nowhere. I called him later, asked him to consider making some changes. Changes that would make it easier to accept the plan."

"What did he say?"

"He promised to make some changes." Stanford's face flushed at the memory. "He made changes, all right. Asking for investors. That was never part of the original plan. It was bad enough jamming a mega-box store down our throat. But to ask us to invest in it. That took the cake."

It would also explain why Stanford was so upset after the presentation. "You told me, after the presentation, not to worry, said you'd take care of everything. What did you mean?"

"I was going to try to talk some sense into him."

"And did you? Talk sense into him?"

"No, I never got the chance." For the first time since Arabella had entered his office, Stanford got angry. "Look I didn't kill him, if that's what you're insinuating."

"Calm down. I'm not insinuating anything. I'm attempting to collect the facts, see if I can figure out who killed him."

"Last time I checked, that was up to the police. Stay out of it and let them earn their paychecks." Stanford stood up. "The man is dead, and his plan died with him. As for who killed him, all I can say is Garrett Stonehaven had it coming for a long time. Now I'm going to have to ask you to leave. I have a client meeting in a few minutes."

Arabella knew there was no point in pushing it. Stanford could be as stubborn as Levon once his mind was made up.

Men.

It wasn't until she was halfway back to the shop that Arabella realized the significance of Stanford's final statement. "As for who killed him, all I can say is Garrett Stonehaven had it coming for a long time." How far did Stanford and Stonehaven go back? And what was it about their past history that caused the normally staid insurance broker to wish someone dead?

Arabella picked up the pace, anxious to get back to the Glass Dolphin. She needed to think, have a shortbread cookie. Or three.

CHAPTER 34

Emily started her day with a five-mile run followed by a visit to the Sunrise Café, where she ordered black coffee, an asparagus and red pepper egg white omelet with rye toast, lightly buttered, and two strips of well-done bacon on the side. She experienced a pang of moderate guilt over the bacon, but dammit, she needed something to calm her nerves, and the run alone hadn't done it.

Michelle Ellis showed up at her office a few minutes past ten in the morning, looking for all the world as if she were ready to attend a high-profile business meeting, her blonde hair impeccably coiffed, her custom-tailored black suit softened by a rose-colored blouse and a strand of freshwater pearls. Even with five-inch heels, she stood a good couple of inches shorter than Emily, and yet everything about her exuded power and confidence.

"Is this the mock-up of the first issue?" she asked, picking up a magazine up from a large stack on Emily's desk before taking a seat on the black leather sofa. "Nice cover."

"Thanks," Emily said, taking the seat at her desk. *Seriously, why did I buy a sofa instead of a couple of chairs?* "That's Arabella Carpenter standing against her wall of clocks in the Glass Dolphin. The owner of Print It! suggested we go with glossy covers and newsprint inside. I think it works."

"It does, and it's a reasonable compromise from a cost perspective." Michelle thumbed through the issue. "Twenty-four pages. Not too shabby for a first run. Nice photography, you have a good eye. I like the way you had the printer color spot some of the photos." She studied the table of contents. "Grand Opening of the Glass Dolphin. What the Main Street Merchants' Association can do for you. Get ready for the Santa Claus Parade." She put the magazine down. "You decided against including anything about Garrett Stonehaven?"

"I was going to include something, but given the recent turn of events, I thought it best to leave it out. I want to create a feel-good marketing magazine. Murder, if that's what it turns out to be, is a bit off-putting."

"You have a point. What's the ad to editorial ratio?"

"About forty percent advertising to sixty percent editorial."

"Not spectacular, but respectable for a first issue."

"I expect it to improve, given time."

"When are you planning to go to press?"

"It's scheduled for tomorrow. We should be able to distribute on Saturday."

"Saturday is a good delivery date. What are your distribution plans?"

"I was conservative with this issue, and as it is we barely broke even. I've decided to start it as a monthly publication. It will give me more time to develop stories and bring advertisers on board. For this issue, I'm having the existing newspaper boxes filled. There are a couple dozen of them in town. I've also asked the merchants and businesses along Main Street if they'd be willing to have a few copies to give to their clientele."

"How was the response?"

"The restaurants were all willing. Lots of customers are looking for something to flip through if they're alone. Most of the businesses were also accommodating. Arabella was, naturally, and Johnny Porter, which was also to be expected." Emily thought about how dismissive Chantal Van Schyndle had been. "Some of the other businesses weren't as keen. I was thinking of offering delivery, by subscription."

"Paid subscription?"

"Hmm. Not initially, but I still think it's worthwhile. You know better than I do that advertisers look at distribution numbers. The greater the distribution, the more willing they are to buy space."

"You've done your research."

"I have. I'm also working on getting the publication online in a 3-D flipbook format, which could offer live links to the advertisers. I'm looking at various software packages."

"It sounds as if you have everything covered. I'm impressed. It makes what I've come here to tell you all the more difficult."

"I beg your pardon?"

"I'm afraid Urban-Huntzberger has decided to terminate your contract."

"Terminate my contract?"

Michelle pushed an invisible strand of blonde hair away from her face. "The reality is you were sent here to find out what Garrett Stonehaven was up to. The magazine was a cover."

"And now that Stonehaven is dead?"

"Your services are no longer required."

"Will you keep it running? *Inside the Landing*?"

"Perhaps."

"But not with *me* at the helm. I assume I'm being punished for finding out about Ambrose? About your past connection with Stonehaven?"

"It has nothing to do with that. I would have been disappointed if you hadn't made the discovery. You're bound to find out the rest, and I owe you the truth, so I'll spare you the research."

"Your generosity is overwhelming."

Michelle ignored the sarcasm. "You know Ambrose is dead. What you don't know is that it was ruled an accidental overdose from a bunch of street drugs. The police called it a Cabbagetown Cocktail. I never believed it. He may have had a troubled youth, dabbled with some marijuana and got caught, but boot camp scared him straight. He'd been clean for five years, finishing high school, taking some college courses, working odd jobs. I would have known if Ambrose was into drugs."

"You suspected Stonehaven was behind the overdose?"

Michelle nodded. "By then, Garry Stone had become Garrett Stonehaven. He hired Ambrose as a sales associate for the first HavenSent Development. At first, Ambrose was thrilled. He idolized Garry, thought the job would be his big break. But one day Ambrose came to me, more than a little bit worried. Said the sales formula reminded him of a pyramid scheme they'd run at Camp Miakoda. A few days later, Ambrose was dead. Stonehaven didn't come to the funeral."

Emily wasn't surprised. He hadn't bothered to attend her mother's funeral, either. "The development? Did it go ahead?"

"It did, and frankly, I could never find any evidence of a pyramid scheme in that project, or any other. Believe me, I tried. And then I heard about his plans for Lount's Landing."

"You suspected with Neighbors Helping Neighbors, Stonehaven might have been up to his old tricks. But how did you find out about it?"

Michelle studied her hands a moment before answering. "You're bound to find out. Ambrose's father was on Team StoreHaven. Stanford McLelland. We never married."

Stanford McLelland. She thought about Arabella, and wondered if she knew. Somehow she didn't think so. "Tell me about it."

"We were just kids when I got pregnant, a summertime romance. My folks had a place on the water in Lakeside. Stan's father worked at an insurance brokerage in Lount's Landing. Stan bought the business a few years back. I met Stan at a party in Miakoda Falls and the rest, as they say, is history. I was already home in Toronto and back in school by the time I found out."

"Did you tell Stanford?"

"Not for a long time. My parents... things were different back then, for young girls who found themselves in 'the family way.' I was in my third trimester when I got the nerve to call him." Michelle gave a short laugh. "He didn't even remember me, kept calling me Michaela. He was full of stories about getting accepted into three universities. I hung up without telling him."

"But you did tell him, eventually."

"I did, but not until Ambrose starting asking a lot of questions, wanting to know who his father was. He was about twelve at the time."

"How did Stanford take it?"

"He was great, although I'm sure it helped that I wasn't looking for any sort of financial support. I sent him some photos, offered him the option of getting a paternity test. He declined. One look at Ambrose and it was obvious. He was the spitting image of his father when he was young."

"So what happened?"

"I started sending Ambrose up to Lount's Landing, one weekend a month, a week or two in the summer. He'd take the train into Miakoda Falls, and Stanford would pick him up from there." Michelle gave a sad smile. "I've always wondered what would have happened if I'd told Stanford sooner. Maybe he could have kept Ambrose on the right path."

"You can't blame yourself. Hindsight is always twenty-twenty."

"You're right, but it doesn't make me feel any less guilty. When Ambrose was fourteen, he started hanging around with a bad crowd. Managed to find one in both places. I suppose I overreacted and became overly protective. Most likely the worst thing I could have done. He and a group of his so-called friends got caught one night breaking into the pawnshop. Long story short, the owner pressed charges but Ambrose was underage, Stanford was respected in town, and my parents had money."

"So he ended up in Camp Miakoda."

"At first, we were relieved. We thought it would be a good place for Ambrose."

"But you didn't count on Garry Stone."

Michelle nodded. "It was as if he'd cast a spell on Ambrose. He followed Garry around like a puppy. There was only one other person Ambrose would listen to."

"Let me guess. Garry's girlfriend."

Michelle's eyes narrowed.

"Levon told you about her?"

"He told us about the pyramid scheme, and Millie's name came up."

Michelle nodded again. "Millie would take the time to say hello, ask how things were going for me. I didn't trust Garry, or appreciate his influence on Ambrose. But I couldn't help but like her. We lost touch after camp ended. But then, after Ambrose died, she sent a lovely card and made a donation in his name to a foundation for troubled youth."

"How did she find out about Ambrose?"

"You know, I don't know. I never thought to question it. Why? Do you think it's important?"

"All I know is we have a bunch of folks who met at Camp Miakoda, and three of them are now dead. Stonehaven, Ambrose, and Graham."

"Surely you don't think there was anything sinister behind Graham's snowmobiling accident?"

Emily shook her head. "I don't know what to think anymore. Look, why don't you let me stay here and report on the murder investigation? It would be easier to do that within the parameters of *Inside the Landing*."

Michelle shook her head. "It's out of my hands. The partners at Urban-Huntzberger have already made arrangements with another reporter."

"Another reporter?"

"Kerri St. Amour. She's checking into the Gilroy Mansion as we speak."

Kerri St. Amour? Now that was a low blow. Emily forced herself stay calm. She wouldn't give Michelle the satisfaction of knowing how much it stung.

"It isn't all bad, dear. Urban-Huntzberger has prepared a generous severance package." Michelle pulled a sheaf of papers from her briefcase and handed them to Emily. "I insisted."

Emily read the paperwork. It was a simple document. Eight weeks pay in lieu of notice, plus an additional twelve months at full salary, with benefits. The bonus she had been promised when accepting the initial assignment. Rent paid in her current house to the end of the month, plus moving expenses back to Toronto or a place of her choosing. In exchange, she would forfeit all interest in *Inside the Landing*, and any future employment with Urban-Huntzberger Publications.

She had to admit it was a generous package, not that it made getting fired any more palatable. But there was something else, something that didn't seem right. Emily looked back over the numbers and realized what it was. The package was a bit *too* generous. It was as if someone wanted her to leave.

"What if I decide to stay in Lount's Landing?"

"Why would you want to do that?"

Because she had made a promise to Arabella. Because she didn't like the idea of someone trying to stop her from finding out the truth. Because she owed it to her mother. If she'd listened to her, if she had believed her allegations about CondoHaven on the Park, her mother might still be alive.

"I like it here."

Was it her imagination or did Michelle look nervous? Emily decided to push it. "There's nothing in the severance agreement that stipulates I have to leave."

"No, I suppose there isn't," Michelle said, her lips pursed ever so slightly. "I'm afraid you'll have to find alternate accommodations or negotiate extending your lease with Camilla Mortimer-Gilroy directly."

"I can do that. So where do we go from here?"

"You sign the papers. The money will be wire-transferred into your account within the next forty-eight hours."

Emily reached into her desk, pulled out her gold-filled pen, and signed the termination papers with a flourish.

I'm not giving up, mom. I'm not giving up.

CHAPTER 35

With Michelle gone—no hugging and air pecking to worry about this time—Emily spent the next hour cleaning out the office of *Inside the Landing*. Not that she had a lot to clean out; she hadn't even gotten around to hanging a single picture on the wall before she'd been fired.

At least she wouldn't have to fill nail holes or repaint. But it would have been nice to have enough time to make the space her own, bit by bit, until it reflected her personality. Or at least some personality. As it was...

Emily shook off the feeling of isolation and emptied a box filled with printer paper—the paper belonged to Urban-Huntzberger, but surely the box wouldn't matter—and slowly began placing the handful of personal belongings inside it. Her "World's Most Honest Golfer" mug. A long-sleeved cardigan for when the office got chilly. Her jersey knit black dress and low-heeled pumps, in case she had to clean up fast. A purple leather-look notebook with a stylized peacock embossed onto the cover. Her laptop.

The printer, paper, pens, and paperclips belonged to Urban-Huntzberger.

So did everything else, with the exception of the used sofa. She remembered the way Garrett Stonehaven sank into the black leather cushions, the way he'd tried to intimidate her. The sofa had cost her less than a hundred dollars. Whoever moved in here next could have it. It and the blank, personality-free walls.

Emily arrived at the Gilroy Mansion at three o'clock. She'd run by it a number of times, but had yet to step a foot inside, partly because there had never been any real need, and partly out of a sense of loyalty to Arabella.

She rang the doorbell. Camilla opened the door less than a minute later. She wore form-fitting jeans, a designer T-shirt in swirly shades of brown, and ankle-high, tan suede moccasins, complete with beaded fringe. Her blonde hair had been pulled back into a careless ponytail, stray wisps and tendrils framing her heart-shaped face. Clear blue eyes, long dark lashes, skin the color of softly tinted porcelain. A woman like that could definitely influence the men in her life.

"Hello, Camilla. I hope I'm not interrupting anything."

"Michelle called. I've been expecting you. Come on in. It's cold out there." Camilla led her into a large, sunlit room filled with Victorian furniture, the kind of room the English would call a front parlor. "I was about to sit down for afternoon tea. Would you care to join me?"

Emily blushed. She hadn't expected Camilla to be so gracious.

"I'm not nearly the nasty witch Arabella has told you about," Camilla said with a smile.

"Arabella didn't—"

"Of course she did. But it's old business between the two of us. It has nothing to do with you and me. It isn't every day a person gets fired. If this isn't a time for tea and sympathy, when is?"

"Tea would be nice."

"I'll be back in a jiff," Camilla said, leaving Emily to assess her surroundings. She couldn't help but admire the detail in the crown molding, the gleaming wood trim, the wainscoted walls, the vintage fireplace with its burnished mahogany mantle, the faint smell of furniture polish permeating the air. Everything about the room spelled old money.

But did it spell new money? A closer look at the furniture revealed patches of threadbare fabric, carefully disguised with pillows and throws. True, a case could be made for maintaining authenticity, but Emily suspected Camilla's financial situation could use a boost. There wasn't a single picture, yet there were faded patches, the odd nail hole, telltale signs that pictures had once hung on these walls.

"I forgot to ask you how you took your tea, so I brought milk, sugar, and lemon," Camilla said. She was carrying a tray laden with a blue and white teapot, matching bone china teacups, and dessert plates. Emily had seen a similar pattern at the Glass Dolphin. Arabella had labeled it "Willow." A tiered platter held what looked to be homemade scones, clotted cream, and strawberry preserves. The woman knew how to put on an afternoon tea.

"It looks wonderful," Emily said. "You needn't have gone to so much trouble."

"It was no trouble. Now, what brings you to the Gilroy Mansion?"

"I suppose Michelle filled you in on my situation. Regarding the house rental."

Camilla nodded. "Urban-Huntzberger has paid up to the end of the month. After that you're on your own. If it's any consolation, the termination wasn't entirely Michelle's decision. She always liked you."

"It's a minor consolation."

"We go back, you know, me and Michelle."

"How far back?"

"More years than I care to admit. My late husband, Graham, was at the same camp as Michelle's son, Ambrose. They were just wayward teenagers back then. Graham was always rebellious. I'm not sure what Ambrose's story was. He was always more of a follower than a leader. When I heard he died, I sent Michelle a card and made a donation in Ambrose's name."

"I'm curious. How did you hear about Ambrose?"

"I can't remember. I suppose Graham must have told me. At any rate, Michelle called to thank me, and we arranged to meet for lunch. She's quite knowledgeable about art. She helped me pick out a couple of nice pictures. They turned out to be a good investment." Camilla smiled. "I'm sure you noticed the fade marks on the wall."

"I assumed you were getting ready to paint," Emily said, pleased with her quick thinking.

"Did you?" Camilla poured the tea. "The truth is I sold every last one of them. Graham's family all but disowned him when he married me. When his parents died in an automobile crash about a year later, he inherited this house and its contents, but all their money was earmarked for charity. I'm afraid Graham's spending habits didn't coincide with a much-reduced income."

Emily wasn't sure quite what to say. She certainly hadn't been expecting Camilla to be quite so forthcoming. It felt oddly embarrassing.

"It's a well-known secret that when Graham died, he left me virtually penniless. I assumed Arabella would have told you some version of the facts. I thought you should know the truth."

"Arabella didn't say anything, but Johnny Porter told me how you transformed the house into a B&B," Emily said. "He was quite exuberant in his praise of Gilroy Mansion, and your accomplishments, including buying and renovating the rental property I'm currently living in."

"Fortunately, I had a few good things to sell, and the Gilroy family name to trade on. I took the money and decided to invest it in real estate. I renovated this house, along with the one you're currently renting. Poppy Spencer has been a wonderful mentor. You might want to consult with her should you decide to stay."

"I'm considering it. Not consulting Poppy—though I might at some point. I'm considering staying. That's why I'm here. I'd like to continue to rent the house from you, on a month-to-month basis. Until I can sort out what my Plan B is."

"Michelle mentioned you might want to continue the lease. Month-to-month is fine, but I'd need at least sixty days' notice in writing before you vacate the property."

"That seems like a reasonable request." Emily took a sip of her tea. Earl Grey. It was one of her mother's favorite blends—but surely Camilla couldn't have known that. "Can I ask you a question?"

"You can ask. I can't promise I'll answer it."

"I'm sure Stonehaven dying here was a dreadful shock."

"That would be an understatement, but yes, it was shock. Is that your question?"

"No. What I wanted to ask was, do you think Stonehaven's death was an accident, a suicide, or murder?"

"What an interesting question. I'm not sure, to tell you the truth—though I'll admit I was surprised when the police told me it looked like a drug overdose. Garrett never struck me as a drug user, though we can never be sure of what goes on behind closed doors."

"What about murder?"

"It would definitely not be good for business if it turns out to be murder," Camilla said. "Even an accidental death is far from desirable from a PR standpoint. But the reality is a lot of folks in Lount's Landing weren't too happy with Stonehaven or his proposal. Your friend, Arabella, for one. Whether she hated him and his plan enough to kill him is something you'd have to ask her directly."

"But you were right by his side on the night of the presentation. You were willing to act as his receptionist. Would you have invested in StoreHaven?"

"I'm beginning to think Michelle made a mistake letting you go. You really are an investigative reporter, aren't you? "

"Guilty as charged," Emily said, smiling. "But you haven't answered my question. Would you have invested?"

This time Camilla actually laughed. "I'm not exactly flush with cash. Mortgaged to the eyeballs, I'm afraid. The white Mercedes you saw in the driveway is a lease. That's why I hired Shakyra. It's important to keep up appearances."

"But you believed in Stonehaven's plan."

Camilla's lovely blue eyes narrowed, and Emily knew she'd pushed too hard.

"Johnny believed in it, and that was good enough for me. Now, if you'll excuse me, I have some other business to take care of. I'll make sure to draw up a new short-term rental contract for you. Swing by sometime tomorrow with your checkbook."

And with that, Emily was summarily dismissed.

CHAPTER 36

Emily left the Gilroy Mansion feeling somewhat battered. First Michelle had fired her, and then Camilla had implied her rental agreement would be short-term. It was for the best, though. As lovely as the house was, it didn't feel like home, and she still hadn't repainted the main rooms with the Hay Bale Johnny had given her. She'd probably end up moving back to Toronto sooner rather than later.

For the moment, however, she couldn't face the thought of moving, or the thought of going back to the house. She decided to swing by the Glass Dolphin and update Arabella on her meetings with Michelle and Camilla.

Emily arrived at the Glass Dolphin to find Arabella hunched over an old clock, a pair of reading glasses halfway down her nose.

"I've been hired to do an appraisal of this antique clock," Arabella said, not looking up. "A fine example of a Sessions Regulator 'E' clock made in Forestville, Connecticut—what collectors would call a square regulator."

Emily sensed a hint of repressed anger, nothing overt, but it was there. She knew it drilled back to not confiding in Arabella sooner.

"What's involved?" she asked, not because she was interested, but because she knew the surest way to Arabella's heart was through her antiques.

"I suppose it depends on the appraiser. I try to provide historical research, along with market comparables, sales on eBay and auctions, for example. What's cool about this clock is that I found reference to it in this 1978 National Association of Watch and Clock Collectors publication called the *Bulletin*."

Arabella pointed to a black and white photo of a clock on page five hundred and ninety. It was a dead ringer for the clock lying on the table in front of Arabella, calendar dial and all.

"I guess being an antiques shop owner isn't much different from being a journalist," Emily said. "We're both investigators of a sort."

"I never thought of it in that way before, but you're right. Look here. The article says these clocks were produced between 1903 and 1908, with a retail price of $7.35 as a timepiece and $8.30 as a striker in 1915. A calendar attachment was forty-five cents extra for either model. This clock would have retailed for $7.80."

"Was $7.80 a lot of money then?"

"I use something called a Historical Currency Conversion calculator, and I have tables to tell me what the average salary was in any given year. Based on the currency calculator, $7.80 would be roughly $200. The average salary in 1908 was twenty-two cents an hour, so this clock would have cost the equivalent of about one week's pay."

"You *are* an investigator."

"Speaking of investigating, how did it go with Michelle Ellis? That's why you're here, isn't it? Not for a lesson in clock appraisals." Arabella gave her a full-on smile, and Emily knew they'd be okay. She felt the tension leave her neck and shoulders.

"Before we get to that, did you meet with Stanford?"

"Yes, I did. He told me Camilla had recruited him to be part of Team StoreHaven, and he'd been led to believe they were sourcing out properties for a condominium, not a mega-box store. He had no idea there would be a request for investors until the night of the presentation."

Interesting. Camilla hadn't mentioned that she'd also been a recruiter for Stonehaven. Emily gave Arabella a quick rundown on her meeting with Camilla.

"I thought you were going to meet with Michelle, not Camilla," Arabella said after Emily had finished.

"I did meet with Michelle first, but I also had to talk to Camilla about my rental agreement," Emily said. "I'll fill you in on the details later, but let's get back to Stanford for a minute. Did he tell you anything else?"

"Nothing of importance, why?"

"Something Michelle Ellis told me."

"Like what?"

"First off, she told me Ambrose died a few years after leaving Camp Miakoda. From what I can gather he was in there for possession of marijuana, but he'd managed to turn his life around."

"Did she say how he died?"

"Uh-huh. The police ruled it as an accidental overdose—some sort of street drug cocktail, but she never believed it."

"Let me guess. Her boy might have smoked some grass, but he didn't do hard drugs."

"I hear what you're saying. But here's the thing, Arabella. Ambrose was working for Garrett Stonehaven when he died."

"Go on."

"He told Michelle he saw irregularities in the HavenSent sales model."

"What kind of irregularities?"

"He said the format reminded him of a pyramid scheme they'd run at Camp Miakoda."

"And a few days later, Ambrose died of an accidental overdose."

"And here's the kicker. Stonehaven didn't bother to attend the funeral."

"Nice guy. Did Michelle find any evidence of a pyramid scheme?"

"No, but then again, she wasn't directly involved in the project, and she would have been devastated by her son's death. There's something else you need to know, Arabella."

"What?"

"Ambrose Ellis had a father."

"Everyone has a father," Arabella said.

"So they do, it's just that this particular father might come as a surprise to you."

"Are you saying I know the father?"

Emily nodded. "It seems his father was Stanford McLelland. I gather he and Michelle were teenagers when she got pregnant. They never married. Stanford didn't know he had a son until Ambrose was about twelve."

"I can't believe Stanford never told me. Do you think Levon knows?"

"I don't know. My guess is he might not. There's no reason he would have known, unless Stanford visited Ambrose at Camp. Or if he connected the dots. You'll have to ask him yourself."

"I'll ask him, all right." Arabella frowned. "Something doesn't make sense to me. Why, all these years later, does Garrett Stonehaven surface in Lount's Landing with a plan sounding suspiciously like a pyramid scheme? Both Johnny and Stanford were part of the Camp Miakoda years. He had to know they'd recognize the formula."

"What if he knew they'd recognize the formula and was baiting them?"

"What kind of person does that? What was he hoping to prove?"

"If we had the answer," Emily said, "we might also know who wanted him dead."

CHAPTER 37

By the time Arabella finished off the clock appraisal, it was after six o'clock—but she knew Stanford would still be at the office. The man lived and breathed insurance. Hungry as she was, she needed information more than sustenance. She went to her cookie stash, took out a couple of shortbreads, and ate them standing up. Dinner could wait.

He picked up on the first ring. "McLelland."

"It's Arabella."

"Is everything okay?"

"I found out about Ambrose today."

Silence. "Who told you?"

"Emily. Michelle Ellis told her."

"By the time you started working for me, Ambrose was already dead. There didn't seem to be any need to tell you about him. What was I going to say? By the way, I have an illegitimate son who is dead?"

"You must have been surprised when Stonehaven arrived in Lount's Landing."

"Surprised? That's one way of looking at it. I was more suspicious of his motives. Michelle always believed Stonehaven was behind Ambrose's death. I was never quite as sure. I figured Ambrose had taken another dark turn. He was easily led."

"Do you still believe that?"

"I'm not as convinced. First Stonehaven arrives in Lount's Landing, sets up the StoreHaven team, and before you know it, the bodies began to pile up. Carter Dixon. February Fassbender. All accidental deaths. I began to wonder."

"You think Michelle might have been right."

"I think it bears consideration. Ambrose had found something suspect in Stonehaven's books. Or so he'd said. I'm ashamed to admit that I didn't believe him at the time. I told him to man up and be glad for the job." Sanford sighed, a sad, deflated sound. "Not my finest moment in parenting, I'll admit. But as I mentioned before, Ambrose was easily led. He had a history of drug abuse. He had lied to Michelle and me on repeated occasions. But I can't help but wonder. If I'd believed him—or at least given him the benefit of the doubt—things might have turned out differently."

Arabella heard the torment etched into her ex-boss's face. Her heart went out to him. "I'm sorry," she said, realizing how inadequate that sounded.

"Thank you, although I don't just mean things might have turned out differently for Ambrose. Maybe Carter and February would still be alive."

"But why would Stonehaven want Carter dead? And why February?"

"The way I figure it, Carter had something Stonehaven wanted."

"The apartment building."

"Uh-huh. Gloria was ready to sell, but Carter was holding out for more money. I think Stonehaven may have hired February to give him a dose of peanut butter. I'm not saying he meant for Carter to die. Maybe he just wanted to scare him."

"So you think Stonehaven killed her to keep her silent?"

"Possibly, though Michelle thinks February might have tried to shake Stonehaven down for more money."

So Stanford had discussed all of this with Michelle. "Did you share your suspicions with anyone other than Michelle? Confront Stonehaven?"

"Hell, no. I had no intention of becoming victim number three, and the reality is both deaths could have been accidental. I wanted to make sure Stonehaven didn't fleece folks with another one of his pyramid schemes. Couldn't do that from the grave."

Arabella nodded. It all sounded plausible, still... "I don't understand why Stonehaven would come here. He had to know that you and Camilla and Levon and Johnny would recognize the pattern. Why not take his plan elsewhere?"

"You didn't know Garrett Stonehaven. He loved playing games, even more than he loved money. He would have thrived on us figuring out his plan, trying to stop him. He just didn't count on dying."

"Who do you think killed him? Someone on the team?"

"I think it's safer not to have an opinion. To let the police do their job. A murderer is out there. They've killed at least once—possibly three times, if Stonehaven wasn't behind the deaths of Carter and February. Promise me you'll stop all this amateur sleuthing and go back to what you know best. Antiques."

"I promise," she said. And she would—as soon as she and Emily solved the case.

Arabella's next call was to Levon. She wanted to fill him in on Emily's conversation with Michelle. But mostly she wanted to know if Levon had once again withheld information.

"Interesting," Levon said. "So Ambrose suspected Stonehaven was up to no good, and a few days later he died of an accidental drug overdose."

"It's more than interesting. But before I get to my theory, do you know who Ambrose's father was?"

"How would I know? Michelle Ellis always came to Camp Miakoda alone."

"Stanford McLelland."

"You're kidding."

After all their years together, Arabella could tell if Levon was lying as easily as she could spot red lipstick on a white collared shirt. And she was convinced this was the first he had heard about Stanford's connection to Ambrose Ellis. "I'm not," she said, and proceeded to fill him in on the details.

"I assume you confronted Stanford?"

"I did, and he confirmed it. He said a few other things that got me thinking."

"Go ahead, Sherlock."

"Don't make fun. I think Stonehaven may have been a serial killer, starting with Jake Porter's drowning at Camp Miakoda. You said yourself Jake would never have gone out in a boat that day unless he was coerced in some way."

"True enough, but the fact remains it was ruled an accident."

Arabella ignored him. "Next up, Graham Gilroy, a veteran snowmobiler goes out on thin ice and dies in a snowmobile accident."

"Graham was always taking risks."

"Carter Dixon, anaphylactic shock, an allergic reaction to peanuts."

"We don't know if Stonehaven was aware of Carter's allergy."

"We don't know he wasn't. Carter was a windbag. He could have mentioned it in one of the team meetings. Then there was the waitress, February Fassbender. A drug overdose, though as long as she worked at the Sunrise Café, nobody had ever seen evidence of a problem. Ambrose, Carter, February. For all we know, there could be others."

"Let's stick to what we *do* know, shall we? There's already enough gossip and fear-mongering going on in town. We don't need to fuel that."

Arabella leaned back and tried not to pout. Levon had a point. According to Betsy, Nigel Watters had been doing a booming business at his fish and chips shop since the news of February's death was made public. "Ghouls," Betsy had told her with a disdainful sniff, "and Nigel lapping up every minute of it."

"Fine. We stick with what we know. My point was that everyone knew about Carter's peanut allergy, and there was no evidence that February was a druggie."

"Yes, Carter's allergy to peanuts was widely known," Levon said, "but we don't know for sure that Stonehaven knew about it. As for February, if she was a druggie, she could have been clean for a while and then gone back to it. It happens all the time."

"Whose side are you on?"

"Side? This isn't a reality TV show, Arabella. I think we should let the police work on this. What if you're right, what if there is a serial killer out there? What if it isn't Garrett Stonehaven who was doing the killing? After all, he is dead."

"You think someone else may be responsible?"

"I think you should let the police handle the investigation. Go back to the safe world of antiques."

What is it with the men in this town? "I've already promised Stanford I'd give up amateur sleuthing."

"Glad to hear it," Levon said. "Did you also happen to tell him when you planned to give it up?"

Damn Levon. He knew her all too well. She hung up without answering.

CHAPTER 38

Emily watched as Arabella dusted the assorted curios scattered about the Glass Dolphin. It was either dust or eat shortbread, Arabella had told her. Dusting had fewer calories.

For her part, Emily was comfortably ensconced in a leather and oak rocking chair labeled, "Gustav Stickley #2603 Rocker, c. 1901." Arabella had finished updating her on her conversation with Levon, and while it was all very interesting, it had done nothing to further their investigation. She hadn't shared the news of her termination yet. There would be plenty of time once the money was in the bank. Until then, it wasn't official.

"MOM," Emily said, starting to rock back and forth.

"Mom?" Arabella stopped dusting long enough to favor Emily with a quizzical glance. "Whose mom are you referring to?"

"Not mom, as in mother. M-O-M."

"Oh, I get it, M-O-M," Arabella said, rolling her eyes. "What the heck are you talking about?"

"M-O-M. Means. Opportunity. Motive. If we want to solve this, we have to consider who had MOM. Starting with the first murder."

"The first murder?"

"The first murder. The more I think about it, the more I'm convinced Carter Dixon's death was not an accident. If that's the case, it stands to reason that neither was February Fassbender's."

"You sound like Stanford," Arabella said, and filled Emily in on her conversation.

"So with Stanford's theory, Stonehaven had means, opportunity, and motive in both cases," Emily said.

"There's one thing you're both forgetting in all this."

"What?"

"Garrett Stonehaven is also dead."

"So what are you saying? That Stonehaven was murdered, and whoever did it was also responsible for the deaths of Carter and February?"

"I think it's possible, and I'm not the only one who thinks that way. Three unexpected deaths in such a short time, in a town this size. People are starting to talk, and according to Betsy, a lot of them are getting nervous, worried they might be next. Nigel Watters isn't helping, either. He's telling everyone who will listen about finding February's body."

Emily could believe it. And knowing Nigel, no detail had gone unembellished, despite cautions from the police.

"Point made. Any suggestions on where we start?"

"Let's assume we can eliminate one another," Arabella said. "I mean, I definitely believe I can eliminate you as a suspect, and I'm hoping that you feel the same way about me."

"Of course I feel the same way," Emily said, making up her mind. It was time to confide in Arabella. "Speaking of MOM, before we go on, there's something I need to tell you."

Arabella put down the duster. "What is it?"

Emily swallowed hard. "My connection with Stonehaven, and my reason for coming to Lount's Landing, it runs a bit deeper than I led you to believe."

"How much deeper?"

"Quite a bit deeper," Emily admitted, albeit reluctantly. "My mom had worked for Garrett Stonehaven for years, most recently as his personal assistant. But a little over a year ago, Stonehaven announced CondoHaven on the Park."

"Sounds swanky."

"Swanky is an understatement. It was supposed to be way more than the usual high-rise building with retail and commercial shops on the ground floors, and condo units above. From the tenth floor up every unit housed one-half of each floor, with views of the city and the water most folks can only dream of. Not to mention the penthouse, which took up the entire top floor. The penthouse balcony encompassed the entire perimeter of the building."

"It sounds spectacular."

"Hmm. The problem was the plan called for a complete loss of the existing public green space. Green space inner city kids and low-income families had used for years. Their tiny bit of nature in the midst of an ever-growing urban jungle."

"So why would anyone want to live there? Views are great, but I can't imagine living somewhere that doesn't have at least a bit of a garden."

"That's the point. *Residents* would have access, but the general public wouldn't be allowed in. Stonehaven wanted to be sure this was an exclusive building, right down to the benches and bougainvillea." Emily's stomach roiled at the memory. "My mother was always a social activist, volunteered at the food bank, did back-to-school book bag drives, that sort of thing. And the callousness of CondoHaven set her blood boiling. She confronted Stonehaven about it."

"That must have infuriated him," Arabella said. "An employee, his personal assistant no less, taking him to task."

"You could say that." Emily looked embarrassed. "At first I was angry with her. For one, my dad had been dead for years and she couldn't afford to lose the job. Plus, I'd been working for *Urban Living* for a while, and folks loved reading about anything to do with Garrett Stonehaven. In Toronto, his name traded like gold, and he'd always been there for me when I needed a quick quote." She thought of past headlines. "Stonehaven's Condos Continue to Sizzle." "More Hot Times at HavenSent Solutions." "Mega-builder Garrett Stonehaven Garners Accolades."

She'd been so proud of her brilliant banners and clever cutlines. "I was afraid if things got too heated, I'd stop getting his cooperation. Not to mention the assignments."

"I gather something changed."

Emily nodded. "The more my mom tried to dig into the CondoHaven details, the more she believed there was something not quite right about it. She asked me to investigate. I'd had a bit of experience with exposing a toxic land brownfield scandal. But I blew her off."

"What did she say?"

"She didn't. Instead she became obsessed with what she called 'finding out the truth.' Even people on the committee to save the green space started backing away. It created a massive rift between us."

Emily bit her lip, tried desperately to fight back the tears threatening to fall. "She was my mom, Arabella. My only living relative, unless you count a couple of cousins, a self-absorbed aunt, and an alcoholic uncle I haven't seen in more than a decade. I should have stood by her. But I didn't. Not until it was too late."

"What happened?"

"Stonehaven went after her with a vengeance. I swear I'd never seen that side of him. He'd always been unfailingly polite and professional with me, but he was absolutely ruthless. Not only did he terminate my mother's employment, he intimated to anyone who would listen that she'd been caught with her hand in the till." Emily's eyes narrowed at the memory. "My mom wasn't perfect, but she was no thief."

"I believe you. It sounds as if Stonehaven tried to crush your mom, emotionally and financially. What did she end up doing?"

"She came to me, more bad luck to her. Told me she was tired of being a victim. She planned to sue Stonehaven for wrongful dismissal, had arranged to meet with a lawyer at the end of the week. I pleaded with her to reconsider, said nothing good would come of trying to cross Stonehaven any further." Emily let out a harsh laugh. "Some days I can almost make myself believe I was trying to save her reputation, instead of my job."

"I assume she didn't take your advice."

"She was furious with me, said I was on the wrong side and one day I'd find out the truth, and then I'd be sorry for ever doubting her. She stormed out of my apartment and I never saw her alive again. Those were the last words we ever spoke to one another." The tears streamed down Emily's face, but she was beyond caring. Telling someone was a relief.

"I'm so sorry." Arabella reached over and took Emily's hand in hers.

"There's more. Something I've never told anyone else."

"What is it?"

"After my mom left, I called Garrett Stonehaven. I told him she was planning on filing a lawsuit against him. I begged him to please reconsider, to rehire her, to tell folks it was all one big misunderstanding. I promised him a front page spread in the next issue of *Urban Living*. Not that I had the clout to pull that off, but Michelle would have gone for it. Stonehaven sold copies." Emily shook her head. "I was so bloody naïve. I thought he'd do it. Instead he laughed at me, this cruel, harsh, mocking sound, tinged with revulsion and dismissal and hatred. As if I meant nothing, as if all the stories I'd written about him had never existed. He told me to grow up, said I was more delusional than my mother. And then he hung up on me."

"But your mom. She was still going to go see the lawyer. It could have worked out all right."

"Except it didn't. My mom was dead by the time the appointment came up. The next night, she mixed too many sleeping pills with too much alcohol. Her death was ruled accidental, but the innuendo of suicide was always there. Ex-employee embezzler kills herself to avoid criminal prosecution by big-shot developer. The headlines practically wrote themselves."

"And you blamed yourself, and Garrett Stonehaven, for her death, regardless of the answer."

"Something like that."

"So when Michelle offered you this assignment, you thought you'd have a chance to get the goods on Stonehaven, expose him as a liar and a cheat, get payback for your mother. Except now you suspect your mother's death wasn't suicide or an accident. Now you think your mother's death might have been murder."

Emily smiled. It was a jaded smile, tinged with regret and sadness and lost hope, but it was a smile nonetheless.

"Exactly like that."

"It might have been helpful if you'd mentioned this to me and Levon when you were telling us about your reason for coming to Lount's Landing. Is there anything else you've been holding back?"

"No, nothing."

Arabella studied Emily through narrowed eyes. Sighed. "Oh, what the hell. I might have done the same thing if I'd been in your position. But we have to make a promise to one another. From this point on, no more secrets."

"Agreed."

"Okay then. Let's go back to where we started. Yes, Carter and February are dead. But Stonehaven is dead too."

"Don't think I haven't been over that, time and again. I don't have the answers."

"But we do have the questions."

"Huh?"

"Who, other than Stonehaven, had a reason to want Carter dead? And I think only one person fits the criteria. Gloria Moroziuk. It would have been easy for her to put something with peanuts in Carter's food. Heck, she might have put peanut oil on the grill for all we know. She definitely knew about Carter's allergy. He was always going on about it."

"She might also have been the one to fill up the jam baskets," Emily said, her face brightening. "That look of surprise on February's face, when Carter went off on her about the peanut butter packets, may not have been an act after all."

Arabella frowned. "Something still doesn't add up. Why would Gloria trust February? That part doesn't make sense to me."

"What if she didn't involve her intentionally? What if February saw something and tried to blackmail Gloria?" Emily tapped her fingers on the rocker's wide oak arm planks. "Here's another theory. Michelle Ellis is the one who suggested Gloria hire February. Michelle must have known about February's drug addiction, past or present, and she would have told Gloria. Which means that Gloria would have had a way of getting rid of February, if it came to that."

"I suppose so," Arabella said, her voice thoughtful. "But the same arguments could be made for Michelle. After all, she hired her to work for Gloria, on assignment, the same way she hired you."

"True, but Michelle had nothing to gain or lose by Carter not selling the maisonettes, at least none that I can think of. Neither did anyone else, with the possible exception of Poppy Spencer, and I don't see her killing someone for the sake of a commission. Mind you, she was at the restaurant, so she definitely had the opportunity."

"She was also the real estate agent of record for the elementary school and Camp Miakoda, which means she had Stonehaven's confidence. What if she did it for Stonehaven, and then killed him when she found out his intentions were less than honorable? I think we have to keep Poppy on our suspect list." Arabella sighed. "Levon and Stanford were right. They both told me to let the police do their job. Being an amateur sleuth is harder than it sounds in books."

"We just need to focus. It might be easier if we ruled people out, instead of trying to rule them in. I need to follow up with Betsy, get the list of who was in the bar when Stonehaven gave his toast."

"I've been replaying that scene in my head, and the more I think about it, the more I think Stonehaven's toast was directed to someone sitting at the bar."

"Didn't Betsy say he had a longer toast planned, one that complimented her?"

Arabella shook her head. "That's not what I mean. Stonehaven may have planned to recognize Betsy. But when he said the words, 'I'm not ashamed of anything I have done,' it was as if he was taunting someone."

"The taunting part certainly sounds like Stonehaven. Do you remember who else was at the bar? Other than Betsy and the wait staff?"

Arabella nodded. "Gloria, Poppy, Camilla, and Johnny." A look of abject misery crossed her face. "And Levon."

CHAPTER 39

Once again, Emily and Arabella arranged to meet Levon at The Hanged Man's Noose at noon the following day. While they both agreed the likelihood of either Johnny or Levon being a murderer was remote, the fact remained: Stonehaven's cryptic toast may have been directed at either one or the other.

"How do we find out?" Arabella had asked. To which Emily replied she'd no idea, outside of coming out and asking them. Not the best plan, but it would have to do.

"I suppose it's possible a message was directed at one of us," Levon said, "but I can't imagine why it would have been meant for me. I hadn't seen or heard from Garry until the day of Arabella's grand opening, which, while unpleasant, was hardly cause to threaten death, his or mine."

"I'm inclined to agree with Levon," Arabella said to Emily. "I can't imagine him killing one person, let alone three. Breaking someone's heart, sure. Killing them, not so much."

"Thanks for the backhanded vote of confidence," Levon said. "And still sitting here in front of you."

"That leaves Poppy, Camilla, Gloria, and Johnny," Emily said, hoping to get them both back on track. "Levon, you call on Camilla, see what she has to say. She's bound to be more honest with you than she was with me. Arabella, maybe you can connect with Poppy Spencer. She helped you find the retail space for the Glass Dolphin, so hopefully she'll open up to you. I'll visit Gloria and Johnny."

"Remind me, why am I doing this again?" Levon asked.

"How about because we asked you to," Arabella said.

Levon sighed. "It's not exactly a reason, but I'll do it—providing Arabella comes with me to visit Camilla. I am not going there alone, only to hear about it for the next ten years of my life."

"I'm supposed to talk to Poppy," Arabella said.

"You can swing by on your way home. We can tackle Camilla in the morning."

Arabella shook her head. "I don't want to go to Camilla's."

"And I don't want the two of you getting involved and dragging me into it. Yet here I am."

"We'll make it up to you," Arabella promised.

"That we will," Emily said. "Let's meet at The Hanged Man's Noose tomorrow at one o'clock to compare notes. We'll even buy you lunch and a beer."

"Lunch and a beer is not exactly my idea of making it up to me, but it's a start."

Emily laughed out loud as Arabella fluffed her curls.

CHAPTER 40

Arabella headed to Poppy Spencer's office on Main Street office, relieved to find Poppy sitting at her desk. It hadn't occurred to her to make an appointment. She stood up when Arabella entered, giving her what could best be described as a wintery smile.

"Arabella. I haven't seen you since the grand opening."

It couldn't hurt to grovel a little. "I may have been a tad judgmental of you that day, Poppy. And I definitely should have thanked you properly for the edible fruit arrangement. It was delicious."

"Let's say we're both at fault and move on," Poppy said, with a slightly warmer smile. "Is everything okay with the shop?"

"Sales aren't exactly rocketing, but I've made a few, and I've done a couple of appraisals. It will take some time to build clientele." Now was not the time to mention that money was already getting tight. She needed to spend more time on business and less on investigating.

"But with the property itself, there are no issues?"

"No, none." Arabella cleared her throat. "I'm here on another matter."

Poppy slid her designer-framed glasses halfway down her nose. Arabella tried not to flinch as the steel gray eyes assessed her. "What sort of matter?"

"It's about the night of the presentation at The Hanged Man's Noose. Stonehaven's toast, to be exact."

"It was odd, I'll grant you that. It certainly turned out to be eerily prophetic. Betsy told me later those were the last words of Samuel Lount, although I understand Stonehaven had more to say before you interrupted him with your toast. What did you say again? Something like, 'let's all drink to the newest traitor in town.' I'll admit to being moderately amused at the time. Stonehaven wasn't a man used to being mocked."

"Glad to have made an impression. Here's the thing, though. I've been thinking about Stonehaven's toast, and I'm convinced he was sending a message to someone sitting at the bar."

"And you think that someone might have been me?" Poppy shook her head. "I can't see why. I sold him a couple of properties, but there was no animosity between us. Quite the opposite. He was going to hire me to lease out the retail and commercial space at the elementary school once we closed on the schoolhouse. We were still working on getting planning permission."

Subject to planning permission, meaning Poppy was without a commission now that Stonehaven was dead. It also meant she had no motive to kill him, and every reason to want him alive.

"You said you sold Stonehaven a couple of properties. What was the other one?"

"I suppose it will all come out with the police investigation. It was an old boot camp for young offenders in Miakoda Falls. A place called Camp Miakoda."

So Levon was right. Stonehaven had been the buyer.

"There was some animosity, there, come to think of it," Poppy said.

"What sort of animosity?"

"It was my listing. I figured it would be an albatross. Who wants to buy an old boot camp for young offenders? But to my surprise, two buyers were interested. I got the distinct impression there was some history between them, but that wasn't my concern. My concern was getting the best deal for my client." Poppy smiled at the memory. "It turned out to be quite the bidding war, with an added bonus. I gained Garrett Stonehaven as a client."

"Who was the other bidder, do you remember?"

"Of course I remember. He barely spoke to me again until recently, when Garrett Stonehaven came to town. Then, all of a sudden, he's like my new best friend. Wanted to be part of things, recommend people to be on the planning committee for StoreHaven. It seemed out of character, but I was never the one holding the grudge. Plus, we needed someone like Johnny to smooth the waters with the merchants along Main Street, get them on board with the plan. Someone folks would trust."

"Johnny?"

"That's right. Johnny. Johnny Porter."

CHAPTER 41

Based on the sulky expression on his face, Levon wasn't any too pleased to be paying a visit to Camilla. *Well, too bad for him.* Arabella wasn't about to go into the lioness's den alone. Never mind that Levon insisted he'd only wanted to rent a room for a week or so and figure out where things had been going wrong. The reality was that couples hit rough patches all the time, and most husbands didn't all traipse off to an attractive widow's B&B looking for a place to stay.

Next thing you know, Arabella and Levon were headed to divorce court, with Camilla gloating in the wings and spreading her malicious lies all around town.

It had taken a long time, but bit-by-bit Arabella and Levon had managed to resurrect their friendship. After all, they'd been friends long before they became lovers, and business associates before that. But she still missed the whole of Levon, even after all this time. She wondered, sometimes, if he felt the same way. Not that it mattered. Arabella knew she could never completely trust Levon again. And without trust, you didn't have a relationship.

They arrived at the Gilroy Mansion just as Camilla was getting out of her Mercedes. She was decked out in black spandex tights and a fluffy white fake fur jacket, a yoga mat under her arm. Arabella couldn't help but notice the toned thighs, flat tummy, and tight ass. The woman probably hadn't had a shortbread cookie in a decade. She glanced at Levon and was amused to find him trying not to look.

"Levon," Camilla said, completely ignoring Arabella. "Don't tell me you're back looking to rent a room? The farmhouse not working out for you?"

"Pull in your claws, Camilla. We're here to ask you a couple of questions about Garrett Stonehaven."

"Why would I want to answer them?" Camilla's eyes flicked over Arabella. "Especially with *her* here."

"Why wouldn't you? Unless you've got something to hide. If you don't, then we can get this whole affair put to rest." Arabella flashed a saccharine smile. "It can't be good for business, people knowing a man might have been murdered in one of your rooms. Whatever would your precious Shakyra think?"

"Low blow, even for you Arabella. Especially after your nasty toast to Garrett at the presentation." Camilla sighed dramatically. "Besides, you'd be surprised at the ghoulishness of people. I've had more interest in that room in the past week than I have in the past year."

"I'm not surprised," Levon said, "which is all the more reason you should be inviting us in. Unless you want us to debate this outside so the neighbors can hear."

That got Camilla's attention. "Come on in. I'd offer you tea and scones, but it's not like this is a social visit."

They settled into the front parlor. Arabella couldn't help but notice that the room was looking a bit sad around the edges, as if Camilla had run into hard times. Levon had told her that the rental unit he'd stayed in had been done up to the nines. Had all the money had been poured into the rentals? Arabella realized she knew nothing about Camilla's financial situation, beyond the rumors Graham had left her without a bean. Not that she was convinced. Camilla had always been good at spinning a yarn. She'd learned that the hard way.

"What was it you wanted to know?" Camilla asked. She was perched in an oversized wing chair, her legs tucked underneath her. She reminded Arabella of a jungle cat, sleek, self-satisfied, superior, and in complete control of every movement.

"We wanted to talk about Stonehaven's toast," Levon started. "He stared right at the five of us. At you, me, Gloria, Poppy, and Johnny."

"How can I ever forget? It was like he was speaking to us directly. Not that I understood the message. I keep thinking I should, but I don't."

"Let's assume his toast was a message to one of us. Maybe whoever understood the message felt threatened enough to kill him. If it wasn't you, and it wasn't me, then who was it meant for?"

Camilla shrugged. "How should I know?"

"Gloria, Poppy, and Johnny," Arabella said, trying to keep the frustration from her voice. "Who of the three was the most likely to pay Stonehaven a visit? And get let in?"

Camilla frowned in concentration. "I have to say any one of the three are possible. Gloria was on his team, and she owned the apartment building he wanted to buy. Then again, a dead man can't exactly buy real estate."

Arabella had to admit she had a point. "What about Poppy?"

"Poppy was his real estate agent, but for her to benefit, he had to be alive. The schoolhouse property wasn't set to close until all the approvals were in place. That was one of the reasons for the presentation. It was one of the requirements from the Cedar County Municipal Board."

"I didn't realize that," Levon said.

"Neither did I," Arabella said.

"I'm not even sure if his team members knew. Regardless, Johnny had nothing to gain by Stonehaven's death. He was lobbying for the Main Street Merchants' Association. You both know as well as I do that Johnny would do anything to get Main Street back to its glory days."

"So we're no further ahead," Arabella said, although she was thinking quite the opposite. Because Johnny Porter *would* do anything for Main Street. Which meant he must have recognized Stonehaven's pyramid scheme for exactly what it was. An elaborate version of the same game he'd played at Camp Miakoda. She glanced at Levon, saw the way his face had drained of all color, knew he was thinking the same thing. They had to get in touch with Emily, warn her about Johnny before she went over there to question him.

She just hoped they weren't too late.

CHAPTER 42

Emily paced the living room, trying to ignore the two gallons of Hay Bale stacked in the corner. Her mind kept flicking back to that first day in the Sunrise Café. Some clue was there, something she was missing, something beyond February's stumble over Carter's jacket.

It wasn't that she suspected Gloria. Because if the deaths of Carter, February, and Stonehaven were orchestrated by the same person—and she believed they were—then Gloria had the best alibi of all. You couldn't sell property to a dead man.

She'd gone over it and over it. A vase of roses had been in the bay window. Yellow roses. She glanced at the cans of paint, thought about the lavender roses from Johnny. He'd mentioned to her, the first time they'd met, that he had a fascination with colors. If the flowers had been meant to signify love at first sight—and admittedly she might be making a bit of a leap there—then maybe yellow roses also meant something.

A Google search revealed several meanings: "Joy; Gladness; Friendship; Promise of a New Beginning; Welcome Back; Jealousy; Remember Me; and I Care." Talk about the all-purpose rose. Could be nothing more than a vase filled with yellow roses, meant to complement the yellow and orange décor at the Café. But Emily didn't think so. The question was what *did* they mean? And had Johnny sent them?

Gloria stared at Emily. "You want to know about the yellow roses that were here the day Carter died?"

"Yes, you see, I'm writing an article on the meaning behind the color of roses." Not true, but certainly plausible. "I think most people know red is for true love, but beyond that, most people don't realize that different colors have different meanings. For example, lavender roses mean 'love at first sight.' Yellow roses have a few meanings, like 'welcome back' or 'new beginning' or 'remember me.'"

"I get you, sure. I guess you journalists are paid to notice every detail. You're right, the yellow roses were sent with a note that said, 'To a Prosperous New Beginning.' But I figured whoever sent them selected yellow because they matched the décor in here."

"You said whoever sent them. You don't know who sent them to you?"

"I have no clue. You see, the card wasn't addressed to me."

"It wasn't?"

"No, the roses were sent to February. I thought it was odd at the time. What sort of prosperous new beginning could a waitress at a small town diner have?"

Emily couldn't begin to imagine, but one person might have the answer. The chairman of the Main Street Merchants' Association.

It was time to face Johnny Porter.

Johnny was on the phone when she arrived at It's a Colorful Life. He gave her a quick wave and hung up a few seconds later, turning his 100-watt smile on her in full force. Once again, Emily was struck by his movie star good looks. She felt her resolve melt a little. *Damn, but this is going to be hard.*

"Hey, Johnny. I wondered if you have a few minutes to spare?"

"Sure." He looked at her, his black-brown eyes filled with concern. "Is anything wrong?"

Every fiber of her being wanted to say, "No, everything's good, I thought I'd take you up on that dinner you were offering." But she couldn't back down now. It was time to find out the truth.

"I've been thinking about Stonehaven's death. I can't seem to think about anything else."

Johnny gave her a sympathetic nod. "You knew him back in Toronto, didn't you? Arabella told me you used to write about him in *Urban Living* all the time. So his death must have come as a terrible shock."

"You could say that." Emily took a moment to consider her options. Like confronting Johnny with her theory in a safer, more public place. Ask him out for dinner at The Hanged Man's Noose. Or Frankie's Fish and Chips. No, Nigel would be sure to eavesdrop and dinner out was simply delaying the inevitable. Besides, It's a Colorful Life was a public place, wasn't it? A customer could stroll in at any moment.

She forged ahead. "My relationship with Stonehaven was complicated."

"Complicated?"

"It's true that he was a frequent source for my *Urban Living* feature articles, but recently there had been some personal animosity between us."

Johnny laughed out loud. "Personal animosity? Who didn't have personal animosity with Garrett Stonehaven? Not to speak ill of the dead, but the man had an ego twice the size of Toronto and the moral compass of a gnat. He had no compunction about crushing anyone who stood in his way."

"Yet you supported his plan, knowing the kind of man he was."

"Ever hear of the old adage, 'keep your friends close and your enemies closer?' The only way I could guarantee Stonehaven wouldn't ruin Main Street was to get involved. That's what I did."

Emily felt a sense of relief. Johnny's explanation made perfect sense.

"What about now that he's dead?"

"A good question. I suspect his plan died with him. He was careful not to divulge all the details. In all likelihood, the schoolhouse will go back on the market. Life will go back to the way it was, at least until Poppy comes up with another developer for the property."

"So you don't believe there's anything suspicious about Stonehaven's death?"

"Suspicious? Nigel Watters told me the police are treating it like an accidental overdose."

"The gospel according to Nigel." Emily grinned, then immediately sobered up. "Look, I won't lie and say I liked Stonehaven. I didn't. But I didn't wish him dead, and I can't buy his death as a suicide or accidental overdose. Neither scenario fits with the man I knew."

"What are you suggesting?"

"I think Stonehaven was murdered, and his death might be related to the deaths of Carter and February."

Johnny folded his arms in front of his chest. "You think there were three murders?"

"I've been going over everything in my head, all the little things I've seen and heard, wondering if any of it meant anything. And then last night I remembered something."

"Which was?"

"The day Carter Dixon died at the Sunrise Café, a vase of yellow roses was in the bay window."

"Yellow roses. Okay, I'll take your word for it."

"I wondered who the roses came from, whether they had any significance, or whether they were meant to match the décor."

"Wow. Investigating roses. You are inquisitive."

Was that a note of thinly-veiled hostility in Johnny's voice? Or had she just managed to hurt his feelings? Emily chose to ignore the faint trace of unease creeping into her gut. Surely the entire town couldn't be wrong about Johnny Porter. He was good people, Arabella had assured her—and Arabella was a reliable judge of character... wasn't she?

"What can I say, Johnny? It's a side effect of the job. Anyway, I spoke to Gloria earlier today. It seems the roses were sent to February, with a note that said, 'To a Prosperous New Beginning.' I thought you might have sent them."

"Did you now?" Johnny's handsome face had taken on an unbecoming look, a cross between a smirk and a scowl. "You make it sound as if something sinister was behind it. So what if I sent yellow roses to February? The poor kid told me she was trying to start over, get a brighter financial future. I thought they'd make her day. Like I hoped the lavender roses might have made your day. Obviously, I misread at least one situation."

"I apologize if I offended you. I'm just trying to make sense of things."

The scowly-smirk faded ever so slightly. "Fair enough. I suppose there's no stopping the journalist in you, even when it comes to roses. But let's suppose your triple murder theory is true, Emily. Suppose there's some sort of serial killer lurking out there. Who had the means, opportunity, and motive to do it? And where's your proof?"

"I may not have proof—yet. But I believe Stonehaven's toast at The Hanged Man's Noose was directed to someone at the bar that night."

"But who? There were any number of people at the bar that evening."

"True enough, but not all of them knew Stonehaven in a past life." Emily swallowed hard. "I know all about your brother, Jake. All about Camp Miakoda. Levon told me about it, filled me in about the pyramid scheme. He said Neighbors Helping Neighbors smacked of more of the same. I think Stonehaven planned to pull the same stunt all over again. Moreover, I think you knew it and decided to stop him. Everyone always says you'll do anything for Main Street."

She didn't know what she'd expected. Would Johnny break down and confess everything to her? Or would he get angry, but vehemently deny any involvement?

As it turned out, he did neither.

"Come take a ride with me to someplace near Miakoda Falls," he said, a trace of tears in his beseeching black eyes. "I need to share something with you. Something important. Something that will make you understand the whole story. It won't take more than a couple of hours. In fact, we'd be back by noon if we left right away."

Emily was a sucker for tears, and she had to admit that she was curious. Could the someplace near Miakoda Falls be Camp Miakoda? Despite her best instincts, she'd acquiesced—but not before sending a text to Arabella while Johnny went to the back to get his jacket.

"Off to MF with JP. Stay tuned."

As if a cryptic message would be able to help her.

And now here she was, sitting next to a silent and sullen Johnny in the front seat of his black SUV, with no way to get a reply, and no way to send another message. Somewhere along the road heading towards Miakoda Falls, they'd lost cell reception. Not so much as a single, solitary bar, no matter how many times she tried.

Every instinct told her this wasn't going to end well.

CHAPTER 43

Arabella checked her phone for the third time in as many minutes. "Emily's late." She'd been waiting with Levon at The Hanged Man's Noose since one o'clock, the prearranged time to meet for lunch and compare notes. Thirty minutes had passed since then.

"Everyone's late now and again," Levon said.

"Everyone might be, but not Emily. She's an absolute stickler for punctuality, claims it comes from living life eternally on a deadline." Arabella rechecked her messages. Nothing since *Off to MF with JP. Stay tuned.* "MF. That must be Miakoda Falls."

"That would be my guess."

"Why Miakoda Falls?"

"You've got me there. What do you suggest we do?"

"How should the hell should I know?" Arabella knew she was getting cranky. She always got cranky when she was worried. Especially when there were no cookies around. Why didn't Betsy sell cookies?

"Maybe you should text Emily back, tell her we're waiting."

"You think I haven't thought of that? I've tried texting her. No reply. I've tried calling her. Goes straight to voice mail. I'm seriously concerned. What if Emily is in danger?"

"I think you're overreacting. The text message suggests she went with him voluntarily. And you know how patchy cell reception is once you get out of town." Levon took a sip of his beer.

"You might be right, but the idea of Johnny taking her somewhere outside of cellular range isn't exactly comforting. I feel as if we should be doing something more than sitting around here waiting."

"You could fill me in on what Poppy told you yesterday. There might be some clue in that."

Arabella leaned across the booth and hugged Levon. "You're a genius," she said, tossing a ten-dollar bill on the table. "C'mon, we have to go. I'll drive, you navigate." She caught his look. "You've had half a beer. I've had club soda."

"All right, already. But where are we going?"

"To save Emily, of course."

"But we don't know where they went. Miakoda Falls might be a small town, but it's not *that* small."

"We're not going to Miakoda Falls. We're going to Camp Miakoda."

"Camp Miakoda?"

"Yes, that's what Poppy told me. She said Stonehaven faced another bidder for Camp Miakoda."

"Johnny Porter?"

"Johnny Porter."

Levon tossed his keys over to Arabella, his face suddenly pale. "Let's go."

On the way to Camp Miakoda, Levon told Arabella that everyone thought Garry had hidden the eight thousand dollars from the pyramid scheme, along with a list of the investors. Once the Camp closed down, there'd been no way to access the building without being seen by security cameras.

"The camp might have been a failed experiment, but no one in charge was about to let the place get trashed," Levon said. "Given the previous clientele, that would have been a very real possibility. Not to mention an empty building off the beaten path would have attracted vagrants and college kids wanting to party hardy."

"So when the property came on the market, Stonehaven and Johnny saw their chance."

"Exactly. The money wasn't enough to make a difference to either of them at this point in their lives—certainly not enough for them to want to invest in an old boot camp for young offenders. But the list of names, however... that would be pure gold."

"Stonehaven didn't want that list to get into the wrong hands," Arabella said. "But why? Surely after all these years, no one was going to prosecute them."

"Unless one of the people on that list was responsible for Jake's death, which is what Johnny always believed."

"It must have gutted him to lose the place to Stonehaven. And then to have him come back a couple of years later and flaunt his pyramid scheme in front of Johnny's friends and business associates." Arabella shook her head. "Garrett Stonehaven was not a very nice man."

They debated back and forth about calling the police. Arabella was for it, and Levon was against it.

"You were the one who wanted to leave things up to the police," Arabella said. Her hands clenched the steering wheel, knuckles white. She glanced at the speedometer; she knew she was driving far too fast for the curvy county road. She slowed down a bit.

"What I said was, let the police do their job," he replied. "And if you and Emily had bothered to listen, we wouldn't be in this predicament right now." Levon rested his hand on her thigh for a brief moment. "Look, I know you're worried. So am I.

But what are we supposed to tell the police? 'Hello, we think our friend may have been taken somewhere against her will by Johnny Porter, the much loved chairman of the Main Street Merchants' Association. We don't know where they might have gone, but we think it might be an old boot camp called Camp Miakoda. You see, there was this pyramid scheme and...'"

"It does sound a bit stupid, when you put it like that." Arabella sped up again. "How much further?"

"Another ten minutes, max—if we arrive alive. Ease up on the gas pedal a bit, okay?"

The warning came too late. Before Arabella had a chance to slow down to something resembling the speed limit, she saw flashing lights in her rearview mirror. "It's an omen," she said, pulling over and rolling down her window.

"Don't even think about it, Arabella. You'll sound like a nutcase. Or someone who's trying to get out of a ticket."

A burly police officer, padded with winter gear and bulletproof vest, made his way to the driver's door. "License and registration."

"We think our friend has been abducted," Arabella said, pulling her wallet out of her purse. "Taken against her will to Camp Miakoda."

"Uh-huh. License and registration."

Levon handed her the registration and shot her a warning look. Arabella pulled her license out of her wallet. She gave both to the officer, ignored Levon, and tried again. "Officer, I realize I was driving over the speed limit, but we're worried about our friend, Emily—" Her voice trailed off as she watched him make his way back to the cruiser.

"Lying nutcase, that's what he's thinking," Levon said. "Probably thinks Camp Miakoda is something out of a computer game."

———

The ticket cost them a delay of ten minutes and a fine for Arabella, though thankfully she hadn't been dinged with demerit points. It also cost her an unwelcome admission: Levon had been right.

"Okay, so I should have slowed down, the officer did think I was trying to get out of the ticket, and he probably thought I was a nutcase with an overactive imagination."

Levon grinned. "I wish I had a tape recorder. Could that be Arabella Carpenter admitting she was wrong?"

"Don't push it. Are we almost there?"

"We turn left on Concession 8, less than a mile up the road, and then we continue on for about five miles, give or take. You'll see a row of jack pines. Keep your eyes peeled. There's a hidden driveway about ten trees in."

Arabella did as she was told, this time careful to stay within the speed limit. When she saw the row of jack pines, she slowed down some more until she spotted the driveway. She pulled in and kept driving, although by now they were down to crawl. The road had been rutted by time; by now it wasn't much more than a dirt path overgrown by years of neglect. About a half a mile in there was a ten-foot high chain-link fence, with a row of rusted barbed wire laced through the top. A hole had been cut out of the fence's gate, large enough for a person to climb through, but nowhere big enough for a vehicle.

"We'll have to get out at the fence," Arabella said, winding her way through the final twist and turn. Fear rose in her throat, and she tried to swallow the bitter bile back down. Because a black SUV was already parked there. And it had a vanity plate that read MAIN*STRT.

"We're in the right place," Arabella said. "The black SUV is Johnny's. I recognize the Main Street license plate."

"You were right. We need to call the police."

"Good to know you're starting to see things my way." Arabella pulled her phone out of her purse and looked forlornly at the unresponsive screen. "No bars. What do we do now? Go back to County Road 37 where we're likely to get reception?"

Levon shook his head. "That will cost us at least another ten minutes each way. By the time the police arrive—if they arrive—who knows what could have gone down? We have no choice. We have to go in. But we have to go about it quietly. We might be able to gain the upper hand if we have the element of surprise on our side."

The element of surprise. Suddenly the game of amateur detective wasn't quite so much fun. The bile rose in her throat again. "Okay," she said. "Okay."

Arabella and Levon trudged wordlessly along the path. There was evidence of footsteps ahead of them.

"How much further?" Arabella whispered, weary of the silence. They'd been walking for fifteen minutes. Her legs ached and her feet were cold. Her riding boots might have made a nice fashion statement, but they had never been made for serious winter walking. Who was she kidding? It wasn't only the boots. *She* hadn't been made for serious winter walking.

"Not too much," Levon whispered back. "We'll come to the main building beyond the next clearing. Red brick with leaded glass windows. Beyond that's the water." He turned to Arabella and gave her a quick, wordless hug.

Arabella felt herself melt into the familiar comfort of his arms, breathed in the dusty denim of his jacket, forced herself to pull away. There would be time enough to sort out her feelings later.

"Let's go find Emily."

CHAPTER 44

Emily had just about convinced herself that Johnny's ongoing silence was nothing more than a man lost in his own thoughts, although she had to admit that the lack of cell reception was disconcerting. She wasn't one of those people tied to their phones as if it was an oxygen tank, but she didn't like to go unplugged, either. It wasn't until they arrived at their destination and she saw the chain-link fence with the seriously barbed wire top and a hole cut out of the double-padlocked gate that she figured she might be in trouble.

"Where are we?" she asked. Her voice had a hollow ring to it, the voice of someone terrified to speak. She didn't care for the sound.

Johnny looked over at her, then looked away towards the direction of the fence. After what seemed like an eternity, he looked back again, a strange expression on his face, then he got out of the SUV, walked over to the passenger side, and opened the door.

Finally, he spoke. His words held no comfort.

"Welcome to Camp Miakoda."

The way into the Camp was a mix of overgrown shrubs, tree roots, and small rocks. The space felt claustrophobic, as if the road had tried to choke out any evidence of its being there. Patches of ice and snow blanketed the shaded trail, making travel both tricky and treacherous.

Despite all of that, Emily was beginning to feel guardedly optimistic. She'd slipped and fallen about ten minutes along, twisting her left ankle. For the moment, at least, it was causing nothing more than mild discomfort, but she suspected adrenaline and endorphins had a lot to do with suppressing any pain. Johnny had picked her off the ground, and since then he'd held onto her hand, lending stronger support when the terrain went from rough to rugged. He'd also become a little more talkative.

"I tried to buy this place three years ago," Johnny said after they'd been walking, hand in hand, for a few minutes. "Stonehaven had deeper pockets."

So Levon's theory had been right. "You're saying this land is... was... owned by Garrett Stonehaven?"

"I don't think he necessarily *wanted* to own it. He just didn't want *me* to own it."

"Why would *you* want to own it? I wouldn't think this place would have happy memories for you after what happened to Jake."

"You wouldn't think so, would you? But the reality is I feel closest to him when I come here." He stopped and took both her hands in his, his jet black eyes wide and serious. "Look, Emily, no matter what happens, I want you to know something. I did have feelings for you. It wasn't an act."

Another glimmer of hope. "And now?"

He didn't answer, just started walking again, pulling her along. Maybe he was holding her hand so she wouldn't run away. But that was ridiculous. Where would she run to with a bum ankle? And why would she have to?

After all, Johnny had brought her lavender roses. That had to count for something.

They reached another fence, this one with a gatehouse and a gate, the kind where a button would be pushed by a gatekeeper to raise the arm up and let a vehicle go through. Emily supposed twenty years ago the road would have been drivable, at least in the summer.

They slid underneath the wooden arm and made their way past a red brick building with small, leaded glass windows. With the exception of random patches of curling shingles, the building still looked solid.

"We're going down to the water," Johnny said. It was the first time he'd spoken since telling her his feelings hadn't been an act. That felt like a lifetime ago, although Emily suspected less than twenty minutes had passed.

"Why the water?" she asked, trying to remember what Levon had told her and Arabella. Something about a waterfall a couple of miles down the fast-flowing river. Someone tumbled over and died every year, he'd said. There was no surviving that open dam. But the water would be frozen by now, wouldn't it?

Besides, the water might not be a bad thing. Emily recalled the photograph in It's a Colorful Life, the one of a young Johnny with his brother, Jake. How happy they had looked, Jake's arm draped protectively around his kid brother.

Maybe Johnny's silent treatment didn't mean anything. Maybe all he'd wanted to do was figure out the best way to share his past with her.

Delusion was the better part of valor.

CHAPTER 45

The first thing Emily noticed was how fast-flowing the water was, with the only visible ice at the edges where the water's movement stilled long enough to let it freeze. The water looked deep, dark, and dangerous.

The second thing she noticed was a dilapidated wooden rowboat tied up to the side of an equally dilapidated dock, both weatherworn and beaten down by time. But it was the third thing Emily noticed that convinced her she'd landed herself into some serious trouble.

"What's Camilla Mortimer-Gilroy doing here?" she asked Johnny. "And why is she throwing those boat paddles and life jackets into the water?"

"Camilla," Johnny said, ignoring Emily. "I didn't see your car. How'd you get here?"

"I parked by the open dam, then hiked along the shore from the waterfalls—not that it's any of *your* business." She waved a leather-gloved hand in Emily's direction. "This is your idea of not doing anything rash? Why did you bring *her* here?"

"What did you expect me to do? She all but accused me of murder. Given enough time, she would have figured out everything—including your insistence on terminating her employment with Urban-Huntzberger. If you had let that be, I'm sure Michelle could have convinced her to stop her investigation."

"And I warned you not to get involved with her." Camilla pushed aside a blonde tendril of hair and sighed dramatically. "I'll have to make the best of a bad situation." She looked at Emily. "Did you tell anyone you were coming here?"

Emily shook her head. She wasn't about to mention her text message to Arabella. "Johnny said he had something to show me," she said, determined to keep the warble out of her voice. "I didn't know that something would be my ex-employer."

Camilla's lovely face tightened into a distorted mask. "Johnny has a big mouth. So what if I'm a silent partner in Urban-Huntzberger? God knows Michelle couldn't run the place without some serious business savvy. All the editorial skill in the world doesn't make the publishing world go round."

"And the other silent partner?"

"No reason you shouldn't know now. Man by the name of Eldon Thornbury."

Emily recognized the name. Eldon Thornbury was the accountant who worked with Stonehaven on the Kraft-Fergusson brownfield land. The man her mother had suspected of money laundering and investment fraud. She wondered how much Michelle knew.

It was as if Camilla read her mind. "Michelle knew Eldon's name, and she knew he was an accountant. But to her he was just the money guy in the Urban-Huntzberger merger. She never knew or suspected the connection between him and Garrett. Nobody did, with the exception of your mother. She got a bit too snoopy for her own good."

"What are you saying?" Emily's fear dissipated, replaced by raw rage. "Are you telling me my mother's death wasn't an accident?"

"You do the math, sunshine. All I'm saying is that I spent a lovely evening with your mom, sipping on cocktails while she told me all about the criminal lawyer she was going to see."

"She told you about the lawsuit? She didn't even know you."

"Michelle introduced us. Of course I completely sympathized with your mother's cause from the minute I befriended her at one of those tedious food fundraisers she was always putting on." Camilla smiled slyly. "Who can fault wanting green space for inner city kids? And bringing a case or two of canned beans certainly wasn't going to break the bank. But her going to a lawyer? Trying to ruin Garry's plans? So a few too many Vicodin landed into her vodka martinis. If it's any consolation, she died peacefully."

"Consolation? You're telling me you killed my mother, and I'm supposed to take comfort from the fact that you didn't bludgeon her to death?" Emily's anger flared. She moved forward, ready to push that lovely face down in the icy water, when a strong pair of hands reached out and pulled her back. *Johnny.* She'd forgotten Johnny was there.

"You'd do best to reconsider your actions," he said to Emily. He turned to Camilla. "What the hell were you thinking, spilling every detail?"

Camilla shrugged. "It's not like she's going to live to tell anyone about it. Now toss me your car keys."

"My car keys?"

"Yes, your car keys. I have a plan."

"What sort of plan?" Johnny asked, but he tossed her the keys.

Camilla put the keys in her parka pocket. "Enough chatter. I'm getting cold and bored—never a good combination. Emily, I need you to get into the boat. You too, Johnny."

Emily figured if going over the falls didn't kill her, it wouldn't be long before hypothermia set in. She thought about trying to make a run for it—might have chanced it, twisted ankle and all—except for one tiny new detail.

There was a gun in Camilla's right hand.

CHAPTER 46

Emily glanced over at Johnny. Based on the glazed expression on his face, he appeared to be in shock.

"Into the boat?" Johnny said. "*Both* of us? I don't understand."

"What did you expect? That I'd take care of Emily and you'd walk away, free and clear?" Camilla laughed softly. "You always were a dreamer, Johnny. No, I'm afraid some unfortunate soul will find your car parked by the dam, and the remnants of a battered rowboat floating in the water. As for your bodies, who knows where and when they'll turn up? By that time I'll be safely ensconced at the Gilroy Mansion, sipping Earl Grey tea and eating scones with strawberry preserves and clotted cream."

"And why would Emily and I be in a rowboat in late November?"

"Why indeed? I suppose I'll have to share my suspicions with that nice Detective Merryfield. Tell him all about how you were responsible for your brother's death. How Emily, fishing for a story, found out and decided it was murder, not an accident."

"You know damn well that I never meant for Jake to drown." Johnny turned to face Emily. "Jake promised to meet me near the falls, help me get out of a spot of trouble. I'd talked some not very nice guys into investing in Garry's pyramid scheme. When it all fell apart, things got ugly fast. But Jake was an incredible paddler. He should have made it, in spite of the storm. Garry must have done something to the boat."

"Maybe Garry did, and maybe he didn't," Camilla said, still waving the gun in their direction. "Unfortunately, that won't be the version I tell the police. Now, into the boat you go, or I'll have to shoot you."

Until that moment, Emily had been staying silent, trying to think up a plan of escape that didn't involve trying to navigate a rowboat without a paddle or a swim in glacial waters. But the journalist in her couldn't let it go. She had finally connected the dots. If only Levon had been a bit more forthcoming, a bit less concerned about pissing off Arabella.

"You're Millie," she said, trying not to think about the gun pointed in her general direction. "I should have realized it when you said my mother was trying to ruin *Garry's* plans. Only people from his Camp Miakoda days knew him as Garry. He made sure to erase all that when he transformed himself into Garrett Stonehaven."

Camilla clapped, her leather gloves dampening the sound. "Bravo. I wondered how long it would take you to figure it out. I'll admit I was starting to give up hope. Then again, I'm surprised Levon didn't mention it, though given his annoying infatuation with Arabella Carpenter I suppose I shouldn't be. And I couldn't entirely trust Johnny here, either. Not once he started falling for you like some pathetic schoolboy with a bad crush."

"I would never betray you," Johnny said. "Unlike *you*, I have some scruples."

"Easy to say with a gun pointed at you."

Emily decided to speak up. What was the worst that could happen? The way she figured it, she was dead either way. "You won't shoot us, Camilla. For one, how can you explain having a gun to the police? For another, it's not your style, far too hands-on, far too messy. You much prefer arranging accidents, hence sending Johnny and me out in a boat without paddles or life jackets. We're sure to die, either from hypothermia or from going over the falls. But before we go, can you tell me one thing? The night he died, how many drugs did you ply Graham with before he decided snowmobiling was a good idea?"

"He was an adult. He knew what he was doing," Camilla said. But something in her expression told Emily she'd hit on a nerve.

"So you say. The same cannot be said for Ambrose Ellis."

"Ungrateful bastard. Garret gave him a job and then he threatened to go to the authorities."

"And Carter and February? Why did they have to die?"

Camilla shrugged. "Neither of them would be dead if they hadn't been so greedy. Everyone thought Carter Dixon wouldn't sell the apartment building, but the reality is he wanted an exorbitant amount for it. Gloria, on the other hand, was perfectly willing to be reasonable."

"So Carter had to die?"

"Carter was never meant to die. All we wanted to do was scare some sense into him. But that moronic waitress took it a step too far and stole his EpiPen. And then she got greedy, tried to resort to blackmail—as if *that* was about to go unpunished! Not the sharpest knife in the drawer, February. Getting the drugs into her was child's play."

"You seem to know a lot about it, for someone on the sidelines," Emily said, trying to stall for time. If Stonehaven was responsible for the deaths of Carter and February, then her suspicions of Johnny were unfounded. There was still a chance if they worked together.

"Do I look like someone who would be satisfied with staying on the sidelines?"

"So you and Stonehaven were a team?"

"From the day we met in grade nine."

"You bitch," Johnny said. His face was contorted with rage. "You told me Stonehaven was back to his old tricks, except he'd learned a thing or two since Camp Miakoda. You told me we couldn't watch him cheat honest business people out of their hard-earned money. You gave me the drugs, told me to go to his room, pour them into his red wine. I stayed and watched him die because of you."

"He was going to leave me, Johnny. After everything I'd done for him."

"He was always a womanizer," Emily said, remembering the way he'd played the room at various housing functions. "Surely you knew that."

Camilla favored her with a venomous glare. "This time was different. He'd managed to fall in love, 'true love for the first time in his life,' the smug bastard told me. With that floozy bartender Betsy Ehrlich, no less."

"Betsy isn't a floozy," Emily said, and immediately regretted the outburst.

"She's worse than a floozy. She's a money-grubbing floozy. He was going to let her in on the ground floor of StoreHaven, and fund her way in! Talk about rubbing my nose in it. But the final straw was the night of the presentation, that ridiculous toast at The Hanged Man's Noose. He stared right at me when he said it, completely unashamed of anything he'd done. Willing to die like a man, was he? Well, he got what he asked for."

Johnny shook his head. "I still don't understand, Camilla. Why not call the police, tell them everything? I would have backed you up, told them all about the pyramid scheme Garry ran at Camp Miakoda. I know it was a long time ago, but I'm also sure he hid the money and the list of investors somewhere in the building. I'm equally positive someone on that list killed Jake. With your word and mine, the police would have been forced to do a proper investigation, not just for the Neighbors Helping Neighbors scam but for Jake's death. Don't you see? You could have gotten your revenge that way."

"Are you seriously that clueless, Johnny? Did you actually believe Stonehaven was behind Neighbors Helping Neighbors? That he would have come to Lount's Landing on his own volition? It was *me* calling the shots, Johnny. It was always me, right from the first pyramid scheme that sent Garry to Camp Miakoda."

Johnny stared at Camilla, his black eyes glassy. "Are you saying that you arranged the pyramid scheme at camp?"

"God, you're slow. Even Jake had that much figured out! He was going to report me to the authorities, the stupid son of a bitch. He said it was best for all of us to come clean. As if." Camilla laughed, a high-pitched, screeching sound that chilled Emily more than the thought of the icy-cold water. The woman in front of her was a certifiable maniac who would stop at nothing to save herself.

"That was why Jake had to die, wasn't it?" Emily said.

"You're too smart by half," Camilla said, waving the gun in Emily's direction.

It was the final blow. Johnny lunged at Camilla, stumbling in the attempt. Camilla lunged back, kicking and clawing and screaming obscenities.

Emily considered her options. She could try and make a run for it, bad ankle and all, and hope Camilla wouldn't shoot her in the back. Or she could get in the rowboat and take her chances navigating the river.

The sharp crack of a gunshot told her she'd hesitated a moment too long.

CHAPTER 47

Emily sat shivering in the rowboat, icicles forming streaks of glitter in her long, dark hair, her left ankle throbbing in pain. Everything was happening so fast. One minute she was standing on shore wondering how she was going to escape, and the next minute there was a harsh, popping sound. Gunshot. The time for deliberation was over.

She stumbled in her haste to get away, then bit her lip to hold back a scream as she went over on her bad ankle. Her body hit the river face first, the mud and the muck of the sludgy bottom sucking her further and further into the icy abyss.

She was a good swimmer—hell, she'd completed an Olympic-distance triathlon this past summer, a one and one half kilometer swim in Lake Ontario with a hundred like-minded individuals thrashing about like clothes in a washing machine. But the water in July had been merely chilly, and she'd been wearing a wetsuit, not jeans and a wool jacket, with goggles instead of sunglasses, and a swim cap instead of a toque.

The water pierced every fiber of her being, saturating her clothes within seconds. The heaviness of the fabric cloaked her skin like a shroud, and she could see the rowboat out of the corner of her eye. Temporary sanctuary. It was a million to one shot, but it was better than drowning in five feet of water. Better than giving in to Camilla without a fight. She sent a silent prayer to her mother and hoped someone up there was listening.

Against all odds she managed to scramble her way out, a survival instinct that somehow managed to kick in when her breath kicked out in ragged gasps. She grabbed the boat's edge and pulled herself up and over, all six hundred pounds of sodden wool and drenched denim. Another gunshot rang out, excruciatingly loud, and the water in front of her splashed as the bullet entered the water.

"It's got to look like you shot Johnny and tried to escape," Camilla said, her voice eerily calm as she leaned over to untie the boat. "Sorry to say the odds of you surviving the falls are slim, but you might get lucky—until you find yourself getting battered and bashed along the rocks in the swirling whitewater." A maniacal look of glee crossed her face. "It might speed things up if I shot you, too."

Emily stared at Camilla, then down at Johnny's lifeless body, his beautiful black eyes staring blankly upward, a thin trickle of blood at the edge of his mouth. She wished she had something clever to say, something that might save her life.

She didn't. But then she heard footsteps, followed by a voice.

The voice of a friend.

"For God's sake, Camilla, put the gun down," Levon shouted. "I'll tell the police that Emily shot Johnny. You and me, we can make this go away."

"Levon? What are you doing here?"

"I had a feeling you were in danger." Levon's voice was soft, soothing, and seductive. "I came as soon as I could."

"Johnny's dead. *I* shot him, not Emily." Camilla looked at the gun. "I shot him."

"We can tell the police otherwise. It's not too late."

"I never meant to hurt him, Levon."

"I know, Camilla, I know." Levon kept walking toward her, arms outstretched, his heart pounding. "Please, give me the gun."

"What about *her?*" Camilla pointed to Emily.

"I'll take care of her. Make sure she gets the boat ride she deserves. Nosey bitch. Come on, Camilla, give me the gun."

Levon figured she might have even done it except for one thing: Arabella entered the clearing—upright and standing, no less.

What part of "best if you stay back" did that woman not understand?

CHAPTER 48

Camilla looked up as Arabella came out of the treeline. "Your ex-wife is here," she said. "Or should I say, your lover?"

"Levon may be my ex-husband, but he's certainly *not* my lover," Arabella said, casting a disdainful glance in his general direction. "Not now, not anytime in the foreseeable future."

"You expect me to believe that? From what Nigel tells me, you two have been spending a lot of time together. You and that snoopy journalist, Emily Garland." Camilla pointed to the boat and the semi-conscious Emily. "You can see where snoopiness got *her*."

Where the hell did Nigel Watters get all his bloody gossip? Arabella wondered. "Levon's been using me to make you jealous. I suspected he was seeing you again, so I followed him here. Frankly, when I saw Johnny's car, I thought I might be wrong." Arabella brushed a twig out of her hair. "I could have done without the scenic hike."

"She's telling the truth, Millie," Levon said, his voice tender. "I've loved you from the first day I met you. I never thought I stood a chance."

Millie? Camilla Mortimer-Gilroy was Millie? And this was how she had to find out? She was going to kill Levon if they managed to get out of this mess alive. Kill him with her bare hands, no gun needed.

Emily tried to focus on the scene between Camilla, Levon, and Arabella playing out before her eyes, but it was getting harder and harder to concentrate. She tried to take her pulse, the way she did after a long run. She knew it had grown faint beneath her increasingly clumsy fingers. *Hypothermia.* She closed her eyes, heard a faint hum.

She was finally going to see her mother again.

Chapter 49

The faint hum was a police boat, which arrived just as Camilla was getting ready to hand the gun over to Levon. Arabella recognized the burly officer who had given her a speeding ticket a couple of short hours before and wanted to run over and hug him. The other officer was Detective Merryfield, who had interviewed her a lifetime ago when she'd discovered Stonehaven's body. Another boat followed with two paramedics on board, who made their way over to Emily.

It was painfully obvious that Johnny could wait.

They were been questioned, admonished severely more than once for trying to take the law into their own hands, and questioned again. Emily spent the night in the hospital and came out the next afternoon right as rain, save for a tensor bandage on her left ankle. Camilla remained in jail, awaiting her day in court and the likelihood of life in prison without parole. As for Levon, as much as she hadn't wanted to forgive him for not 'fessing up about the whole Millie business, she couldn't seem to hold a grudge.

She'd found herself reassessing a lot of things about her life. The next thing you knew she'd be accepting consignments from local artisans. Not reproductions, mind you; that wasn't *ever* going to happen at the Glass Dolphin. Authenticity still mattered. But selected handmade arts and crafts? When she thought about it, what could be more authentic than that?

"I didn't think you believed me," Arabella said to Constable Aaron Beecham. After all the hours of interrogation, she'd gotten semi-friendly with the burly police officer that had saved their lives.

They were sitting inside the Sunrise Café, sipping coffee. The diner wasn't quite the same now that Gloria had left town. Nigel Watters had closed down Frankie's Fish and Chips and taken over. Then again, change took time.

"I honestly didn't think you believed me," Arabella said, again.

"I didn't," Beecham admitted. "At least not at first. But you were so determined to tell me something. I knew Detective Merryfield had his doubts about all the recent accidents in Lount's Landing. So I called him, told him you'd mentioned a place called Camp Miakoda and a friend you thought might have been abducted. Turns out Merryfield's partner grew up in these parts. She remembered the local outrage when it opened. Unfortunately, we didn't get there in time to save Johnny Porter."

"Everybody always said Johnny was good people," Arabella said. "He'd spent his entire adult life in Lount's Landing trying to live up to that reputation. No matter how pure his intentions, I don't think he would have been able to live with everyone knowing he was a cold-blooded killer."

"Not many people can," Beecham said. "Not many people can."

CHAPTER 50

A couple of weeks later, the tensor bandage gone, Emily walked into the Glass Dolphin carrying a large, gift-wrapped box. "The elementary school is back up for sale," she said.

"I saw that on my way in this morning," Arabella said. "I notice Poppy didn't get the listing this time. Can't blame the school board for that one. What's in the box?"

"I brought you a shop warming gift."

"A shop warming gift? Sweet of you, but I've been open for a while."

"At first I bought it as a Christmas present, but I didn't want you to think you had to buy me a Christmas present. Then I thought, I'd call it a New Year's gift, but then I'd have to hold onto it, and people don't give gifts on New Year's and that might start another gift exchange. So I decided to call it a shop warming gift."

"I'm certainly not one to look a shop warming gift in the mouth. Can I open it?"

"You can."

"It's heavy," Arabella said.

Emily waited impatiently while Arabella slowly peeled off the silver wrapping paper. After what seemed like an eternity, she got around to opening the box.

"A wine refrigerator. I love, love, love it, Emily. You shouldn't have. But thank you."

"You did save my life. Plus, I fully intend to help you consume the contents."

"You stocked it with wine?"

"Hell, no. A bottle of Courvoisier and a half dozen miniature carrot cake cupcakes with cream cheese icing."

Arabella opened the refrigerator door and laughed. "I always did like your style." She sauntered over to the filing cabinet and grabbed two brandy snifters, then poured a healthy shot of Courvoisier in each. "What shall we toast to?"

"Before we get to that, there's something else I have to tell you. I've been waiting for the right time. Urban-Huntzberger has terminated my contract."

"They're going to stop publishing *Inside the Landing*?"

"Not exactly. They've hired Kerri St. Amour as the editor."

"Nice."

"It's okay, they were more than generous with their severance. Seems I never had a chance once you and I became friends. It turns out Camilla was one of the silent partners, along with Stonehaven's accountant, a slimeball by the name of Eldon

Thornbury. Urban-Huntzberger has been quick to divorce themselves from their association with Camilla, and the accountant will be doing some serious jail time once Revenue Canada takes a look at his books."

"Do you think Michelle knew about Camilla?"

"Camilla said she didn't, and I'm inclined to believe her. Why lie about that and not everything else? And Michelle assures me she never meant me to come to any harm. Not that it changes anything. I'm still unemployed."

"You were too good for that job."

"I'm not sure if that's true. But thank you for saying so."

"What will you do?"

"That depends on you."

"On me?"

"You've got a great shop here, Arabella, filled with amazing merchandise. But you aren't getting the sort of traffic you should be."

"It is still early days, and I have been a wee bit distracted," Arabella said. "But I'll admit I'm better at buying than I am at selling. And it's a lot harder than I thought it would be, running a place all on my own. Every time I want to leave, I have to close the shop. I can't imagine trying to go on a vacation."

"What if you had someone to help you? Someone to do the online stuff, keep the website updated with fresh merchandise, write a monthly newsletter. Start a blog."

"You mean, educate folks? Let them know antiques are green, that they're the original recyclable. That antiques aren't scary things you have to treat with kid gloves. That people have lived with these pieces for decades and decades."

Emily laughed. "Yeah, like that, although a little less intense."

"Wait a minute, are you volunteering to do the online stuff and the newsletter? Because I can't afford to hire you."

"I'm not volunteering, and I'm not looking to be your employee. I have some money from the Urban-Huntzberger buyout. I could put a down payment on a modest house in Lount's Landing and still have some left to invest as a partner in the Glass Dolphin. Provided there aren't any pyramid schemes involved."

"Ha, ha, very funny," Arabella said. "But I have to admit, I'm intrigued. What would you do, as my partner?"

"Marketing. Take care of the web presence, work at getting tour groups from the city to visit historic Main Street, get other businesses and associations to link to the website." Emily grinned. "I would never have told him so, but not all of Garrett Stonehaven's ideas were bad."

"You've thought this through?"

"I have. And there's more. I could write feature articles for antiques and consumer interest publications, include the website. I used to eke out a decent living as a freelance writer. I could do it again. I still have some connections, and I can build more."

"It all sounds good, but are you sure you don't want to go back to Toronto? Don't let the past few weeks fool you. This town is usually beyond sleepy. And as you pointed out, business isn't exactly booming."

"I'm positive. With the right marketing strategy, the Glass Dolphin could become a huge success. Besides, I've always wanted to write a historical romance. What better place to write a historical romance than in a town filled with history and hangings?"

"You'd have to learn more about antiques."

"I'm a fast learner, and I'd have a good teacher."

Arabella sipped her cognac and considered Emily for a long moment before answering. "We'd have to have a lawyer draw up the paperwork."

"Absolutely."

"And we'd have to be sure of who was responsible for what."

"Naturally."

"So, I would be in charge of Sales and Acquisitions, and you'd be in charge of Online Sales and Marketing."

"That's what I was thinking."

"We'd have to have an open and honest relationship. No more secrets."

"Agreed."

Arabella smiled. "Then I can't imagine anyone who I'd rather have as my business partner. Shall we toast to becoming partners, work out the details tomorrow?"

"I have a better idea."

"What's that?"

"How about toasting to the power of friendship instead?"

"To the power of friendship," Arabella said, and clinked Emily's glass.

Levon pressed his nose against the window of the Glass Dolphin, watching the scene between Emily and Arabella. He couldn't make out what they were saying, but it had been a long time since he'd seen Arabella look that happy. He fingered the tiny velvet box in his left jean jacket pocket and sighed.

Maybe he had misread things. Maybe you couldn't go back.

He turned away from the window and walked up Main Street towards The Hanged Man's Noose. There was a Sleeman Honey Brown lager there with his name on it.

-THE END-

ACKNOWLEDGEMENTS

All stories have to start somewhere, and in the case of *The Hanged Man's Noose*, that somewhere was a short story written for a creative writing class. At the time, there was no murder or mayhem, but there was a small, fictional town, Lount's Landing, and there was an antiques shop owner by the name of Arabella Carpenter. Long after I put that short story to rest, Arabella and the town rattled around in my head. And so, work on what would become *The Hanged Man's Noose* began in earnest.

But writing is a solitary pursuit, sometimes lonely, sometimes so all consuming you start to forget there's another world out there than the one you're immersed in. That's where friends and family come in; they serve to remind us of reality, share in our angst over rejection and blank pages, and help us to celebrate every victory, however minor.

While there are far too many people to recognize here, there are a few that must be mentioned. They include my first editors, Lourdes Venard and Marta Tanrikulu, as well as my early readers: (the late) Lou Allin, Janet Bolin, Dorothyanne Brown and Marcus Trower. My "tea and sympathy group" includes Barry Dempster, Sharon Wilston, and Christine Barbetta, and, in alphabetical order, Carol Dee, Donna Dixon, Vicki Gladwish, Charlotte and Larry Owen, and Nina Patterson. For your support, encouragement, and unfailing belief in me, and my story, thank you.

I'd also like to acknowledge the writing associations and members that have become an integral part of my life: Crime Writers of Canada, Sisters in Crime, and Sisters in Crime – Guppies (especially James (Jim) M. Jackson, who told me about Barking Rain Press).

To my editor, Narielle Living, and to my publisher, Barking Rain Press, thank you for taking a chance on me, and for your hard work and suggestions to help make *The Hanged Man's Noose* the best it could possibly be.

Last, but certainly not least, to my mother, who instilled my love of reading, and to Mike, who encouraged me not only to follow my dreams, but to believe in them.

— Judy Penz Sheluk —

ALSO FROM JUDY PENZ SHELUK

"Plan D" (*The Whole She-Bang 2* anthology)

"Live Free or Die" (*World Enough and Crime* anthology)

COMING SOON FROM JUDY PENZ SHELUK

Skeletons in the Attic

WWW.JUDYPENZSHELUK.COM

JUDY PENZ SHELUK

Credit: Jen Short Photography

Judy Penz Sheluk's short fiction has appeared in literary publications and anthologies, including *The Whole She-Bang 2* and *World Enough and Crime*. She also contributed to Bake Love Write, a dessert cookbook featuring recipes from 105 authors.

In addition to writing mysteries, Judy works as a freelance writer, specializing in art, antiques and the residential housing industry; her articles have appeared regularly in dozens of U.S. and Canadian consumer and trade publications. Past editorial responsibilities have included the roles of Senior Editor, *Northeast Art & Antiques*, and Editor, *Antiques and Collectibles Showcase*. She is currently the Editor of *Home Builder Magazine*, and the Senior Editor for *New England Antiques Journal*.

Judy is also a Professional member of Sisters in Crime International, Sisters in Crime — Guppies, Sisters in Crime — Toronto, and Crime Writers of Canada.

You can find out more about Judy on her website/blog and sign up for her quarterly newsletter. She can also be found on Facebook, Pinterest, Twitter, Goodreads, or on her Amazon author page.

WWW.JUDYPENZSHELUK.COM

ABOUT
BARKING RAIN PRESS

D id you know that five media conglomerates publish eighty percent of the books in the United States? As the publishing industry continues to contract, opportunities for emerging and mid-career authors are drying up. Who will write the literature of the twenty-first century if just a handful of profit-focused corporations are left to decide who—and what—is worthy of publication?

Barking Rain Press is dedicated to the creation and promotion of thoughtful and imaginative contemporary literature, which we believe is essential to a vital and diverse culture. As a nonprofit organization, Barking Rain Press is an independent publisher that seeks to cultivate relationships with new and mid-career writers over time, to be thorough in the editorial process, and to make the publishing process an experience that will add to an author's development—and ultimately enhance our literary heritage.

In selecting new titles for publication, Barking Rain Press considers authors at all points in their careers. Our goal is to support the development of emerging and mid-career authors—not just single books—as we know from experience that a writer's audience is cultivated over the course of several books.

Support for these efforts comes primarily from the sale of our publications; we also hope to attract grant funding and private donations. Whether you are a reader or a writer, we invite you to take a stand for independent publishing and become more involved with Barking Rain Press. With your support, we can make sure that talented writers thrive, and that their books reach the hands of spirited, curious readers. Find out more at our website.

WWW.BARKINGRAINPRESS.ORG

Barking Rain Press

Also from Barking Rain Press

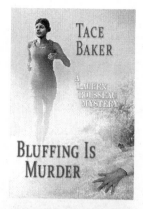

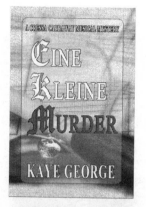

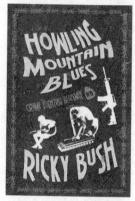

Made in the USA
Charleston, SC
01 August 2015